GOOD WITCH HUNTING

DAKOTA CASSIDY

GOOD WITCH HUNTING

BY DAKOTA CASSIDY

COPYRIGHT

same name or names. Any similarities to real persons, situations, or incidents is purely coincidental.

ISBN: 9781720222804

Imprint: Independently published

ACKNOWLEDGMENTS

My darling readers,

Please note, the Witchless in Seattle series is truly best read in order, to understand the full backstory and history of each character as they develop with every connecting book.

Especially in the case of the mystery surrounding Winterbottom (I know it drives some of you crazy. Sorrysorrysorry!). However, his story is ever evolving and will contain some mini-cliffhangers from book to book. But I promise not to make you wait too long until I answer each set of questions I dredge up.

And, too, I promise the central mystery featured in each addition to the series will always be wrapped up with a big bow by book's end!

Also, forgive me for being so late with this install-ment of Witchless In Seattle. I know I promised book 7 at the end of October, but alas, that didn't happen. Yet, this is not without reason. As some of you may know, if you follow me on social media, I've had a pretty rough year, medically speaking, and I'm just now recuperating.

So as not to dwell, I'll just say I'm much better and hope to have many adventures with the Ebenezer Falls crew, while introducing you to a new gang in the Nun of Your Business Mysteries! I hope you'll check out Stevie and Win's new friends, ex-nun Sister Trixie Lavender (her voice is based on my amazing narrator, Hollie Jackson, who sounds like a Disney princess and Mary Poppins all rolled into one fab package!), and Coop, her demon straight from hell, as they solve mysteries from their tattoo shop in the heart of a fictional town in Portland, Oregon.

Thank you for your emails, your prayers, your kind words while you've waited for this book. You're the best readers a girl could ask for!

Dakota XXOO

GOOD WITCH HUNTING

BY DAKOTA CASSIDY

"*I*sn't it beautiful, Win?" I breathed out with a dreamy sigh, folding my fists under my chin.

"'Tis indeed beautiful, Dove. Like white frosting on a cake," he whispered back in his raspy-sexy British accent. His words so close to my ear, I shivered.

Arkady sighed with me in obvious longing. "Is like home. Sometimes, I miss home, *malutka*."

My smile was one of understanding and sympathy. I knew what it was to miss home. "I know, my Russian spy. Someday, when the time is right, we'll pay a visit to your great country and you can show me all the greatness. Except for the cabbage soup greatness. No cabbage soup. Twinkie soup? Maybe. But no borscht for your *malutka*," I teased.

Arkady's laughter rumbled deep and hearty. "*Nyet!* No soup. But I think my little artichoke dip would be pretty as picture in babushka. Don't you agree, Zero?"

Win barked a laugh, obviously at the image he'd called up in his mind of me in a babushka. "Without doubt, bloke."

Again, I smiled into the darkness of the kitchen as we sat at the table by our big bay window and watched the heavy snowfall. We didn't get the white stuff by the tons here in Ebenezer Falls, a small suburb of Seattle. Usually it was just a dusting and then it melted away. Rain was our bread and butter, in the way of bucketsful during the winter months.

But on this fine evening in mid-March, snow had been falling for hours; thick and crystalline, shimmering on our backyard lawn like sparkling fairy dust as it wisped over the water rolling by in choppy froths. We'd stopped everything to appreciate the beauty of the snowflakes after a long day of thorough inventory at our shop, Madam Zoltar's.

The winter months were slow in our tourist town, and my readings for those seeking confirmation of their loved ones from the other side were sporadic until at least May.

Belfry hummed his approval, snuggling deeper into the thick hair on our dog Whiskey's back. "Never thought I'd say this—I'm a southern climate boy through and through for obvious reasons—but it's really beautiful to look at. As long as we don't have to go out in it again. Last time my little buddy here almost suffocated me, rolling around in that stuff like our lawn was covered in steaks and sprinkled with jerky."

I chuckled at my tiny familiar and ran my hand over our extra-large St. Bernard's head with affection, loving the velvety feel of his ears. "Well, he's a cold-weather dog. They used to carry around those barrels of booze and save people in the mountains—isn't that what you told me? His breed lives for weather like this. He also loves you. It only stands to reason he'd want to share his joy with you."

Whiskey harrumphed his pleasure. Almost as if he knew we were talking about him. Strike, our most exotic and unexpected pet turkey, nudged his way between my leg and Whiskey's big body, looking for love.

Turkeys are surprisingly sweet and gentle, and we'd found our Strike, who'd become ours quite by accident, was a hugger. He loved nothing more than to snuggle up against a warm body. In fact, he and Whiskey often slept cuddled together on the rug by our fireplace while we watched television.

"I haven't seen snow like this since I was in Siberia in 2012," Win recalled.

Belfry shivered, his tiny body shuddering in fluffy white ripples. "Was that the mission you told me about involving a beautiful princess from Uzbekistan and a vial full of anthrax?"

"'Twas, good man," Win confirmed.

As the men in my life rehashed the mission Win referred to, I fought an outward cringe at the mention of a beautiful princess. Since last summer, when Win had finally told me the details of his death—and

3

Miranda, his ex-lover's alleged involvement—I still felt a little raw.

Now, every time he mentioned another woman, whether he'd legitimately been intimately involved with her or not, I experienced pangs of ridiculous jealousy. These annoying pangs had increased in frequency and grown in size. In fact, maybe it was fair to say they threatened to turn into a tsunami of green-eyed monsters, raining down from the sky in a crashing swell of water, moments before metaphorically drowning me.

Win's love for Miranda (his *spy* ex-lover) has always been clear, her alleged betrayal and how deeply it hurt, clearer still. But after this past summer, when he'd revealed all, when every emotion connected to Miranda had been stripped naked, I saw how deep his feelings truly were.

And I was jealous. And I hated it. Nowadays, all he had to do was mention any woman at all, and it was like a pile on of jealousy. Rather like when you're irritated by someone's mere existence, and everything they do, no matter what it is, makes you insane? That's how I've been feeling.

I know why, too. There was no more mystery to Win. Not in the realm of his love life, anyway. We'd laid it bare, and I couldn't see a way he'd ever be able to love or trust anyone in quite the way he'd done with Miranda.

He'd never put himself out there like that again, and who could blame him? He believed she'd betrayed him.

His feelings were fair even though I had my suspicions about what happened that day.

So where did that leave *me*?

Unrequited. That's where. And it had begun to eat at my insides like a Pac-Man game. Sometimes I swear I hear the actual sound the video game used to make on my TV when it chewed up the ghosts.

Yet, I'm not sure what difference it would make if I told Win how I felt about him anyway. We can't ever be together. Yes, sure, he'd possessed a couple of bodies since we'd met, but he'd never lasted very long in them. That aside, I didn't want him to possess someone else's body.

I liked him exactly the way I'd seen him in the picture with Miranda in Paris. It was the picture of the man I'd fallen so deeply in—

"It is good night for snuggling on couch, yes? Warm and cozy by fire with hot toddy to keep insides warm, too? Maybe we watch marathon? I see *Psych* is on. You know how much I love the crazy Guster and his Blueberry." Arkady's deep laugh resonated in my ears.

I winked up at the ceiling. "I'll get the *Twinkies* and the *Pepsi*."

"Bah, Stephania!" Win chastised, the way he always did whenever I mentioned my beloved junk food. "Must you eat like you're a twelve-year-old boy? Have I taught you nothing about proper snacking? Surely we have some cheese and crackers. Maybe some prosciutto?"

I let the darkness of the kitchen hide my smile. "I

have Cheez Whiz. Oooo! Now that sounds good, don't you think, Mr. Pretentious? Cheez Whiz and some of those fancy stone wheat crackers you're so fond of. C'mon, boys. Shall we adjourn to the living room by the fire?"

Win scoffed in my ear as I took one last look outside at our lawn furniture, now totally covered by glistening snow. "Cheez Whiz," he admonished with a cluck of his disapproving tongue. "If it can't be sliced with a sharp knife, it should not be consumed. Otherwise, it's unseemly, Stephania. What sort of monster thinks to put cheese in a spray can anyway?"

I went to the fridge, my trail of pets and assorted ethereal beings right behind me. "The same monsters who named a sponge cake spotted dick?"

Win's laughter followed me as I grabbed my unseemly spray cheese and some crackers and headed toward the living room to settle in for some deep couch sitting.

Hopefully, watching some mindless television would take my mind off my woes about Win.

～

"*S*tephania!"

I rubbed my eyes with my knuckles and fought to open them, briefly wondering what the heck was going on with Win. He never woke me up unless it was an emergency.

That thought made me sit straight up in my bed.

As my eyes adjusted and a glance at my bedside clock told me it was three in the morning, I frowned. "Are you okay? What's wrong, Win?" I asked, my hand instantly reaching for the warmth of Whiskey's fur where he was snuggled beside me.

"Oh, Dove. My deepest apologies. Your name burst from my lips before I thought to remember it's three a.m. Go back to sleep. We'll talk in the morning," he soothed in gentle tones.

I pulled my comforter tighter around my chest and cocked an ear. There was something in Win's voice. Something distracted, something faraway, something stricken that made me pay attention. "Spill, Win. Everything you do or say has a reason. That you called out my name in the middle of the night means something urgent is going on with you. Talk to me."

"Not now, Dove."

He was brushing me off, and I didn't like it. I'd had enough with his secrets and his flat-out avoidance of all things Win the Spy Guy.

So I threw my legs over the side of the bed and instructed Alexa, our home device, to turn on the lights, crossing my arms over my chest with a shake of my head.

"Nope. Don't tell me not now. I've had it up to my eyeballs with your secrets—"

"Secrets?" he gasped his outrage at my response, his voice filling my bedroom. "We have no secrets, Stephania."

"Oh, suuure," I drawled with a little more sarcasm

than intended. "We have none now, after a year of mostly nothing *but* secrecy."

His aggravated sigh grated a rasp of air in my ear. "I've explained that, Stephania."

I hopped off the bed and slid my feet into my fuzzy slippers, reaching for my bathrobe and slipping it on, giving a glance to Strike, who was sound asleep on his heated dog bed. Yes. Our turkey has a heated dog bed to rest his head upon, and yes, he sleeps in the house.

Would you expect anything less from the crazy lady who talks to ghosts?

"Yep. You've explained it, and that's all well and good, but here's the thing. You never wake me up in the middle of the night—"

"I was simply deep in thought, Dove. Your name fell from my lips unintentionally as I pondered. You're just the first person who comes...to my mind when..." Then he scoffed. "This is nothing that can't wait until tomorrow morning over coffee. It's certainly not worthy of your rapt attention at this late hour."

The first person who came to Win's mind, eh? Not Arkady. Not even Belfry, whom Win had become quite close with. It was me. I was the first person who came to mind when he had something important to share.

My heart warmed around the edges just a smidge— before I reminded myself there was nothing to be pleased or warm about. Sure, I was Win's confidant. His *friend* confidant. His *earthly* friend confidant.

"Which tells me it's important, and if it's important,

I want to know what made you call out my name at three in the morning. So spill."

"I remembered something," he muttered quietly.

A slither of ominous chills slipped along my spine at his tone, making me tuck my clenched fists to my sides. "Okay. What did you remember?"

"A tattoo."

I tilted my head in question. "Of?"

"It's more like *on*. What the tattoo was on."

I scratched my head and sighed. "Don't make me pull teeth, Win."

He chuckled his teasing gurgle of a laugh. "If this is pulling teeth, I'll take it. Once, deep in the Andes, I lost my bicuspid to a group of—"

"Win! It's three in the morning." I narrowed my eyes at the ceiling. "I don't want to hear a spy story tonight. I think I have a Cheez Whiz hangover, and I'm just not up to your avoidance tactics. Now tell me what the heck you mean by a tattoo and stop going off topic with tales from the MI6 Crypt!"

"All right then. Fine. I had a memory of the night I was killed."

Then there was a long silence.

Like, really long.

As per usual, he stopped just when things were getting juicy. I shook my fist at the ceiling. "You are the most frustrating man!" I growled as I began to pace. There was no way I was going back to sleep now. Not a chance. "So the memory involved a tattoo? Explain. Please. Without wading into your spy-capades or stopping just shy of telling me the whole story. Now, let's start over. What does a tattoo have to do with the night you were killed?"

"Do you recall my mentioning the shadow I thought I saw just before Miranda allegedly killed me?"

I did. I also noted he was now using the word "allegedly" when linked to his death and Miranda. Interesting.

So I answered him, driving my hands into the pockets of my flannel pajama bottoms. "I do remember. What about it?"

"There was a hand attached to that shadow, Stephania. I just recalled it clear as day."

My heart jumped in my chest. For as long as I'd known Win, he'd been pretty sure Miranda had been the one who'd killed him. And this past summer, he'd finally confessed why he thought she was his murderer. To have this type of recollection was enormous.

Thus, I treaded carefully. I strolled to my bedroom windows overlooking the driveway, pretending interest in the still falling snow, and cocked my head as though I were paused for thought.

"Any thoughts on who the hand belonged to?"

"Not a one."

"Male hand? Female hand?"

"Definitely male, if the hairy knuckles are any indication."

Pushing my hands behind me, I wove them together and stretched my arms upward before letting them swing at my sides. "And the tattoo? Was it on the hand?"

"'Twas…" he offered. But that was all he offered.

I fought the roll of my eyes. "And what did the tattoo look like? Do you remember it clearly?"

"I do…"

I whipped around, forcing myself to stay calm even though I wanted to scream at him—shake him—make him part with this new information before, oh, I dunno, sunrise.

"And what do you remember about the tattoo, Win?" I said from teeth clenched so hard, I was destined to need a visit to my dentist when they crumbled from the pressure of clamping them together with such force.

"It's very specific. Very detailed in its finery."

My shoulders sagged as I made my way back to the bed and hopped up into it again, careful not to disturb Whiskey and Belfry. Maybe he was right. Maybe this could wait until morning coffee—or a fishbowl full of tequila—because that's how frustrating having a conversation about the night Win died can be. It drives me to consider drinking—a lot.

Resettling myself under my toasty comforter, I cuddled into my delightful bed specifically designed for me by Win himself. He'd created a nook in the wall of my bedroom in almost the shape of a hexagon, rather like a place for me to nest. My gorgeous bed nook featured a fluffy mattress and tons of pillows, with a stained-glass window overlooking our side yard, and it had shelves above my head for my books. I plumped those very pillows Win endlessly complained about and yawned.

Maybe if I pretended this revelation was no big deal, much the way Win had, he'd cough up the information. But I really had overdone the Cheez Whiz, and I needed some sleep to wash away my carb frenzy.

Tucking my hand under my chin, I muttered, "Okay. Well, when you want to talk with more than three- or four-word sentences, lemme know. Until then. Sweet dreams, International Man of Mystery."

Closing my eyes, I feigned the beginnings of sleep—which wasn't a difficult task, considering the hour and my processed cheese hangover.

"It was a snake. The tattoo was of a coiled snake, with a very detailed collar around its neck. Who puts a collar on a snake, I ask you? Regardless, the snake had a collar—a vividly royal-blue collar with a diamond in the center, and upon the jewel, the initial R."

My entire body stiffened at this new batch of information, but I fought for a literate, composed response. "And it was on this shadow person's hand? Like the back of his hand? Or his palm?"

"Yes, Stephania. It was on the back of his hand just below his hairy knuckles. I saw it very clearly." His tone held that rigidness I'd come to know so well because despite the fact that we were openly talking about the night he'd died, that never happened without stiffness in his words and the underlying anger I was sure he must still feel.

"And you're certain the hand and this tattoo were present on the night you were…" I couldn't say it out loud. I could never say it out loud.

But Win could. "*Murdered*. Yes. I'm quite positive."

"Does the initial R mean anything to you? Could it have something to do with Inga Von Krause?"

Inga was one of the last people Win had spent time with before he'd died. Granted, he'd been undercover and she was the daughter of a horrible man she ended up escaping, so there'd been no romantic involvement between the two.

But I'd had a taste of what his life had been like, after meeting Inga and falling wildly in love with her son Hardy…er, Sebastian. In fact, they'd visited us just this past Christmas for a long, wonderful weekend, where I was able to collect gooey baby kisses to my heart's content.

But I digress. Suffice it to say, Win's life had been chaotic during that time. Maybe Inga knew something about this shadow and a tattooed hand?

"No. It had nothing to do with Inga," Win confirmed with an air of surety.

"Did you have any R people in your life at that point in time? Is it like a gang thing, this initial? You know, like a representation of gang membership—an initiation or whatever. Because gravy knows you've been mixed up with all manner of mafia, drug lords and the like in your time as a spy. Could that be what the R represents? A group of some sort? Or does it represent someone's name?"

Clearing his throat, his voice invaded my ears. "I've racked my brain about just that, Stephania, and come up with nothing. I don't know anyone with a tattoo like that. Certainly not a fellow spy from MI6. We do our best to hide any blatant identifiers such as tattoos and piercings for fear of being recognized when in deep cover. A tattoo that obvious would never be allowed simply due to its in-your-face nature. As spies, we were very careful to keep our true identities hidden."

"So wouldn't that lead one to believe this wasn't a good-guy shadow but a bad one?"

"Quite possibly."

"Know any bad guys with the initial R?"

"Maybe it wasn't the tattoo owner's initial, Stephania. Maybe it represented someone in his life. In memorandum of someone who'd died. Someone he loved."

"Maybe. Or maybe he just has a thing for the letter R. Who can say for sure? All I know is, this is huge, Win. You've remembered something crucial and maybe you've exonerated Miranda," I offered around the lump in my throat.

I often wondered if I wanted Miranda to have been the one who killed Win. It's an awful guilt I carry around. At least if she really were the one who'd killed him, he'd only continue to suffer her betrayal. He'd still be angry with her.

But if she wasn't his killer, then he could go on loving her from way on high, and that was a hard pill for me to swallow. She'd return to reverent status in his heart, and he'd never let go.

Then I berated myself for even considering such a thing. What difference did it make in the end? He was there and I was here and never the twain shall meet and all.

Period.

"I don't know that I've done that just yet," Win said, his voice cutting into my dreadful, ugly thoughts, but I heard the hope in his words. "I *do* know we need to go to that tattoo shop in town and further look into this."

Running a hand over my eyes, I gave them a good scrub to keep them open. "You mean the one that just opened? Inkerbelle's, is it? Such a cleverly cute name. I've been meaning to go welcome them to our quaint 'hood."

"That's the one."

"And why do we need to go there?"

"Because while the letter R implies the tattoo is personalized, maybe the design isn't. Maybe it's a standard universal design one can find anywhere. I'd like to know one way or the other."

That was fair, and he was right to want to look deeper. It's exactly what I'd do. Maybe we could solve this once and for all. If nothing else, despite my feelings on the subject, Win might finally find some peace. I wanted that for him more than I wanted to forget Miranda had ever existed.

"Then it's a date," I replied sleepily. "Tomorrow we storm the castle."

Win's chuckle, light in comparison to his tension-filled, evasive tone earlier, made me smile. "Tell me, Stephania, have you any tattoos?"

Giggling, I burrowed under the warmth of my comforter, pressing the tops of my thighs to Whiskey's bulk. "I'll never tell." I don't have any tattoos, but he doesn't need to know that. "Do you?"

"What's good for the goose is good for the gander, as they say. So never you mind, Mini-Spy. Rest well, Dove. See you in the morning," he whispered on another laugh, leaving me to wonder about tattoos and very personal things I had no business wondering.

CHAPTER 2

"Is this what you're thinking?" I held up my doodling pad to the ceiling (even though I know he's not hovering above me. It's a habit I can't seem to break) to show Win my sketch of the tattoo he'd described in great detail over coffee this morning.

He gasped with exaggerated flair. "The likeness is so distinct, it's almost uncanny. Who knew you were a regular twenty-first century Picasso? Right here in modern day, as we live and breathe. Surely, it's as though you're in my head, Stephania."

Scrunching my nose, I sipped my coffee, tilting my head to the right. "Really?"

"Erm, no, Stephania. Not at all. I'm using sarcasm as a means to deflect from how truly horrible that sketch is."

I frowned and toyed with my scarf, throwing down my colored pencil. "Not even close?"

"Not unless kindergartners have taken to drawing tattoos these days," he teased in his dry British way.

Looking at my sketch, I kind of had to agree with him. It *was* pretty bad. My coiled snake looked akin to a big green blob of goo.

Okay. It was *really* bad.

In my defense, I stuck my tongue out at him. "I'm just trying to help, Fussy Pants."

"And a splendid job of that you're doing, Stephania. How will I ever repay your diligence?"

I batted a hand at him. "Just you hush. So I'm not going to win any art scholarships. I was only trying to get an image in my mind's eye to work with, is all. Next time, I'll keep my doodling to myself." I took a long gulp of my coffee while he and Arkady laughed.

"The roads look pretty good, Boss. I think it's safe enough to go out now that they've plowed. You guys about ready?" Belfry asked on a violent shiver as he flew into the kitchen.

We'd sent him to scout the condition of the roads after so much snowfall. We lived on the edge of a cliff a few minutes out of town, and we were always the last to see any clearing of the roads. I didn't want to risk losing yet another car to an accident should they be dangerous.

I was 2 for 0 in the car department, in case you're wondering. I'm still trying to put the last incident out of my mind.

I patted my shoulder, signaling Bel should settle there and cuddle up against my neck to warm himself.

When he landed, I tucked my new scarf (a vintage, lavender Hermes, and heck of a find) around him and asked, "Would you rather stay here with Whiskey and Strike, pal? I know you hate this weather, and we won't be gone long. Promise. We're just going to ask a couple of questions, and I might grab a coffee before heading back here to spend the afternoon by the fireplace."

Belfry's breed—a cotton ball bat, for those wondering—are warm-weather lovers. To say his tiny body wasn't used to this weather is to say the least.

"Not a chance, Petunia," Bel chirped, tucking himself against my skin with a ripple of fur. "You don't think I'd miss this, do you? We're finally onto something about our man of mystery, right, old chap?"

"Indeed, this could very well be a lead to something bigger, old friend," Win agreed, but again, he had that distracted hint to his tone. His voice held a forced cheerfulness I couldn't miss.

If I knew Win, he was thinking ahead rather than staying in the moment—something he always told me was imperative to solving any good mystery. Yet, I couldn't blame him. He'd waited a long time for even a small clue that could lead to some answers.

"Well, I'm ready if you guys are." I rose, taking one last gulp of Enzo's special brew of coffee before dropping my mug in the sink and heading toward the coatrack at our entryway to grab my coat and boots. "Are you ready, too, Arkady?"

"*Dah*, my crunchy granola bar. On with this, I say! I,

too, am wondering about this tattoo and the mystery hand."

I chuckled as I headed out our stained-glass front door and down the steps Enzo's sons had so kindly shoveled and salted for me while I was in the shower. "Then buckle up, Buttercups. Let's go meet the new people and do some digging."

"Dare I say that lilt I hear in your tone is giddy joy, Stephania?" Win asked, laughter lacing his words.

Beeping my car, I popped the driver's side door open with a shiver before sliding in. Dang, it was cold. "Joy? Explain."

"Well, we haven't had a mystery to solve since this past summer, when Inga brought baby Sebastian here and had you believing he was mine."

I nodded my head, started the engine, and turned the heat in the car to high. "You have to admit, her note was pretty convincing, and truth be told, he could have passed for your son."

"Fair enough," Win acquiesced. "But still, you sound positively capricious despite the early hour and the frigid temps. You don't even make appointments at the shop before ten a.m., Dove. Yet, here you are at nine sharp, showered, dressed—in a lovely frock, I might add—and ready to take on the world with only one cup of coffee and a store-bought cream puff to your name. Whatever am I to think other than you're excited at the prospect of solving the mystery of the shadow and his tattoo?"

Win knew me well. Too well.

Yep. It was true. It had been exceptionally quiet here in Eb Falls for quite some time now. Maybe too quiet for someone like me who, when faced with too much idle time, filled up that time with broody thoughts and projections about Win.

Absolutely nothing of interest had gone down since the summer and my brush with death via Heinrich Von Krause, an arms dealer, and the man Win had spent a good deal of time in deep cover with before his untimely death.

My heart still stung just a little over baby Sebastian, but Inga, his mother and Heinrich's rebel daughter, made a point of keeping in close contact with me, due to the nature of the attachment I'd formed with her son —who really didn't turn out to be Win's child, by the by.

Since then, there hadn't been a murder or even a burglary in Eb Falls—a place we were beginning to think was the Hellmouth for murder central. Since I'd moved back here from Paris, Texas, we'd solved six mysteries and murders in as much as two years.

But lately? Nothing. Not unless you counted the heated argument between two soccer moms at a hot yoga class, and even that was nothing to write home about.

Preparing to back out, I took a moment to enjoy the beauty of our house wreathed in freshly fallen snow and reflect on Win's statement. Was I one of those murder hounds? Like Aurora Teagarden on The Hallmark Channel?

Did I salivate at the mere suggestion of a mystery while rubbing my hands in glee?

"To answer the question I see behind your lovely green eyes, yes. You do enjoy a good mystery—be it murder or otherwise. Surely you recall Gladys Pepperton's hunt for her brooch at bingo a month ago?"

As I backed out of the driveway, taking my time— even after a good salting, it was still slick—I thought back to bingo night at the VFW. I love bingo, and in a town this small, sometimes that's all a girl has to look forward to—Tuesday night bingo.

Clearing my throat, I replied, "I remember finding her brooch for her..." It was easy to find, too. A little too easy. I needed more of a challenge.

Belfry snorted. "Do you remember yelling at the top of your lungs about finding her brooch in the middle of the VFW hall like you'd just found Jimmy Hoffa's skeletal remains?"

Rolling my eyes, now *I* snorted, mostly in discomfort. "I did not. Don't exaggerate."

"Oh yes, my little sunflower seed. You did," Arkady assured.

"And you drooled a bit, Dove. Right at the corner of your mouth for all to see. 'Tis just the truth."

"Then you declared yourself the winner of this made-up game in your mind right to Officer Nelson's face, like he even knew he was playing," Belfry added with a chuckle at the memory.

Dana Nelson is one of the police officers I frequently deal with when one of these murders occurs. We've become friends of sorts—sharing a cup of coffee from time to time, and sometimes even a burger. There's no physical attraction between us. In fact, he's so far my polar opposite, I'm surprised we're even friends. At first, when I returned to Eb Falls, we weren't. But we'd come a long way. Which is why I knew it was okay to tease him about finding the brooch before he did.

And listen, January is always a sad month for me. Christmas and the New Year were over, my mother and father had gone home, all the fun parties had ended, everyone had gone back to their lives, we'd taken down the decorations I love so much, and my endless cookie/eggnog binge came to a screeching halt because Win makes me exercise. Finding Mrs. Pepperton's brooch made me feel better, okay?

Taking off along the road to town, I shrugged. "Officer By The Book should have stepped up his game is all I'm saying. There was a lost brooch on the loose. It needed to be found. I found it. He's an officer of the law. Finding a brooch should have been easy-peasy-lemon-squeezy. My coup deserved some crowing."

"Did it?" Win teased.

"Oh, all right. I like a good mystery, and it's been months since we've been able to sink our teeth into something worthy. Not that I'd wish murder on anyone. I'd be just as happy to find buried treasure as I would a murderer, BTW. Maybe even happier."

Win cleared his throat. "As I said—"

"So, about this tattoo," I deflected away from my

alleged fixation on solving mysteries. "Anything specific you want me to ask?"

"I'm simply curious about its origins. Maybe it's a common design."

"I know next to nothing about tattoos, but the only common design I see usually has to do with cartoon characters. The one you're describing seems pretty specific, Win."

"Thus, we must ask. Who knows if it's a universal tattoo with the artist's personal flair thrown in for good measure? Also, tattoo artists sometimes know one another's work merely by sight. 'Twould be helpful if they knew the tattoo artist, would it not? Not to mention, we haven't properly welcomed them to the neighborhood. They're just four doors down from you and they've been lodged there for almost three weeks. It will do you good to get to know your neighbors and fellow friends in commerce."

Nodding, I took my time around the sharp bend in the road leading to town, slowing to take into account possible icy patches. "You're right, Spy Guy. It's not like we've been busy with much else but inventory anyway. Maybe I should stop and grab some pastries for them? I feel so rude for not extending a hand sooner, but I guess I've just been preoccupied."

Which is the truth. I just couldn't tell Win what kept me so preoccupied.

"Is okay, *malutka*. Yesterday when we were in town at Madam Z's, Arkady see they are still moving into their shop. Boxes and more boxes. They looked too busy for pleasantries."

"Pastries would be a brilliant welcome gift, Stephania."

"Pastries it is then," I agreed, parallel parking without much fuss two stores down from the bakery.

I sat in the car for a moment and enjoyed the stillness of Ebenezer Falls after an unexpected snowfall. It was nestled in a suburb of Seattle, and I loved my quaint town—the town I'd grown up in and left for a job as a 9-1-1 operator in Paris, Texas, so many years ago. It was bright and cheerful with colorful awnings on each shop, and it sat in the arms of Puget Sound with the mountains for its backdrop.

Blanketed in snow, it was idyllic.

The enormous pine trees were covered in heavy tufts of white on green and icicles hung from the big maples' winter-bare branches like icy fingers.

It was abnormally quiet today due to the unexpected snow—which was what made parking such a breeze. Clearly, everyone had hunkered down for the snowstorm and decided to sleep in. Pushing my car door open, I took a deep breath of the tangy air, raw and damp from the heavy precipitation. I loved the scent of Puget Sound—I loved the seagulls flying above on this overcast day.

I even loved the gray sky with its swollen clouds, and for the first time since the holidays had ended, I felt a little better. Scooping Bel from my neck, I dropped him into my latest vintage purse find, where a microwaved hand warmer awaited him.

I heard his low moan of gratitude and smiled as I scooted into the bakery to grab some welcome-to-the-neighborhood pastries, so I could well and truly extend my hand to the people who owned Inkerbelle's.

~

The bright neon sign with the words Inkerbelle's Tattoos, with a picture of a skull's head—made even brighter by the gloomy skies —blinked cheerfully at me. As I peeked inside, I saw movement.

Gorgeous movement, as a by the by. A beautiful dusky redhead, long and lean in a bulky off-white sweater and leather pants, moved boxes, her hair cascading down her back to her waist in rippling waves. As she bent and picked things up, I noted her sculpted features were near perfect in every way.

Arkady wolf-whistled his appreciation at that movement, seconds before Win chastised him.

"Good man, behave yourself! Have you no impulse control? Especially in this day and age, where women have finally risen up against such blatant philandering. For shame, Spy!"

Arkady let out an embarrassed chuckle. "I slip. Old habits die hard. My apologies, my *malutka*."

I flapped a hand at him as I balanced the box of yummy pastries in the crook of my elbow. "No worries.

Just don't let it happen again. And I admit, she's certainly not hard to look at. If I were a misogynistic cad, I'd whistle, too."

My admission made Arkady laugh. "Then I am forgiven for being dirty, lowdown pig?"

I nodded, catching a glimpse of myself in the store's glass door and feeling very inadequate when up against this ethereal creature. "You're forgiven. Now let's go make friends."

I tried to push the door open, but it was locked. So I wiped the condensation collecting on the glass and knocked, catching the stunning tall woman's gaze.

Or should I say glare.

Yes. Glare was the right adjective when aligned with this beautiful woman. She was sleek and supple, like oil on water, as her face turned to a mask of clear suspicion when she slinked toward the door.

But I smiled reassuringly and waved, holding up the box of pastries, hoping to abolish that "you owe me money" look from her face.

And then another woman appeared—a curvier woman than the one who looked like she belonged on a billboard in Times Square in a pair of Victoria's Secret angel wings. She was shorter than the glamazon, and wore a holey red sweatshirt with fashionably ripped jeans, and a black knit beanie covering her straight reddish-brown hair.

She, too, was pretty in an understated way, as though she didn't want anyone to know she was attractive—or rather, she didn't know how attractive her clear porcelain skin and bright eyes were.

I pointed to the box of pastries again and smiled, and she paused for only a moment before she put a hand to the other woman's shoulder and squeezed, then nodded with a smile of her own, coming toward the door.

She flipped the lock and opened it, her eyes bright with curiosity. "Hi there! How can I help you?"

Her voice struck me in the strangest way. A right-in-the-gut way. It was so warm and comforting, sort of one part Mary Poppins-ish without the accent and two parts Disney princess. Instantly, I felt soothed and comfortable with her. How odd.

I stuck my hand out, the smile still on my face even as my teeth chattered. "I'm Stevie Cartwright—your neighbor in commerce. I own Madam Zoltar's just down the block. I'm sorry it took me so long to drop by, but I wanted to personally welcome you to Eb Falls. We're thrilled you're here."

"Are you?" the sleek woman asked, hovering behind the lady who'd opened the door. Her nostrils flared momentarily, like a cat smelling a stranger who wasn't supposed to be in her kitty condo.

But the curvier woman nudged her in the ribs and said, "Coop, this is our neighbor, Miss Cartwright. She owns Madam Zoltar's—you know, the psychic reading place just down the block? I'm Sist— Er, Trixie Lavender, by the way. And this is Coop."

I waved a hand at her as she took a step back, her

body language inviting me into their shop. "Just call me Stevie, please, and I'm not a psychic. I'm more of a medium. We just never changed the sign out of respect for the old Madam Zoltar. Pleasure to meet you both."

Coop swung her lustrous hair over her shoulder and looked me up and down with critical green eyes, her finely boned hands on her slender hips. "You're a medium?"

I fought a sigh. I was used to this kind of skepticism, but sometimes it rankled me. Tucking my purse under my arm, I handed the pastries over and forced a smile. "I talk to dead people."

Coop's jaw, sharp and well defined, pulsed before she sniffed the air again and finally stuck out her hand —or more like jammed it under my nose, but whatever. The move was aggressive, which I found odd, but who am I to judge? I talk to ghosts and have a pet turkey.

As though she hadn't heard my answer, Coop waved her fingers under my nose again to indicate I'd better shake it or die. At least that's what it felt like— the threat of death. And I took her slender fingers in mine because I didn't want to die. No, sir.

She gave my hand a good, hard pump and sort of wince-smiled. "Nice to meet you, Stevie Cartwright."

"Just Stevie is fine, Coop. Remember what I told you?" Trixie whispered to her friend with a pat on her arm then plastered another smile on her pretty face before looking me directly in the eyes. "How lovely you've brought us pastries. Are they from the local bakery?" She motioned for me to follow her, and I did, stepping over boxes and such to walk to the back of the store with Coop hot on my heels.

"They are! Are you familiar?"

Trixie threw her head back and laughed as she led me to a small table and chairs in their makeshift kitchen by a small white Formica countertop with a coffeepot. "I'm convinced I've gained at least ten pounds in a week from her bear claws. Oh, and those honey-almond muffins they mix with her angel's wings and the tears of the goddess of baked goods? I'll never be the same! I think we've had breakfast there at least every other day since we moved here."

I giggled. No one knew those heavenly creations better than I did. "Where did you guys come from, if you don't mind me asking?"

Trixie grabbed a worn chair with a spindle back and motioned for me to sit against the backdrop of some posters with famous celebrities and their tattoos. "Oregon. Deep in the backwoods of Oregon. Coffee?" she asked before she was at the small counter, reaching for a mug from a worn cardboard box.

Nodding with gratitude, I pulled my scarf off and set my purse on the tiny table, all while Coop's eyes followed my every move. "I'd love some, please. So what made you choose Eb Falls?"

She shrugged, her hair swishing across the tops of her shoulders in a silk curtain. "We needed a change of scenery, didn't we, Coop?"

A change of scenery—in Eb Falls? Sure, the tourist

season was great, but it might not pay the rent come winter.

Maybe tattoos were a better financial bet than mediums. Surely the business was brisker. Still, I was curious at her short, almost dismissive explanation—I couldn't help but get the feeling she was skirting the subject.

Or maybe I'm just itching to create a mystery where there is none. I'm mystery-starved, people—seeing shadows in dark corners that don't exist. Don't judge.

Coop pulled up a box and plopped down on top of it, her long legs sprawling out before her when, out of nowhere, she agreed with Trixie. "Yep. New scenery."

I couldn't tell if it was just me, but I felt as though Coop were vetting me. And I don't mean what I look like or my hair or even what I was wearing—I mean, digging around in my soul. Her gaze was frightfully intense until Trixie put her hand on Coop's shoulder and patted, almost like one would do when they were attempting to soothe an anxious pet.

"My, this Coop's quite edgy, eh, Dove?" Win asked, something he usually doesn't do when I'm interacting with other people so as not to distract me. For him to have noticed it as well meant I was right in my assessment. And then he added, "I vote we tread lightly."

And I hummed my agreement before I spoke. "Well, either way, whatever the reason, welcome to the neighborhood. If you need anything, anything at all, here's my card. Call me anytime. I'm happy to help." I dug in my purse, nudging a sleepy Belfry around before finding the ivory vellum business cards I'd recently had made for the store.

Coop snatched it from me with such force, the air whizzed with the snap of the printed card, making me blink, until Trixie once more put her hand on Coop's shoulder and squeezed without saying a single word.

Coop seemed to respond best to that, as though it were a secret signal between the two of them. She leaned back, looking at my card before tucking it into the back pocket of her leather pants, her almond-shaped green eyes never leaving my face.

I licked my suddenly dry lips. The vibe between us had gone all wonky and I wasn't sure where to take the conversation without this strange, beautiful creature named Coop chewing my face off. So I tied knots in my scarf and floundered awkwardly. Very unusual for me...I can make conversation with almost anyone.

"The tattoo, Stephania. Lest you forget why we're really here," Win prompted with a whisper.

And as he spoke again, Coop cocked her head, scanning the store's orange and yellow walls like she'd heard Win speak. But that was impossible, right?

She'd thrown me off my game is all. Everything appeared suspicious now.

It was time for a diversion. I wanted to get this conversation back on track to Pleasantville. We were to be neighbors. I wanted to keep it neighborly. "Anyway, would you mind if I asked you a quick question?"

Coop pushed off the cardboard box, using her hands for leverage on her thighs as she rose. "Yes. I would mind. I have work to do. I can't get work done if you're asking questions."

I blinked again. Er… I was at a loss for words, but Trixie passed a stern look to Coop before she said, "Why don't you go empty the boxes in the storeroom, Coop, and I'll help Stevie. Okay?"

Coop appeared to think about that for a moment before she turned on a booted heel and headed toward the back of the store, her hair swaying about her trim waist.

Instantly, Trixie's pretty face and sparkling brown eyes went apologetic. "I'm sorry. Coop spent a lot of her time isolated. She still does with the exception of the time she spends with me. Nuances to a conversation, even polite responses, elude her sometimes. She means no harm. She's just very direct and honest to a fault. Creative geniuses, you know?" was the explanation she gave for Coop's short demeanor. "I hope she didn't offend you."

I wondered how that was going to work out with a customer-oriented business. I also wondered why Trixie's explanation sounded so down pat. As though she'd rehearsed it in a mirror. Or again, maybe I was digging around for something that wasn't there.

Although, maybe Coop was autistic. That certainly could explain her odd behavior and her stilted social skills. And if that were the case, I'd make an extra effort to pay closer attention to her needs from this point forward. In fact, that I hadn't considered the notion beforehand left me disappointed in myself.

But I truly didn't think that was the case. I think she's just surly.

Still, I shrugged off Trixie's explanation and sipped at my coffee with a vague smile, still processing Coop in all her Coopness. "That's totally fine. Not a worry in the world."

Trixie tilted her head, her sweetly soft voice easing my agitated state. "So that question?"

"Oh, yes! Forgive me if I go about this the wrong way. I know nothing about tattoos. Anyway, I have a... friend who has a memory of a tattoo he once saw. I can only describe it, but I was wondering if you maybe had a book of designs I could look through—for reference. I've had no luck on the Internet so far. Or maybe if I describe it, it'll ring a bell? I wondered if it could be a universal tattoo. You know, like a beloved cartoon character that's popular? One you can personalize with an initial."

Trixie was up and moving toward a particularly large box labeled with Coop's name. She pulled out a big black binder and hauled it over to the small table while I glanced at my surroundings.

I'd been so caught up in figuring out Coop, I hadn't really given the place a good once over.

It needed work, no doubt. The walls were a bit off-putting in their orange and yellow, and the real wood floors, a light oak in color, needed a pass with a sander and a coat of gloss, but when the sun shone through the enormous picture window once summer came, it would be fantastic.

The space was large, with plenty of room for tattoo stations or whatever you called them.

Trixie dropped the binder on the table and told me to take a peek while she dug up more design books. "Some of those are Coop's personal designs, and some of the sketches are mine. Some are tattoos every artist in any shop from here to Hoboken can ink. They're called flash art—the ones that are, as you called them, universal."

Good to know…

As I flipped through the hundreds of pages in the book, I mused, "Ever seen a tattoo of a snake with a collar around his neck and a diamond in the center of it? I might be able to eliminate some of this hunt if you've seen something similar—"

Coop's guttural howl from the back room cut into my words, stopping all sound and motion from either of us. I was up on my feet in an instant, my heart thrashing in my chest, but Trixie put a hand to my arm and called out, "Coop? You okay back there?"

Yes, I prayed. *Please be okay back there. Please don't let that agonizing howl be the one you let out after a fresh kill.*

Stephania Cartwright! You take that back. Coop's shown no signs of violence.

But no sooner had I chastised myself for being an awful person than Coop was calling out to Trixie.

"You better come back here right now, Sister Trixie Lavender!" she bellowed.

Sister?

Yet, I had no time to ruminate over that strange title

before I was following Trixie, who was power walking to the back room.

Stopping short of the room's door, I heard Trixie gasp on a sharp, wheezing breath.

"*Coop?*" Trixie whispered in what definitely sounded like horror, her hand over her mouth.

When I peered over her shoulder, I gasped, too.

"That's Abe Levigne's stepson, Hank Morrison!" I blurted out, taking in the scene before me. My mouth fell open as I attempted to parse what to do next. And then I sprang into action, setting Trixie aside and kneeling down amongst the boxes and clutter to see if I could help him in some way.

But Coop grabbed my wrist before I could check for his pulse, her glittering eyes pinning me to the point of discomfort.

I pulled up my big girl britches and took control, because control needed taking. I looked up at her flawless face and managed to squeak, "Is he…?"

"Dead," Coop answered without so much as a bat of her luscious eyelashes. "He's definitely dead."

And just like that, this mystery lover finally had another puzzle to solve.

CHAPTER 3

I gulped as I rose to my feet and continued to lock eyes with Coop, who stood over Hank's crumpled body as though he were just another box she needed to unpack.

I glanced away only briefly and noted there were specks of blood on the front of her tan boot, but then I didn't see much blood around Hank at all. Maybe it wasn't blood? Maybe it was some sort of tattoo ink. There was a box labeled ink just behind her, after all. Could tattoo ink kill you if injected and how much did you need to do the job?

And why was I asking myself that question when I didn't even know what the murder weapon was yet?

Slow your roll, Stevie.

Trying to focus, I quickly glanced at Hank's immobile form. He was on his back, his expensive but casual tan suit jacket without so much as a wrinkle. Yet, his legs were positioned as though they'd crumpled beneath him, still bent at the knees. And the fake brown leather loafers he wore sported the white, chalky residue of the salt used to keep the sidewalks outside free of ice.

His sandy-blond hair had nary a strand out of place, still slicked back in that outdated pompadour he was so fond of, but that was all I was able to process before things got sticky.

Suddenly, Trixie was all sound and motion, reaching for her friend and taking her hand. "Coop! *What happened?*"

What happened? I couldn't believe she was asking what happened. Here's what happened: Glamazon went rogue and snuffed a guy out. That's what happened, coo-coo pants.

Admittedly, Hank wasn't the nicest guy and most of Eb Falls wasn't too fond of him, myself included. But we'd all loved Abe, who'd only just died a couple of months back. So we tried to be pleasant toward his stepson in honor of him—sort of a goodwill gesture. Yet, no matter how disagreeable he had been, he certainly didn't deserve to end up dead.

"We need to call 9-1-1," I urged, digging in my purse for my phone.

"No!" Trixie cried out, pushing Coop behind her in a protective gesture I found odd as all get out. Coop didn't need protecting. She'd cut your heart out and serve it on those snobby tasteless crackers Win was so fond of. I didn't doubt that for a second.

But Trixie's face, stricken with fear, spoke volumes.

Which I suppose I could understand if your BFF is a cold-blooded killer and she was caught in the act. But why would she want to protect a murderer? Unless…

"Stephania!" Win's harsh tone cut off my thoughts. "I see the wheels in your head turning. What's the first rule of Spy Club?"

I wanted to answer him with my typical snarky reply, which was, "What happens in Spy Club stays in Spy Club, except when dead spies refuse to share their secrets with their earthly contacts and let new members join their stupid club." But I refrained because I didn't want Trixie to think I was crazy as a bedbug.

"You must not jump to conclusions," he reminded with authority. "You must take in all the information around you before you simply assume this woman is guilty, and while she's quite antagonistic, you have no facts to place Hank's death at her doorstep. That's what the first rule of Spy Club is."

Blah-blah-blah. But he was right. So as I held my phone close to my chest, I eyed a terrified Trixie and an utterly unrepentant Coop. "We have to call the police, Trixie."

But she held up her shaking hands in a frantic gesture. "Wait! Please. Just wait a minute and let me find out what happened before we involve the police. *Please*. I'm begging you."

Okey-doke then. I know I openly gaped at her. Yet, there was something so raw about her plea. So desperate, and when she made the request sounding like the

American version of Mary Poppins, I had trouble denying her. How could such a warm, sweet-spoken woman be knee-deep in this abrasive Coop? Talk about opposites attracting.

On a deep, steadying breath, I looked her right in the eye. "Okay. I'll wait. But I want to know what happened, and I want to know right now. I knew Hank. I knew his stepfather, Abe. How did this happen, Coop?" I waved my hand in the direction of Hank's body and took a step back out into the hall.

But Coop just shrugged her slim shoulders, as unaffected as ever, and said, "I dunno. I came back to empty the boxes just like Sister... Um, just like Trixie asked, and when I moved that pile over there," she pointed to a stack to her left, next to a shelving unit, "I found him all crumpled up like a piece of paper. I almost tripped on him."

Why did Coop keep calling Trixie *sister*? Maybe they were sisters? I hadn't thought of that, though they looked nothing alike. But then maybe they were adopted?

That puzzle was for a much later conversation. For now, we needed to establish what had happened to Hank.

My eyes darted from Hank's body to Coop and back again. "Does that explain the blood on your boot? You tripped on his body?" I asked, forcing my terror to the furthest recesses of my mind.

I realize it's not like I haven't encountered a killer, but there was something about Coop that truly frightened me on a deeper level than some murderer with a gun.

"Probably," she said casually, daring me to say otherwise with those amazing eyes of hers.

"Probably?" I squawked, waving my phone around like a samurai sword. *"Probably?"*

Okay. The waiting game was over. I was going to call the police. Hopefully, Officer Foreign Object Stuffed Up His Butt was on duty and he'd handle this. I began to dial a very familiar number.

But Trixie took a leap toward me, grabbing my wrist, her face red, her eyes full of unshed tears. "Please wait, Stevie. *Please*. I need you to listen to me. If Coop says she found him like this, I know she's telling the truth. It's not in her to lie."

Now that was rich. I fought barking a laugh as I yanked my arm away and took another step backward. "That's insane. No one ever really knows anyone, and there's no way you can possibly convince me it's not in her to lie. I'm sure Jeffrey Dahmer's parents thought he didn't lie either, and look how that turned out." Speaking of Dahmer... "And wait one minute," I hissed. "How do I know the two of you weren't in cahoots?"

Now, that was the dumbest question ever uttered by an amateur sleuth. Why would they murder Hank and wait until I showed up to announce his death? It was about as likely as the notion *Vogue* was going to call and ask me to be on their cover.

But what can I say? I was a little rattled. Not just by

Hank's death, but by Coop's nonchalance about a dead man in their storage room.

Trixie took in a ragged breath, her chest heaving up and down, her neck a mottle red. "I'm begging you, Stevie. *Please listen.* Coop isn't... She's not like most people. She—"

"And that's her alibi? She isn't like most people? Most people aren't like the Zodiac Killer either, but lookie there—a serial killer! A killer's a killer. Period." I backed away until I was almost pressed up against the orange and yellow wall of the hallway.

Out of nowhere, Coop suddenly straightened, her spine stiff, her face no longer aggressive but quite passive and, dare I say, confused.

She shook her head with a vehement motion, making her hair swing. "Kill Hank H. Morrison? Oh, no, Stevie Cartwright the medium. I would never kill someone who didn't deserve to be killed."

"*Coop!*" Trixie hissed, her eyes flashing all manner of signals to her friend who, hand to heart, looked about as confused as a mouse in a maze.

"Something is amok here, Dove. Something deep below the surface of this woman. I almost smell it. I know you'll think me bananapants, as you so crassly point out when I make an observation you don't like, but I find I believe her."

Ooooo! I hated when Win had a point to make, and he made it at a time when I couldn't defend my own point of view. Which was, this was nuts and I could be in danger.

"Coop," Trixie pleaded, turning back to face her friend. "Stop talking. Please. Just let me handle this."

Coop snapped her mouth shut, turning her lips into a thin line and crossing her arms over her chest.

My gaze narrowed in her direction and it took everything I had not to turn tail and run.

So what made me stay? Win and his stupid spy gut. Sure, I could chalk up his notion to the idea that maybe he was on Coop's side because she was flat out a stone-cold fox. And yes, I'm going there because that's always where I go these days. I can't help but take the jealous route. It's pathetic, but in the interest of honesty, I'm not playing games with myself.

However, Win wouldn't put me in danger no matter how appealing Coop is.

So, taking into account Win's gut, I decided to fish around a bit. I only knew a little about Hank, but one thing was for sure. He owned a lot of real estate via his stepfather Abe's passing.

"Do you know Hank? Isn't he your landlord? Didn't he inherit this place after his stepfather passed?"

If that were true, it would explain why he'd been in the tattoo parlor. Hank wasn't the kind of guy who had tattoos, or at least not any visible ones. But he *was* the kind of guy who liked money.

Just ask the Thursday night poker crowd of middle-aged men in Eb Falls. Hank liked to win, and he was a notorious sore loser, but tattoos? Not his thing.

Trixie inhaled a gulp of air and bounced her head.

"Yes. He owns this building and several others on this block, I think."

"He was mean," Coop added for good measure, rocking from foot to foot, two bright spots of red on her cheeks.

"Coop!" Trixie fairly screamed before she appeared to gather herself and shake off her panic.

I cocked my head, eyeballing the front door and trying to remember if Trixie had locked it behind me in case I needed to make a quick escape.

Yet, I couldn't resist asking, "Mean how, Coop?"

But Trixie intervened before Coop had the chance to open her mouth. "When we originally rented the store, the price was much more manageable. But we rented it from Abe, and by the time we got here, Abe had died and Hank was in charge. He upped our rent. It's no big deal. We'll make it work."

"You're not telling the truth, Sister Trixie," Coop crowed like a child who catches their parent fibbing. "He lied and said he couldn't find any paperwork on our lease and that must mean it didn't really exist. *Then* he charged us more money."

"Didn't you have a copy of the lease Abe signed?" I asked, avoiding looking down at Hank's body, though I knew I'd have to if I intended to figure out his murder.

Trixie's shoulders slumped in defeat as she jammed her hands into the pockets of her jeans. "I looked everywhere and couldn't find it when the time came to defend our position and prove he wasn't being truthful. I'm usually so careful about things like this, but I have no idea where it went. I had a copy of it on my laptop, but then my laptop crashed and, well…it was just easier to let things be."

Coop's perfectly arched eyebrow rose. "You said we shouldn't make a fuss because we didn't need any more troub—"

"Coop! Honest to gracious, I'm going to put a dirty sock in your mouth if you don't can it!"

I watched the silent warning conversation between Trixie and Coop play out via their eyes, and I was left feeling uneasy. If Hank was going to raise their rent, and it made Coop angry, she had motive to kill him. So did Trixie for that matter. But would they be so care-less as to do it here in their own store while I'm here?

How long had Hank been dead, anyway?

But none of that made a difference. The police still had to be called. And I said as much.

"You do realize there's no escaping calling the police, don't you, Trixie?" I kept my voice as sympa-thetic as possible. Trixie's panic was truly troubling me.

"Stevie Cartwright is correct," Coop offered without so much as a pause. "The police must be called. It's the rules. I saw it on the television. I think the show was called *Snapped*. And we can't wait too long or they'll become suspicious."

Trixie let her head fall back on her shoulders in clear frustration. "Coop! No more!" she growled.

I didn't know what to say to Coops assessment, but I was calling the police anyway. Looking to Trixie, I sighed in resignation. "I have to call the police, Trixie. *I have to*. But most of the Eb Falls Police Department is pretty decent. If Coop just explains—"

Trixie's breath shuddered in and out, fear written all over her face, cutting off my words. "But they'll have no choice but to question Coop ,and she's, as you can see, very direct in nature. They'll twist her words and—"

"It's going to be all right," Coop reassured her friend, grabbing her by the shoulders and forcing her to focus. "I'm going to tell the truth, and you always say the truth will set you free. They won't have a choice but to set me free because I didn't do anything wrong."

I couldn't get a clear read on the dynamic of their relationship, but I knew the ride home with Win and Arkady was going to be filled with speculative conversation. Sometimes it came off as though Trixie were the moral compass helping Coop understand the world around her, and at moments, Coop didn't appear as though she needed anyone to guide her. Yet, she always deferred to Trixie.

And why was Trixie so worried about Coop being misinterpreted? She appeared pretty straightforward to me.

Trixie hugged Coop and patted her cheek. "You're right, friend. I know you are, but..."

I looked to Trixie, my eyes sympathetic. I saw how torn she was, and I wanted to give her the benefit of the doubt, but I had to call the police. It was my duty to justice for all.

Plus, when I didn't call the police, I ended up with

the sour disapproval of Officer Stodgy and an angry, very vocal Detective Sean Moore who still wasn't over the fact that his partner had been a cold-blooded murderer who'd almost killed me. Sometimes, I almost thought he blamed me for Detective Montgomery's criminal shenanigans.

I put a hand on her arm. "Trixie?"

A tear slipped from her eye, but she nodded in resignation, using her thumb to swipe at the salty drop. "I know you mean well, Stevie. I just wish I could..." Then she paused and sighed. "Never mind. Go ahead, Stevie. Call them."

I hated the defeated tone in her voice. I hated that I was the reason she was defeated.

"I think you guys should step out of the room. Just in case of contamination," I advised.

As I dialed 9-1-1, Trixie drove her hand under Coop's arm and pulled her away from Hank and out into the hallway, while I explained to the operator the scene that lie before me.

And as I spoke to the operator, my heart grew heavy and my stomach turned.

CHAPTER 4

"*M*iss Cartwright."

"Officer Inflexible."

Dana Nelson, my friend and foe, tipped his sharply defined, clean-shaven jaw in my direction, pushing his way inside past the small crowd that had gathered just outside Inkerbelle's.

He came to stand in front of me, his eyes cheerful as he perused my face. "That's a new one."

I nodded and grinned, pleased with myself. Tucking my purse strap around my shoulder, I moved back to let him enter the store, lifting my face to let the frigid air that swept in when he came through the open door cool my hot cheeks. "I looked up synonyms for rigid with you in mind. You like?"

He tamped down a smile and popped his lips. "I'm not unhappy."

"Oh, good. Because just when you think you're

getting used to it, I'm going to find a new adjective and then poof—mind blown."

He pulled out his notepad from the pocket of his crisply perfect uniform and eyed me, still not smiling, but his eyes were twinkling. "I await the blowing of my mind. Until then, you wanna grab some coffee tonight? My treat. I'd like to talk to you about something."

I drove a playful knuckle into his upper arm and chuckled. "Only if it includes a cupcake at Strange Brew—a strawberry one with that hazelnut chocolate frosting on it."

He sucked in his cheeks, his gaze pensive. "Will we make Forrest uncomfortable?"

I shook my head. Forrest was no longer a concern—he'd found a new love. A freshly divorced physical therapist he'd met when his grandfather, Chester (and one of my favorite people in the whole world) had some knee surgery recently. I'd seen them canoodling when I'd gone to visit Chester in the rehab department of our local hospital, and had taken a huge sigh of relief at the sight.

Chester was one of the first people to embrace me when I came back to Eb Falls—he was the first to defend me when I was accused of murder, too. And he was a curmudgeonly, sweet, elderly gentleman I adored as though he were my own grandfather. That I found myself too distracted by Win to date his grandson with any sort of end goal in mind didn't trouble Chester at all. He never gave me a moment's grief over it when he realized I wasn't interested.

But Forrest had been distant for a few months or so after our breakup, and I respected that by keeping my distance from his coffee shop—even if I missed the coffee and cupcakes. So I was thrilled to see him so happy with his new ladylove. They made a lovely couple and I wished him well.

Rocking back on my heels, I said, "Nope. He's moved on, and so have I. So cupcakes and coffee tonight?" I admit, I was very curious to know what he wanted to talk about, but I didn't dare delve into that now.

"Deal." Then his face went all police-officer-ish severe and hard, the way it does when things are about to get serious. "And now, I have to do my job. Which means you have to answer some questions."

As though the gods of detecting heard Officer Nelson, in strolled Detective Sean Moore, a.k.a. Starsky (the one I mentioned had lost his Hutch to prison essentially because of me), and Melba Kaepernick, Officer Nelson's squeeze.

I mean, I *think* she's his main squeeze. He'll never confirm or deny, but I can tell you this, they sure looked cozy in my living room when Dana babysat little Sebastian for me over the summer.

I loved Melba. She was irreverent and funny and just the breath of fresh air I needed in an earthbound friend. We'd spent some time together these last months, having dinner here and there when her crazy schedule allowed, and occasionally vintage thrift shopping, and while she was closed-mouthed about Dana, her cheeks always turned red if I mentioned him in passing.

Melba waved to me, pushing her way past the onlookers and coming to stand beside Detective Moore. She no longer dressed like she was headed to the club. She'd gone all professional and serious since she'd joined Eb Falls PD, in her dark slacks, black fitted shirt and black blazer. Her piercings in her eyebrows and lower lip were gone, too, and her braids, while still in cornrows on her head, were now smoothed back into a neat bun at the back of her head.

"Heyyy, Stevie-B!" she chirped, her infectious grin infiltrating the serious atmosphere. "I hear you have trouble. Yep. That's what I heard." Then she looked to Dana, her pretty eyes revealing nothing about their relationship when he cocked his head in inquiry. "I got it from here, Officer Nelson."

He nodded his head with a curt bounce and said, "I'm sure you do."

I smiled because they were cute—so cute. No one would ever know they were involved if they didn't know them unprofessionally, they were nothing if not decorous around their fellow officers. But *I* knew, and I couldn't help but be secretly pleased because I love love.

When Dana took his leave, Melba turned to me, her eyes searching mine. "So, trouble, yeah?"

I nodded, noting through the big picture window, some shop owners had also begun to gather outside and mingle in the crowd of Eb Fallers who'd been willing to risk the snow and come into town—Forrest among them.

Meeting her eyes, I agreed then looked away and hitched my jaw in Coop's general direction as she talked to Detective Moore to our left. "Yes. Definitely trouble."

Melba latched onto my arm and whispered, "Who's the supermodel? Does she own the place?"

Good question. Who *was* the stunning Coop? I just shrugged. "I'm not sure, to be honest. I came in to welcome them and then whammo. Dead guy."

"Who's the dead guy?" Melba asked as she pulled out her pad and began to write.

I gulped. I've seen a lot of dead bodies since moving to Eb Falls, but it's something I'm never going to get used to. "Hank Morrison."

"Egads. Poor guy. Didn't his stepfather just die?"

Eb Falls was a small town—everyone knew everyone, and if Melba knew of Hank, she also knew he was rather surly. I hope that was taken into account. "Yes. Abe died a few months ago and left him all of his real estate holdings, apparently."

Melba circled her now-ringless index finger around the room. "Did he own this place, too?"

I winced. It wasn't like I could hide the facts, but I knew I was helping dig graves here. The police would get wind of that bit of info Trixie had revealed about the lease agreement. I didn't doubt it for a second. But they weren't going to get it from me.

So I nodded again, tucking my hair behind my ear. "He sure did."

"Ahhh," she muttered, scribbling on her pad. She didn't need me to tell her anything else. "Any clue how or what happened?"

"Nope."

Melba ran her tongue along the inside of her cheek, her eyes skeptical. "What's with the one-word answers? You always have a theory, Stevie. What's your theory?"

My theory was shut my yap before I dug a deeper hole for Coop and Trixie. Call it intuition, but I believed *Trixie* believed Coop was innocent. Whether she was or not—and I didn't want to be the one to sway Melba in one direction or the other, because I needed solid facts before I tarred and feathered Coop—was still unclear for me.

I didn't have any facts, and I think we all know how bad it can look if the facts are misinterpreted. After the mess with Madam Zoltar, I'm the perfect example of an alleged suspect who'd have never made it out of that interrogation room alive if not for Win's lawyer.

So I kept my face passive and my spine relaxed, toying with the strap on my purse. "A theory? I don't have one."

Melba nudged me in the ribs, the sound of her crisp suit jacket rustling in the store's hushed vibe. "Do too. You have a theory about who keeps mixing the oranges with the lemons at the grocery store, so I know you have one about this. You were right here, Stevie."

I flapped a hand at her, but I didn't look her in the

eye. "I do not have a theory about the lemons and the oranges. I do not."

That wasn't necessarily true. I *did* have a theory. Mr. Gorman thought the lemons and the oranges should be side by side for ease of shopping. Plus, they were both citruses and right next to the grapefruits—all citruses, yes? Mr. Gorman made a good point.

Yet, Ansel Feldman, our senior citizen green grocer, disagreed, and refused to move the lemons. But who else was that invested in the lemons? I sure didn't care where they were.

It had to be Mr. Gorman. And I'd shared that theory with Melba in my desperation to create a mystery needing solving. I'd even asked her to inquire about the store's security cameras and whether she could look at them in an official capacity.

Of course, she'd refused to entertain me and abuse her power as a detective, and she's right not to give in to me. But again, in retrospect, I guess I'm hungrier for something other than mooning over Win than I thought.

Melba made a face at me, her brow furrowing. "You do so, and I'm not going to go into it now, but you were pretty close to tipping right over the edge when I told you I wouldn't ask to see security-camera footage. And don't deny it, because you sure were. Yep-yep, you were. So what do you know, Stevie? Don't hold back anything and forget we're friends for the moment." She leaned into me. "Also, be grateful Starsky's questioning the supermodel and not *you*."

My disdain for Starsky…er, Detective Moore, was known far and wide. "Small favors and all," I muttered to her. "Well, what do you want to know?"

Winking, she pointed to the chair I'd sat in earlier while Trixie made me coffee. "Good Stevie," she teased. "Play nice with the detective. Have a seat, and let's get down to the biz."

An hour later, my one-word answers and vague relaying of finding Hank's body were pushing all of Melba's buttons. In other words, she was going to kill me once she was off duty and could get her hands around my throat, if the two bright crimson spots on her cheeks were any indication.

Rubbing her temples wearily, Melba's usually unruffled feathers were officially ruffled. "Are you sure that's all you know, Stevie? This isn't like you. You know every detail about everything you lay eyes on. I'm not buying this song and dance you're giving me." She tapped the near-empty pad with her pen.

Leaning back in the chair, I yawned, hoping Melba wouldn't hate me for my evasiveness. I just couldn't feed Coop to the wolves with Trixie so upset. Not yet. Something held me back—that something was probably Win's doubt, but whatever.

Besides, I'd truly told her everything I saw. I just left out the panic in Trixie's voice and her warning to Coop to keep quiet.

As a diversion tactic, I looked toward the bunch of police officers milling about with yellow tape and caught a glimpse of more snow falling outside.

Melba tapped an unpolished nail on the table's surface. "Stevie? Talk to me. Tell me what you saw."

"That's it. I told you everything. I think I was distracted by the pastries and coffee. You know how much I love the bakery's éclairs, and I was especially looking forward to the yummy, chocolatey goodness on such a cold and blustery day…"

Pushing back the chair until the legs scraped on the wood floor, Melba rose, her eyes narrowed in suspicion in my direction. "I don't know what you're up to, Stevie, but—"

"I already told you, Hank was a bad, bad man!" Coop yelled from the far corner of the room just opposite where I sat with Melba. Her slender but strong form was pressed up against the orange wall near the big picture window, the wall where all the celebrity tattoo posters hung. Starsky was being Starsky by breathing down her neck, his face a blotchy red, his stance antagonistic.

They'd separated Trixie and Coop, which was standard procedure, and that left Coop defenseless. Somehow, that bothered me.

But why?

She rose up on tippy toes to yell in Detective Moore's face—still as beautiful as she'd been when she'd placidly refused to answer my questions. "He told lies! Sometimes when you tell lies, you end up punished. The wrath of Beelzebub is waiting for him in—"

"*Coop!*" Now *I* was the one yelling her name. To my

credit, I moved pretty quickly in my boots and winter gear, getting her attention before she said anything else.

Detective Moore used slimy tactics to get the answers he wanted, and I wasn't sure if Coop would react violently when what she really needed to do was keep her cool and her answers succinct.

I managed to get to her and give Detective Moore a stern look. "She's not answering any more of your questions until she has a lawyer present, Starsky. So lay off the interrogation tactics and back up, please." Putting myself between him and Coop, I attempted to shoo him away.

But he was having none of it. His nostrils flared and his chest pumped up and down under his dark blazer as he gave me a look of disdain. "You just can't keep your nose out of things, can you, Miss Cartwright?"

I smirked a smile and shook a finger up at him. "Aw, Detective Crabby Patty. C'mon. Don't be like that. I'm not sticking my nose anywhere. I'm just keeping you on the straight and narrow. And you know as well as I do this lady can ask for a lawyer at any time and you have to let her have one. Don't make me break out the *Cops for Dummies* book and show you where it says when a suspect is being questioned—and I think we both know by the way you're grilling her like a piece of chicken, you think she's a suspect—she can request a lawyer. Them's the rules, Starsky. I didn't make 'em, but they exist."

He seethed down at me. Yes, he sure did. Literally

seethed. "She didn't ask for one. *You* asked for one for her."

I turned my back to him with purpose and looked to Coop. "You want a lawyer, don't you, Coop?" I prayed the signals I sent her with my eyes were easy to read and she'd pick up on them.

But she looked down at me with such confused vulnerability, I actually wanted to hug her. Where that had come from, I don't know, but she looked so lost, I immediately wanted to comfort her. "What is that, Stevie Cartwright?"

Now *I* was confused. "What is what, Coop?"

"A lawyer. What is a lawyer?"

Oh, dear. What had I done?

"Oh, that's real cute, lady. Pretending you don't know what a lawyer is," Detective Moore sneered over my head right in Coop's face. "Funny. Funny. Just like our Miss Cartwright with the wisecracks."

As he spoke, in his anger for me, he moved too close to my back for my comfort. I gritted my teeth, fighting for composure. "*Please* back up, Detective Moore."

"What Stevie Cartwright said. Please back up, Detective Moore," Coop parroted my words.

"I'll do no such thing. Now, move along, Miss Cartwright, before I move you myself. You're inter-fering with police business!" he grated out stubbornly, his breathing ragged.

His hand grazed my shoulder, making me turn to bark at him, "I will *not* move out of the way, and if you don't back off right now, Detective Moore, I'm going to—"

I never finished my sentence. Coop finished my interaction with Detective Moore by virtually leaping past me, grabbing Starsky by the neck and hurling him across the room to the floor as though he were light as a feather—where she proceeded to raise her fist high in the air and aim right for his nose.

"*Cooooop, noooooo!*" I bellowed, but I was too late. Man, she was quick, I realized as crimson blood gushed from Starsky's nose where she'd popped him one but good.

I'm pretty sure in the *Cops for Dummies* rulebook; you can get in big, big trouble for assaulting an officer of the law.

Which meant, Coop was in big, big trouble.

Oh, heavens. So big.

CHAPTER 5

*A*s Detective Moore was being scooped off the floor and half-carried, half-walked out the door by Officer Nelson, who'd shoved a tissue in his hand to thwart his bloody nose, Trixie approached Coop with a calmness I don't know I would have possessed, were I in her shoes.

Sandwich had arrived, and he was busy getting his cuffs out to secure Coop, who had to be pulled off Detective Moore by no less than three officers.

She'd howled up a storm as they'd attempted to pull her from his face until Trixie ordered her to stop. Everything went silent with Coop from that moment on.

"Coop? What the hay happened? Do you have any idea how bad this is?" Trixie asked on a ragged breath, her soft, comforting voice rising just a hair in her anguish.

She looked harried, making my heart clench tighter.

She'd pulled her knit cap off to reveal a streak of blue in her hair I hadn't seen earlier, the shiny strands tousled from her running her fingers through them, and her eyes were positively haunted.

Coop's face crumpled, as if disappointing Trixie would bring about her very own emotional apocalypse. "He was going to hurt Stevie. I know it. I *felt* it. He was very, very angry with Stevie Cartwright. I like her. I couldn't let him do that, Trixie! It's not nice or polite at all. When a lady asks you to back up, you back up," Coop vehemently insisted, her stance on how a man should treat a lady clear and firm. "You said so yourself. You must always treat everyone with respect."

Was Trixie Coop's life coach? It appeared as though she was always coaching Coop on how to react to situations. I just wasn't getting the connection between them—the thread that tethered them together. What had brought these two very different women together and made them open, of all things, a tattoo shop?

And what did she mean by she *felt* Detective Moore was going to hurt me? The hackles on the back of my neck rose. Was she an intuit? Empath? I'd known a couple in my time.

No. That was crazy. Wasn't it? What were the chances someone with abilities like that would land in Eb Falls?

Trixie was beside herself as Sandwich cuffed Coop and directed her to sit in the chair I'd just vacated. "I'm going to ask you nicely to sit and remain calm, Miss...?"

"Coop. It's just Coop," Trixie provided as she put a protective hand on Coop's shoulder.

Sandwich nodded, his broad, normally cheerful face and typically happy demeanor suddenly quite serious. He looked down at Coop, who'd done as he'd asked. "Okay, Coop it is. Can I count on you to stay seated for me?"

She nodded solemnly, but she didn't speak, making my heart ache. Her confusion was killing me, mostly due to the fact that I didn't understand it, but she'd attacked Detective Moore in my defense.

In my book, that meant something, as misguided and strange as it appeared. She'd been looking out for me. I believed that much, even if I was still on the fence about whether she'd hurt Hank Morrison. Clearly, she was capable of serious bodily harm, and that didn't work in her favor.

"Will you come with me, Miss Lavender?" Sandwich asked, motioning she should head away from Coop.

Trixie looked to me, her eyes filled with tangible fear, but I quickly reassured her. "You go with Sandwich. Um, I mean Officer Paddington. He's a good guy. Swear it. I'll look after Coop. Promise, she's in good hands." I gave her an encouraging smile, even though I was feeling anything but encouraging.

But it was enough to set her into motion. Twisting her hands together, Trixie squared her shoulders and nodded. "Thanks, Stevie."

I knelt down in front of Coop, putting a hand on

her knee and looking up into her ethereal face curtained by her glorious hair. "Coop, are you okay? Are you hurt anywhere?"

"Am I in trouble?" she asked, and the first hint she was afraid showed up in the way of her lower lip trembling. "I didn't mean to make trouble, Stevie Cartwright. I'm supposed to lay low, but hitting the angry detective isn't laying low, is it?"

Oh, she was in so much trouble, and as I tried to understand her, and to understand how she'd managed to throw a grown man twice her size down on the ground as though he were a limp fish, I tempered my words.

Squeezing her knee, I patted it and said, "I don't know what's going to happen, Coop. But I can assure you, I'll tell Detective Moore's superiors he was becoming quite cross with us and using unnecessary force to get answers from you. But forget that for a second. Will you promise me something?"

"I don't know. Promises are tricky things," she answered honestly, her green eyes unsure.

This just kept getting odder by the minute, but I pushed forward anyway. "Well, this is an easy promise. Don't say anything more to the police until we can get you someone to make sure your rights are protected, okay? That's what a lawyer does. Promise me right now, Coop."

Looking directly at me, her eyes honed in on my face with such depth in them, such honesty, I almost lost my breath. "I promise."

"Repeat it," I demanded. "I promise not to answer any more questions from anyone unless it's Stevie or Trixie until I have a lawyer present."

She repeated my words verbatim, satisfying me just before Melba came to take her to the station for further questioning. As I followed them toward the door, Melba holding her arm with care, I had already begun reaching for my phone seconds before Win suggested I call our lawyer, Luis Lipton.

"We can't allow this, Stephania!" Win whisper-yelled in my ear. "Get Luis on the phone posthaste."

"On it," I muttered under my breath, my eyes swerving to Coop being led away.

The way Coop's head hung between her shoulders, her chin almost touching her chest, the way her spine nearly collapsed as she walked with Melba as her guide, made my heart writhe painfully.

And I had no explanation for why. I only knew she suddenly looked like a vulnerable child, lost and alone, and I couldn't bear that.

I made my way out of the store and onto the snowy sidewalk, stopping to see if there was anything I could do for Trixie, who wasn't letting Coop very far out of her sight as she was placed in the police car. All while everyone stood around and gawked.

I loved my Eb Fall folks, but sometimes they were too dang nosy for their own good.

First, I glared at my neighbors and fellow shop owners under the gloomy glare of the sky. "Give the girl a break, lookieloos, would you? Nothing to see here. Go on about your business." I shooed them with my icy hands as they began to scatter.

Forrest put a hand under my elbow and looked down at me, his eyes full of concern, his handsome face sharp and angular. "You okay, Stevie?"

I patted his arm. "I'm fine, Forrest. Say hello to Chester for me, would you? Tell him I can't wait to see our hydrangeas this year." Then I reached for Trixie's arm, pulling my jacket off as I did. "Take this. You'll freeze to death if you don't."

Her eyes began to water as the snow pelted her porcelain skin and she took the jacket from me. "You've been very kind, Stevie," she said on a hoarse, tear-filled whisper. "Thank you."

"Tell me what I can do, Trixie. How can I help right now? Do you want me to come to the station and stay with you while they question Coop?"

"*No!*" she fairly hissed. But then she straightened and visibly regained her attempt at composure. "No, thank you. I don't want you to get any further involved, Stevie. Please. I'm sorry you're involved in this mess to begin with."

Without thinking, I ignored her plea. "Well, I'm coming anyway. So how do you like them apples?" I zipped the jacket, tucking it around her neck, and dug in my purse for my keys, beeping my car open. "But first, do you even have a way to get to the police station?"

She swallowed hard, her throat working up and down before she spoke. "I don't know..." Her eyes wandered to Coop in the back of the police cruiser, totally distracting her as she placed a hand on the frosty back window to let her friend know she was there.

"Trixie!" I yelped on a shiver. "Stay here with me and answer the question. Do you have a car to get to the police station? If not, I'll drive you."

She pointed to the parking lot by the food trucks, as yet unplowed, and nodded. "Yes. I have a car. It's..." she gulped in more air. "It's the rust bucket of a Caddy."

My eyes veered to the parking lot, where I saw an old, beat-up white Caddy, maybe a late-seventies model, with more rust than I'd ever seen on a car still capable of running. "Does it work?"

"Yes," she said, suddenly in motion as she pulled a pair of keys from her jeans, her brow furrowed. "Thank you again, Stevie. But I really have to go now." And then she was off and running across the road to get to her beat-up car.

I ran to mine, desperate to get inside and turn up the heat. As I pulled the driver's side door open, I jumped inside and set my purse on the passenger seat, my teeth chattering violently.

Putting my hands on the steering wheel, I leaned forward, resting my head on my icy digits, tears springing to my eyes. "What a mess," I groaned on a sniffle.

"Indeed, Dove. Now let's talk this out, yes?"

"*Dah, malutka*. Let us put our brains together. I have many questions."

"Heads, good man. It's put our heads together, and we must do exactly that. Surely, amongst the three of us, we can figure this out."

I sure hoped so because seeing Coop and Trixie like that had torn me up.

Bel climbed up the interior of my purse and poked his precious head out with a shiver. "Something ain't right about that Coop, Boss."

"Explain, Bel," I prompted, scooping him up in the palm of my hand to tuck him into my neck, rubbing my cheek against his fur to ward off the swirl of emotions I was trying to parse.

He burrowed into my hair and shivered. "Well, besides the fact that she's unnaturally gorgeous, I just have a feeling. And I don't mean she's off as in her rocker, she's just not like everybody else, and I can't explain why I think that aside from the fact that she's as strong as Hercules. But I know I'm right."

"Yes! Yes, mate!" Win praised Bel. "That's exactly how I feel as well. The impression I get of the fair Coop is she doesn't understand social cues and body language. Thus, her blatant honesty becomes abrasive to the rest of us who hide behind propriety. And she is *unnaturally* strong. I almost cheered when she hurled Detective Moore across the room. He deserved no less for his appalling behavior. Though, she's paid a pretty price for doing such."

I thought about Coop's insane strength for a moment while the heat gushed from the vents in my car. True, she was unnaturally strong. But the kind of strength she exhibited didn't come from doing P90-X.

Yet, that fact didn't faze me as much as others. "Do you think what Trixie said is true? That Coop doesn't have it in her to lie?"

"It was a strange thing to say, yes, my pickled herring?" Arkady surmised. "Who is not capable of lying? No one I say! But her behavior is so peculiar. I am still figuring out this enigma named Coop. Little ball of fluff is right. There is something more to her than just pretty face."

My sigh was ragged as guilt ate up my guts. "Okay, so yes. Everyone is capable of lying. But it's a curious thing to say, don't you think? And what's the relationship between these two women, and... Why the heck do I feel like I just helped send a lamb to slaughter?"

"You did the right thing, Dove," Win whispered in my ear, instantly easing my stress. "You only told Melba the facts. Most of them anyway. I know you hid some of the emotional reactions you had to the very strange proclamations Trixie made, and that Coop didn't seem at all troubled by Hank's body at her feet. But those aren't necessarily needed in an investigation. Don't your lawyers here in the states throw out anything but the facts anyway?"

I bounced my head, running a finger over my suddenly aching temples. "Sometimes they do, unless they can somehow twist the information to their advantage. But Melba knows something's up, Win. She's right about my theories, and she's right that I can't help theorizing even the smallest mystery. But no one can prove I heard what I heard. I'm hoping I can leave it at that without getting in too deep because what I heard…"

"*Dah*," Arkady mumbled.

Dah, indeed.

Pulling my phone from my purse, I clicked the camera icon. I'd taken pictures of the crime scene while we'd waited for the police to arrive.

I'd been so caught up with Trixie's explanations and Coop's strange behavior over Hank, I hadn't had time to pay attention to the details of Hank's body and the condition of the storage room.

Also, for a few minutes, I'd been afraid they'd had a hand in killing him, so I panicked. But I managed to get it together, and I was grateful I had, feeling the way I did now about Coop.

"I took pictures of the crime scene. We need to take them home, load them on my laptop, blow them up, and see what we can see, because you do know there's no chance we'll get back into that store until forensics has cleared the scene."

"Well done, Dove, but first, I think we should head to the police station and see if we can't lend Trixie some moral support, eh? I get the feeling she and Coop are alone in this world. I think we both know what that particular feeling is like."

Nodding, I looked in my side-view mirror to be sure it was clear to pull out, and headed to the Eb Falls Police Station, lost in my thoughts.

None of us said a word, likely due to the fact that this was all so strange. Coop was strange. Trixie's reactions were strange. Hank's death was strange.

A very normal, mundane day had turned strange, but I was taking no pleasure in this. None at all. Yes, I know I've been a bit bored without some kind of crime to solve, but I didn't want innocent people to get hurt in order to do it.

And I was leaning toward the idea Coop really was innocent.

As I pulled into a parking space, I watched poor Trixie run toward the entrance, her face wet with tears I could see from where I was sitting, and my heart turned over in my chest again.

Deciding it was better to wait a moment or two to compose myself before I went in waving my flag of justice, I scrolled aimlessly through the pictures I'd taken of Hank's body.

Surprisingly, I'd managed to take decent enough shots, getting all angles of not only Hank's body, but the room as well.

One of Hank in particular caught my eye. He was sprawled out on the floor, his legs at an awkward angle just like I remembered, but there was something near his shoulder, almost tucked under it. I used my fingers to make it larger and narrowed my eyes.

And then we all gasped.

"Are you seeing what I'm seeing, Mini-Spy?" Win asked, his tone filled with the shock coursing through my veins.

Swallowing hard, I nodded, turning my phone sideways to be sure. "I think I am. I wish I wasn't, but I think I am."

"Holy Toledo!" Bel chirped, pushing his way from behind the hair at the nape of my neck. "Is that what I think it is, Winterbutt?"

"*Dah.* Is what you think it is, Fluffybutt," Arkady retorted in somber tones.

Yep. There it was. Right there on the floor.

A tattoo gun.

And I'd lay bets, it was also the murder weapon.

CHAPTER 6

"So do we still think she's innocent?" I squeaked out the question, but just barely.

Win scoffed as I stared at the front of the Eb Falls Police Department building, the brick façade made brighter maroon by the oppressive gloom of the day. "We don't know the tattoo gun is what killed him, Stephania. It could have been anything. They have to test the ink first. And as a by the by, the tattoo gun alone couldn't kill him. People get neck tattoos all the time, and they don't die. There would have to have been some kind of poison involved, Dove."

Yeah, yeah. As though poison were out of the realm of possibility. *Suuure.*

As the snow began to really fall again, I conceded, staring aimlessly out into the curtain of white. "So then I vote killer unicorn. They're rampant here in Eb Falls, you know. Literally everywhere, always jumping over rainbows and shooting glitter from their butts. Messy stuff, glitter."

"Bah! Don't talk such nonsense. You have no proof the tattoo gun is what killed him."

Running my hand through my damp hair, I conceded again. "Nope. I sure don't, but I've come to the conclusion where we're concerned, Murphy's Law prevails, and if it looks like a duck, and quacks like a duck—wait for it—surprise! It's a *duck*. I'd bet a year's worth of Twinkies something was in that ink in *Coop's* gun."

"What is this duck? This is not a duck. Arkady does not understand what you mean. Is this code for something? You can clearly see it is tattoo gun. Beautiful angel lady from Heaven stab bad Hank with tattoo needle, not duck."

I'd laugh at Arkady's observation if not for the fact that none of this was funny. "It's just an analogy, Arkady. Or a metaphor...or something. What I mean is it's an easy explanation for who murdered Hank, at least for the police. Coop's a tattoo artist, there's a tattoo gun on the floor right next to his body, if they discover Hank was killed with some sort of poison in that gun, it kind of all adds up, you know? It's a nice neat package with a big shiny bow on it. Ten to one, that gun's what killed Hank. Aside from the fact that it's just the way our luck goes."

"And I'll say it again, we have no proof that gun is what killed Hank," Win insisted, clearly aggravated with me.

I stared harder at the picture. I couldn't see any puncture wounds, but then the pictures weren't *that* great, and certainly not the quality I'd need if Hank were killed by a tiny needle laced with poison. Which had me wondering how possible that was? But I didn't have time for that right now. I'd research tattoos and deadly needles later.

"You're right, Win. We have no proof the tattoo gun is the murder weapon."

But I had a feeling it played some vital part. Where were we if we weren't stuffed into a corner with our backs against the wall?

"Fair enough. Stranger things have happened," Win agreed.

Pushing the car door open, I took a deep breath. "We'll look at the rest of the pictures at home later. For now, let's go see what we can do for Trixie and find out whether Luis has shown up yet. I have a bad feeling Coop's going to need help." Then I cupped my hand over my eyes to ease the glare the snow wrought and took a look around the parking lot. "Do you guys see his car?" I asked, pushing my way out into the cold without really listening for an answer, cursing myself for wearing fashionable boots rather than practical ones on today of all days.

Scanning the parking lot, I didn't see Luis's expensive car, so I trudged inside anyway. Weather being what it was, his trip in from Seattle was bound to be difficult at best, but he never disappointed, and I didn't expect him to now.

I don't know how Win had managed to make the lawyer so available to me, but I was glad he was always at the ready.

As I peeked through the glass doors of the station and watched civilians and officers alike mill about, I caught a glimpse of Trixie talking to Officer Nelson, who had his arms crossed over his chest. Her hands were flying in the air and her cheeks were pink.

Which was my cue to get my backside in gear and get in there and be supportive—because this wasn't looking good for Coop.

~

Six hours later, long past my lunchtime, I sat with Trixie in the sterile waiting area of the Eb Falls Police Station while Detective Moore—whose nose was broken and cheekbone fractured—grilled poor Coop. We hadn't seen hide nor hair of her since they'd hauled her off to a room for questioning, and I was beginning to become worried.

Thankfully, Luis had shown up a few hours ago and was in there with her. Hopefully, he'd be able to at least get her out on bail—which was where I had a bad feeling we were headed. My gut said they'd charge her due to so much evidence pointing in her direction.

The tattoo gun, the beef the ladies had with Hank raising the rent, the spots on her boots, likely blood though as yet unidentified, all damned Coop.

As business as usual prevailed and people came and

went, their slushy feet leaving a mess on the concrete floor, I thought about the events of the morning. The more I thought, the more questions piled up. I'd spent a little time looking up tattoo guns on my phone, and Win was right, it was more like a sewing needle than a deadly weapon.

Unless someone had laced the ink with some kind of poison. But then that would lead one to believe there was premeditation involved. So why would Coop plan to kill Hank? Over a raise in rent? Or worse, if someone else were responsible, why would they try to frame Coop for murder?

As the scent of burnt coffee and stale donuts filled the air, I fought to sit and simply stay a silent support.

But it wasn't easy.

"Have I said thank you for calling your lawyer, Stevie?" Trixie finally asked in her dulcet tones after a long silence.

"About ten times in the last few hours," I assured her with a laugh and a smile. "But you don't have to, Trixie. Luis has helped me out of a jam more than once. He's an amazingly brilliant attorney, and seeing as you're new to town, I figured you could use the recommendation."

"How...how much does he cost?" she asked, her voice tentative and almost shy, but it was her hands that really gave her away. She kept wringing them, twisting her fingers together over and over.

"Nothing. He costs nothing. He owes me a favor, so

don't you worry about a thing, okay? Just focus on Coop and Coop alone."

Her hands fluttered around her face before she straightened in an obvious gesture that indicated her resolve was back intact. "I can't let you do that, Stevie. It's very kind, but I can't let you. You don't even know us."

But I knew what this felt like. To be up against something so much bigger than me and not know where to turn because I was broke and alone with only Bel. When Win came along and changed my life, he didn't just change me emotionally. He changed me financially. I didn't go to bed worried about how I'd pay the bills anymore, and that kind of security makes for a good night's sleep. I wanted to pay that forward. So did Win.

So I gave her my best point-blank look. "You can and you will. Unless you want to be the one to go into that room and tell that mean jerk, Detective Moore, that Luis isn't Coop's attorney and let the chips fall where they may?"

Trixie squeezed my hand, her response soft. "You have a point."

I held out the bag of salt and vinegar chips I'd bought. They were the only thing in the vending machine that looked remotely enticing to me at this point and no way was I drinking precinct sludge. "Hungry?"

She blew her hair from her face and shook her head. "No. But thank you."

Trixie was one patient lady. I was impressed she hadn't lost her cool by now. Were it me, I'd have been rattling some cages, but of course, I'm impatient and sometimes impulsive. She'd also been eerily quiet about everything that was going on around us, and I was trying my best to respect that, despite the fact that I had a million questions rolling around my brain.

"You need to eat, Trixie. It's well past lunchtime. We can't have you passing out before they release Coop, can we? She'll need you to be strong."

"I'm used to fasting from time to time. It's no big deal, really. I'm fine with just this water," she replied, holding up the almost-empty bottle I'd bought her.

Used to fasting, huh? Trixie intrigued me almost as much as the odd Coop, and I found it impossible to keep my thoughts to myself anymore.

Sliding to the edge of my flimsy plastic seat, I turned to her. "You're used to fasting? Do you mean like juice cleanses and stuff? I swear, I envy people like you who can stick to something like that. I'd lose my mind if I didn't have a Twinkie every day."

Win snickered in my ear and Arkady boldly laughed.

Her eyes lifted to meet mine, shiny and soft. She tinkled a laugh, a laugh as sweet and gentle as she appeared. "No. Not a juice cleanse. I just mean using moderation. But I get what you mean about Twinkies. Though, my personal favorite is a Funny Bone."

"And you'd give up perfectly good food, why?" It was unfathomable to me. Who gave up a Funny Bone?

"For Lent, of course."

Okay. So she was religious. That made sense. Oh, but wait—Coop had called her sister. Was she...? No. A nun? Seriously? With a tattoo shop? Hardly likely.

"That might explain Coop calling Trixie sister." Win suggested the very thought I'd just had, making me nod my head.

I placed a hand on hers and smiled. "Can I ask you a personal question?"

"You've been sitting here with me for six solid hours after knowing me for thirty minutes, you can have my social security number if you want it."

I giggled and patted her hand. She had a sense of humor even in the midst of this turmoil. That was good. "Did Coop call you *Sister* Trixie Lavender? Or did I mishear her?"

Now her smile went a little sad and even forlorn, something I hadn't meant to make happen. But she bobbed her head. "You did hear correctly. I used to be a nun. Coop forgets to just call me plain old Trixie most times."

No way... Trixie was a nun. Or used to be a nun. Huh.

But this was yet another odd quirk about the lovely Coop to add to her multitude of quirks—her formal way of addressing people. However, forget that. I wanted to know why Trixie wasn't a nun anymore. And I *really* wanted to know what made a nun leave the church to open a tattoo shop?

But that wasn't to be right now. In a burst of sound

and motion, Coop finally came out from behind the ugly gray door of the same room where Starsky and Hutch had interrogated *me*, with a frowning Luis hot on her heels.

And the poor thing looked frazzled and exhausted. Trixie was the first to hop up and rush to her, throwing her arms around Coop's shoulders and giving her a hard hug. "Are you okay, friend?"

Coop nodded, patting Trixie awkwardly on the back with a stiff hand. But her green eyes told a different story. There was relief in them when she saw Trixie, clear as day.

As Trixie and Coop talked quietly, I approached Luis, who looked quite serious in his dapper Brooks Brothers pinstripe suit and new glasses. "So what are we up against? How bad is it?"

"Forgive me for being so bold, Stevie, but *who* is this woman?" he asked, looking down at me from behind his glasses.

I knew that look—the one that made people shrink, but it was usually reserved for meanie-butt Detective Moore. Thus, I was taken aback. "What do you mean?"

He tightened his grip on his expensive leather briefcase. "I mean, there is no history *anywhere* of any Coop With No Last Name. The moment you summoned me, I had my secretary set about the task of finding any information we could on Miss Coop because I don't like surprises. Yet, there's not a word about either her or Miss Lavender anywhere. They aren't online. They're without a Facebook page—in fact, there's no social media for either one of them. How, I ask you, can I defend someone without so much as an address, let alone a social security card? Everything about this woman is fishy, Stevie. Even the way she addresses me as 'Luis Lipton Esquire' is indeed odd. What's going on here?"

I blinked before I tugged his sleeve and pulled him to the nearest corner while Sandwich watched us with curious eyes. "Are you telling me they don't have a Facebook page? The horror," I mocked, pretending to clutch my pearls.

He sucked in his sagging cheeks, pushing a hand into his trouser pocket. "This is not a joke, Miss Cartwright."

I was a little bit peeved. Luis was the best criminal defense attorney in the Pacific Northwest, and we paid him an enormous amount of money on the off chance something should come up—as in, anything from scams to murder—and suddenly he couldn't function because Coop had no Facebook page?

"But that's why I pay you so much money in retainer fees, because even if she doesn't have a soul, it's your job to find her one and *fix this*."

"Stephania," Win soothed in my ear. "Luis is a good bloke. Clearly our problem is bigger than we thought. Don't sass the man. Find out what to do from here."

Win was, as always, right. I think my blood sugar was low at this point, and it was making me cranky.

There was a small silence between us before I broke it by saying, "I'm sorry, Luis. I'm just hungry and tired.

Tell me what we're up against and what we can do about it."

"First, we need to find out where she comes from. Her full name, where she's been before coming to Ebenezer Falls and so on. Your Detective Moore was quite pleased with himself when he, too, found out she had no history to speak of. It doesn't make for an easy defense if I can't refer to her past good behavior or lack of criminal record when she doesn't have anything to refer to. That said, miraculously, she hasn't been charged. But I fear she may if her fingerprints come up on that tattoo gun they found at the scene, and the gun proves to have something lethal in it—like poison? In my experience, that's the first thing they'll look for. The evidence against her isn't exactly over-whelming, but the motive they've created about the raise in her rent and her violent nature is a perfect storm."

Dang it all. "So the tattoo gun...? It's what they think killed Hank?"

"Oh, we played a fine game of possum about that gun, Detective Moore and I did. So, possibly. I believe that is the instrument they think was used to kill Mr. Morrison. And yes, it is in fact Coop's tattoo gun. But as expected, the detectives were quite evasive. They also have an anonymous source who claims to have heard a rather loud disagreement she had with Mr. Morrison over their rent, wherein she mentioned killing him."

Well, it wasn't as though I couldn't see Coop, what

little I knew of her, threatening to kill someone, meaning this made things look very, very bad.

"I wonder who the 'anonymous source' is?" I asked.

"That's why it's called anonymous. But the caller claimed Coop argued with Hank Morrison—quite animatedly, in fact. However, all the police questioning revolved around the subject of that tattoo gun. Also, the spatter on her boot, which I'm happy to report, turned out to be paint. Not blood. Still, it doesn't look good. He was killed in their store. The tattoo gun is hers, and worse, she's shown clear signs of violent tendencies. She assaulted an officer of the law, Stevie."

I winced. Yes. She'd knocked Detective Moore around a little, but he'd deserved that broken nose, and I said as much. "He deserved that. He was pretty pushy. She was just looking out for me, Luis."

He nodded his head, pushing his glasses up on the bridge of his nose. "To the tune of a broken nose and fractured cheekbone? That takes some doing, and some rage."

I rolled my eyes and blew out an exasperated breath. "He's still breathing, isn't he? He didn't lose a limb."

Luis's eyebrow rose. "I hardly think that's the point. That they didn't charge her with assault still has me scratching my head. We need to know what makes Miss Coop tick. I had only a brief meeting with her before the detectives began questioning. But I had a great deal of trouble getting anything out of her."

My head was whirling with questions, and it was a

fight to stay focused on anything like hope when everything appeared so bad. Luis was a shark, and if he was stumped, that meant trouble.

"Explain what you mean by trouble getting anything out of her? She wouldn't talk to you?"

His sigh was ragged. "If one-word sentences and the occasional grunt is 'talking,' we have a long way to go. She denies harming Mr. Morrison. In her very brief words, she told me she 'found him that way' and that was the most in only a handful of words I could wring out of her. I don't know what she's frightened of, but we must dig deeper into her, Stevie. That she's so tight lipped is to her detriment. Though, I didn't have to fret over the notion she'd say anything incriminating, which can be quite helpful in some situations, but refusing to even answer Detective Kaepernick when she asked if Coop would like something to drink is too far."

I tamped down a snort. Coop had taken my words to heart when I told her to keep quiet. "That's because I told her not to say anything else to anyone unless you were present. Our wires crossed."

Luis frowned at me, the wrinkles in his forehead deep lines of frustration. "Oh, they've more than crossed. Now, I must head back to Seattle. I anticipate dense traffic the entire way in this weather. But I have my work cut out for me, and I must get to it before Ebenezer Falls' finest get back the results of the fingerprinting and DNA that I'm desperately worried will match Coop's. In the meantime, she cannot leave Ebenezer Falls. She's not under arrest, but she's certainly under grave suspicion. Also, they'll need to find somewhere else to stay due to the fact that the entire building has been deemed a crime scene, and their living quarters are in a room at the store."

My disbelief was real. "So you managed to get her out without bail?"

I'd been harsh with Luis, and now I felt like a real jerk because he'd somehow kept Coop from ending up behind bars.

Brushing the front of his suit, he squared his shoulders and cleared his throat. "And that, my dear Miss Cartwright, is why you pay me the big bucks."

With those parting words, he marched out of the police station and into the swirl of falling snow, leaving me flabbergasted at his ability to keep Coop out of jail with so much working against her. Not that I doubted Coop could hold her own in jail. She'd probably chew her way through someone's intestines before she'd take any guff.

Regardless, I deserved nothing less than Luis's ire for doubting him, and that only added to my ever-mounting pile of guilt.

Still, I sighed with relief as I made my way over to Coop and Trixie. I reached for Coop's hand, which was ice cold, and squeezed it. "Coop, are you okay? You must be hungry. Let's get you and Trixie something to eat, yes? A nice warm meal and a quiet place to talk are in order."

"The poor thing, Dove. She looks positively broken," Win muttered in sympathy.

"*Dah*, Zero. It's a pity," Arkady agreed.

Coop's head whipped around, her eyes confused as she scanned the interior of the police station.

Trixie gripped her arm, her eyes alarmed. "What's wrong, Coop?"

But Coop pulled from her grasp and instead looked to me with wide-eyed fear—her next words stunning me into complete silence. "Who is Dove, and why is Dove broken, Stevie Cartwright?"

CHAPTER 7

I gasped sharply, and so did my ghostly friends from above. Was it possible Coop could hear Win? Maybe Arkady, too?

Holy cats!

But I had to be very careful here. Very careful indeed. As much as I hated to do it, I played dumb. Don't get me wrong, I know almost everyone in town thinks I'm bananapants and I don't really talk to ghosts, and I'm okay with that. I've made my peace with it, but to those who've come to me, searching for answers from the Great Beyond, I know I've brought them a modicum of peace.

However, they can't hear what I can hear. What if Coop is someone Adam Westfield is using to get to me? He's not just the man who stole my powers, but ruined my entire life and had me run out of my coven on a rail—and he didn't just do it once. He possessed a body just to get to me. I'm not ever going to forget that, or forget that he has connections and powerful spells no dead person should—not even a dead warlock.

So forgive me if I proceed with extreme caution.

Calling on my only brush with acting from my fifth-grade play, wherein Miss Castelano (our phys-ed teacher) cast me as the "third street urchin from the right" in the chorus of our disastrous rendition of *Les Mis*, I cocked my head with an exaggerated tilt and lifted my shoulders with a dramatic heave. "Whatever are you talking about, Coop?" I asked, my words stilted and choppy as though I'd forgotten how to construct a sentence.

Win groaned in my ear. "That was dreadful, Stephania. Painful, even."

Now Coop's eyes zipped about the room, her lips parting, her fists clenched as though she were ready to go into battle. "Who is that and why does he talk funny?"

"*Who is who*, Coop?" Trixie asked, panic in her voice, gripping her friend's arm again and forcing her to look at her.

Okay. We had trouble. Right here in River City. Coop could hear Win. I knew it as sure as I knew my hair was nothing without caramel highlights and a trim every six weeks, and that meant I had to do something fast. I didn't have time to figure out the how or why of Coop.

Leaning into her, I whispered in conspiratorial fashion, "Coop, come with me and I'll explain everything. Okay? And I think you know what I mean by *everything.*"

Her fear didn't exactly lend to her being here because of Adam Westfield, but maybe she was a better actress than I'd ever be. So I was willing to take the chance she was like me and could hear ghosts. Otherwise, this was an elaborate ruse just to get to me, and those dots didn't connect.

But Trixie held up her hands and frowned, firmly shaking her head. "Okay. Hold on here. I'm not going anywhere until someone tells me what's going on, and neither is Coop." Gripping her friend's hand, she pulled her close to her side and huffed for good measure to prove her point.

Trixie's reaction sealed the deal for me. I didn't think they had anything to do with Adam.

I blew out a breath and smiled at them both reassuringly. "I promise to explain everything if you'll just come with me. You can't go back to the store anyway. It's officially a crime scene, and if you two are living there, as I suspect you are, you have nowhere to go until forensics clears the store. Why don't you come back to my place, we'll order in an early dinner, and I'll explain. I have plenty of room, but," I paused, looking around as the entire police department watched us, "I can't explain *here.*"

Coop nodded, pushing her hands under her armpits. "She's right, Trixie. We can't go back to Inkerbelle's. Mr. Luis Lipton Esquire said so."

Trixie's brown gaze was pensive at best when she

sent signals with her eyes to her friend. "Are you *sure* you're okay with going to Stevie's? Because if not, we can figure it out."

When Coop looked at me, assessing me from head to toe as though she'd be able to see if something was awry on my person just by way of a glance, she nodded curtly. "Yes. I'm sure. I trust her." Then she patted Trixie on the shoulder with one of her awkward gestures and headed toward the doors of the station.

Trixie shuddered a sigh of resignation. "If Coop says she trusts you, then your house it is. We'll follow you in our car."

I heard her hesitance, yet the signals she'd sent to Coop with her eyes suggested her friend had some sort of lie-detecting ability, and that was even wackier than hearing ghosts.

But hey, I have two ghost friends and a talking bat. Who am I to say she isn't a human lie detector?

$\sim$

"She heard you, Win! I know she did." I pulled out of the police station's parking lot, watching in my rearview to ensure Trixie was right behind me in her rusty Caddy.

"I'm afraid you're probably correct, Dove."

"How is that possible, Win?"

"How is it possible *you* hear me—or Arkady, for that matter?"

"Because I'm a witch, International Man of Mystery! A witch with medium abilities."

"No. You're a *former* witch who's been stripped of her powers. Yet, somehow, the fates have allowed you to hear us. Who's to say Coop isn't one of your kind?"

Yes. That was true. I'd had blips now and again since my powers were slapped out of me (literally slapped), but nothing concrete, and come to think of it, nothing at all these last few months.

"No," I denied fervently. "I'd know if she were a witch, Spy Guy."

"*How* would you know, Stephania?"

I gripped the steering wheel tighter, still shivering without my coat as splotchy snowflakes spattered on the windshield. "Because we know our own kind."

"And how is that? Do you have a particular scent? Is it like when dogs sniff each other's derrieres? How can you know?"

I tried to focus on the road, but my mind was in overdrive. "Never mind. We just know. She's not a witch. The community is small. Everyone pretty much knows everyone. Just trust me on that. Think of it like Plane Limbo. You know everyone there, right? It's similar but different."

"Then she must be a medium, Boss," Bel chirped from my purse. "A scary, violent, really pretty one, but a medium nonetheless. Something's going on with her. I don't know what, but you mark my words, she's got a creep factor that's adorable, but still creepy."

"Mediums are baloney, Bel. You know that. They're

shysters looking to prey on the bereaved. And she's not creepy. She's just... Odd." Yes. Odd. That was an appropriate word to describe Coop. Beautifully odd.

"Is that what you consider yourself, Stephania? A shyster?" Win crowed.

"You are not oyster, my *malutka*. You are honest and good lady. You do not take money for you. You give away to people who have none."

I could always count on my Arkady when I needed an ego boost. It was true. We gave away my medium fees to all manner of charities. We didn't need it, but I *did* need to help people. It'd just who I am.

"The word is *shyster*, Arkady, and yes. That's true. We don't keep the money people pay to contact their loved ones. And no, Win. I don't consider myself a shyster. I consider myself rare. It's very, very rare to find another true medium."

"Yet, here you are," he pointed out once more.

"But I'm a witch."

"No, Stephania, you are not. You've lost your abilities to witch. But you haven't lost your abilities to hear the dead. The two are apparently not mutually exclusive."

"But I only hear you and Arkady. You guys do the rest of the listening for me at Madam Zoltar's. It's not the same." Shrugging, I kept one eye on Trixie behind me and the other on the road as more snow fell. "I don't know. Either way, Coop can hear you, Win, and that terrifies me."

"Whatever for, Dove?"

"Because I don't know what it means, and it means *something*. Maybe something not good. Maybe it has to do with Adam Westfield? There's always that possibility. Though, Coop looked terrified when she heard you call me Dove. Of course, Adam is terrifying. So maybe that explains her fear."

I had to throw that out into the universe so the notion could be tossed about and ease my inner turmoil. I didn't want to be wrong about these women, but I needed to say the words out loud just in case.

"Do you really believe that, Stevie?" Bel asked. "Let's rationalize here. You're bringing these women to our *home*. If you felt in any way they were in cahoots with Adam "Maniac from The Great Beyond" Westfield, you wouldn't do that. I know you well enough to know that much. You're bringing them back to the house because you have a good heart, you know they have nowhere to go, and likely no money to go anywhere with. Oh, and let's not forget, you love a good mystery. They brought the mystery."

"I just felt like I had to put it out there as a suggestion so I could get it out of my system is all. But it also means Coop knows our secret. Or she will when I tell her. We have no choice but to be honest about it. She already knows because she can hear you. If she knows, she can tell other people."

"*Who?* Who would care? Everyone in Eb Falls already thinks you're one bon-bon shy of a box when it comes to talking to the afterlife, Stephania. How is Coop's confirmation going to change any opinion that doesn't already exist? Do make note, it sounds quite ridiculous when repeated. All that aside, I have a feeling about Coop. A good one. I don't think she'll have any problem with you hearing ghosts. But she also has some explaining to do. She did lob Detective Moore across the room as though he were a mere box of tissues. I imagine that's her secret, and I'd like to know the explanation."

There was that. Among the million questions I had, that surely was one of them. "Are you just saying all that because she's insanely beautiful and you want to keep her around?" I teased.

Win's answer growled in my ear. "That she is indeed. But nay, Dove. I'm looking at this objectively and rationally—and rationally, I believe Coop, though peculiar, has good intentions. And I do not believe she murdered Hank Morrison. If there was some kind of poison in the ink of the tattoo gun, that would suggest premeditation. I don't believe Coop's anything but black and white."

"I hope you're right, Win. Otherwise, we could be getting ourselves into something we can't get out of," I reminded him, pulling onto our street and praying Enzo had plowed the driveway so Trixie could get her very old car up our steep drive. "Not to mention, we need to find out when and why she argued with Hank. In the meantime, just stay quiet until we can figure this all out, okay?"

"Of course, Dove."

"Arkady, are we in agreement?"

"*Dah-dah*, my sugar snap pea. I will zip my lip."

The sight of our house, blanketed in snow, the lights in the gardens just coming on at dusk, warmed me from the inside out. A toasty fire and some pepperoni pizza were in order, and then we needed to get down to the business of figuring out who killed Hank Morrison.

Before the police had the chance to pin it on Coop with their "overwhelming evidence."

As I exited the car and raised my hand to wave Trixie into a parking spot that wouldn't interfere with Enzo's plow, Win's warmth (or his aura, as we mediums say) encompassed me, wrapping around my shoulders as though he'd loaned me his coat to keep me warm.

And that was some comfort as I headed into what we both knew would be a difficult conversation.

～

"Ohhh, your home is beautiful, Stevie!" Trixie said on a sigh, her hand absently running over Whiskey's head as we landed in the kitchen, the last stop on our tour.

I'd somehow managed to divert all suspicion and fear by showing them the house. I have to admit, the house formerly known as Mayhem Manor was a fabulous diversion when one wanted to avoid the inevitable.

"So you did the renovations yourself?" Trixie asked,

her eyes tired and red, but wide with curiosity as she looked at our kitchen.

I barked a laugh and went to grab some wine glasses. "Um, no. I hired people to do it for us... Er, *me*. I picked colors and pointed my finger and wrote big checks. Lots of big, big checks."

Trixie breathed in again, closing her eyes before she opened them and gave me a warm smile. "Well, you did a lovely job, didn't she, Coop?"

Coop cleared her throat and straightened, inching closer to Trixie as Strike pecked at the floor near her feet. "Yes. This is quite lovely." She repeated the words woodenly before looking to Trixie for approval.

And I know that's what she was looking for. *Approval.* And still, I didn't know why. But that was all about to change.

Coop blanched when Strike brushed against her to get to me, nearly climbing into Trixie's arms. For such a warrior, she sure was easily spooked.

Reaching down, I stroked his head and smiled with affection. "He won't hurt you, Coop. He's quite friendly. I promise."

"*What* is he, Trixie Lavender?" she whispered to Trixie, her voice trembling, adding to her cache of bizarre questions.

Trixie chuckled and held her hand out to Strike, who quite willingly rubbed up against her. "He's a turkey, Coop. You know, like cluck-cluck—or something like that. I've never seen one as a pet, but if Stevie says he's okay, I'm sure it's fine."

Grinning, I grabbed some feed from the cabinet and scattered it on the floor. "He's sort of a rescue. Long story, but suffice it to say, he's just another whacky addition to my family."

Trixie knelt in front of Strike then, grabbing Coop's hand. "Hold out your hand, Warrior Princess," she teased. "He's really very sweet."

As Coop very tentatively let Strike closer, I went to find refreshment. Some much-needed libation.

"Can I interest you in some wine with our dinner? I sure could use some after today. Coop? How about you?" I asked as I popped open our industrial-sized refrigerator and pulled out a bottle of cabernet.

Trixie shook her head. "None for me, thanks, and Coop doesn't drink."

Coop agreed as I held up water bottles instead. "Yes. She's right. So no thank you, Stevie Cartwright. I don't drink."

I was just going to let this bizarre habit of Coop running everything she did past Trixie go for the moment. "So let's have a seat in the living room and call for our pizza, yes? Enzo, my amazing handyman and dear friend, built a fire, and it's lovely and warm in there. You both look like you could use a moment's peace."

But Trixie hesitated, pulling her cap off and tucking her reddish brown hair with the blue streak behind her ears. "Hold on for a sec. I don't mean to come across as rude after all you've done for us, Stevie, but...what's the catch?"

"The catch?"

Holding her phone up, she scrolled the screen. "Yes. Er, as in, the lowdown, the shakes, the gist." She paused and squinted her eyes. "And the shimmy?"

I stood on tippy toe and looked over her hand to the screen of her phone. "Did you Google that?"

Trixie blanched, her pale skin getting paler. "I did. I'm not really up to date on things of this nature."

I laughed and headed into the living room anyway, motioning them to follow. I stood in front of our stone fireplace to warm my hands and sighed a happy sigh. It was good to be home. "I know there's a story there, Trixie, but for now, we need to clear other things up first, don't we? And there's no catch or lowdown or anything else. I want to help because I know what it's like to be unjustly accused of murder."

Coop hissed while Trixie stopped dead in her tracks, putting a protective hand at Coop's waist. "You were accused of murder?" she squeaked.

I grinned and winked, passing it off as no big deal. "Yep. But I was cleared. Promise. Just like I hope Coop will be. But we can't do that unless you tell me what the heck is going on. Let's start at Coop javelin-throwing Starsky across the room as though he were a ragdoll. I think that's a good place. And please, don't insult my intelligence here. I know what I saw. I also know Detective Moore outweighs Coop by at least seventy-five pounds—minimum. Sweatin' to the Oldies won't give you that kind of workout."

Coop looked to Trixie, an eyebrow raised. "What is Sweatin' to the Oldies, Trixie Lavender?"

"And then there's that," I pointed out, using a finger to punctuate the air with a warm smile. I didn't want to upset them. I wanted to understand them. "Maybe I could let the reference to Richard Simmons go because Coop doesn't look much older than twenty-five."

Inching through the doorway behind Trixie, scouring our enormous space with those ever-inquisitive eyes, she took in the cool-colored walls in shades of beige and cream, the crown molding, and the big comfortable furniture we'd so carefully chosen before she addressed her age.

"I'm not twenty-five. I'm thirty-two, Stephania Cartwright," she offered with all seriousness.

Of course she was, and naturally someone as ethereally beautiful as her wouldn't look her age. Not to mention, she'd used my full name. She'd heard Win, all right. No doubt.

"Right," I said with a nod, snapping my fingers to invite Whiskey into the room. "But no one calls anyone by their first *and* last name. And how did you know my full first name? At first I thought you might be from another country, but there's no sign of an accent. Then, in all honesty, I wondered if there was some medical reason—which you don't have to divulge at all, if you don't want to. Yet, those solutions don't explain Coop's undeniable strength."

Coop looked at me with that gaze that shot right

through my flesh to my very soul. "I'm not from another country."

"Then where are you from, Coop?" I asked gently, taking a seat in my favorite wingback chair and hoping they'd do the same on our couch with its jillion throw pillows Win complained about endlessly.

She didn't hesitate. She didn't bat a luscious eye. Rather, she looked deeper into my soul and said, "I'm from Hell."

CHAPTER 8

$\mathcal{I}$ pulled a pillow over my chest and thought about that, refusing to react to her answer if that's what she hoped for. Yet, the look on Trixie's face didn't appear as though she were pleased with Coop's answer. She hadn't said it for the shock value. She looked at me in all seriousness.

Knowing her penchant for bizarre answers, I tried to interpret what she meant, and it was reflected in my next question. "Do you mean you're from a bad neighborhood, Coop?"

"Coop. I can't let you do this. Stop. *Please*," Trixie begged, her eyes growing glassy with tears.

But Coop flashed angry eyes right back at Trixie and stomped into the living room in a huff. "You said it's wrong to lie, Trixie. I read it's a sin on the Internet. I will not do wrong, sinful things. I'm a good person now. I will always be a good person. I promised you."

Trixie's sigh filled the living room when it escaped her throat. It was a weary sigh of pent-up fear. Of aggravation. Of worry. "I know what I told you, Coop. But sometimes, there are things better left unsaid—"

"Yes!" Coop intervened with more emotion than I'd seen since we'd met—more than even when she'd been put in handcuffs and arrested for a possible murder. "You told me that. But I don't have to leave things unsaid with Stevie Cartwright, do I? She wants to know the truth. I want to tell her the truth because I know she'll understand. I can smell she'll understand."

Smell... How peculiar.

I held up my hand to thwart any more disagreement and sat forward on the chair, making Whiskey lift his head and rub it on my leg. I reached down to scratch him between the ears to let him know everything was all right. "Listen, ladies. I only want to know the truth so I can help you. Luis was very clear about a few things he needs to represent you—like Coop's last name, for starters. Sure, I'm curious. I won't lie. There are some things that have happened today I simply don't understand. But beyond those concerns, you could be in a great deal of trouble, Coop. I'm not sure you understand just how much. So giving me all the information is crucial to helping you. Not to mention Luis. He says you can't be found anywhere. Not online, not anywhere. And you have no last name? Why is that?"

Trixie rocked from foot to foot, her movements

jerky and nervous. If she were planning to lie about the reasons for these strange happenings, she was going to bomb. Her body language said as much.

But Coop? Yeah, Coop wasn't nervous at all. She took Trixie by the hand and led her to the couch, pointing to the seat next to her as she sat down. "We have to tell Stevie Cartwright everything. I can tell she'll listen and believe. I told you, I smelled it on her."

There it was again. My smell factor.

Still, her trust astounded me, but I didn't want to spook Trixie, who was less enthused, and I was choosing to ignore the bit about her smelling me. Coop waters were murky at best; I wasn't ready to wade into the deep end yet.

Silence prevailed momentarily until I finally said, "Let's start here—did you hear someone call me Stephania, Coop? Can you hear that voice…but you're unable to see the person the voice belongs to?"

Coop looked to Trixie, who smiled at her, even though it was evident she was terrified. "It's your story to tell, Coop. It's up to you how you want to tell it. Just like we talked about on the car ride over. But I hope you'll remember what I said might happen."

Coop licked her lips but her stare never wavered. "Yes. I can hear that voice. I heard the other one, too. At first it scared me until I realized they were talking to you. You are Dove."

Indeed, I am. "So then you're a medium? Like me?"

What the fluff? That left me stumped. When I'd first

mentioned I was a medium, she'd looked at me as though I had two heads and one eye.

"No. I'm not a medium. That's not what my title is. I have a title."

Her title… "What do you mean by title, Coop? Are you some kind of royalty? Like a princess or something?"

Now *that* I could believe. First, she was gorgeous. Whoever gave birth to her hit the lottery gene pool. Second, she held herself like someone had taught her to walk with a book on her head—long, tall and seductive.

"No. Where I come from, there's only one ruler. The rest of us are just minions created to do his bidding. And we must do it right or we're punished. Severely."

My mouth fell open at that point.

"Stephania, wipe the corner of your mouth, Dove. You have a bit of wine there," Win said on a laugh.

Coop leaned forward and did just as Win instructed, using her thumb.

But I brushed her hand off and asked, "And where are you from again?"

"I told you, Stevie Cartwright. I'm from Hell."

Did she mean Hell, Michigan? I'd heard of it. That had to be what she meant, right?

"Do you mean like Michigan? Hell, Michigan?" Did Michigan have a ruler? Maybe in her muddled miscommunication she meant the governor or the mayor.

Coop shook her head, the curtain of her dusky red hair falling around her face. "No. I mean from down there." She pointed to the gleaming hardwood floor.

Nope. She didn't mean the mayor.

Swallowing, I reached for my glass of wine and took a long gulp followed by a deep, deep breath. "Okay, and what's your title in Hell, Coop?"

"*Demon.*"

Forget my glass—I blinked and grabbed the entire bottle of wine. In fact, I might even hunt around for some whiskey before all was said and done, because that confession called for some hard liquor.

Instead, I took a long swig and said, "Ah. I see."

Coop, however, didn't miss a beat. "Unless you care to count head tattoo artist. Then I'm a demon head tattoo artist. I tattooed all new entrants to Hell with a special insignia. Everyone gets a unique tattoo so if they escape Hell, they can be caught and dragged back. Escapees make Satan very angry."

Dragged back to Hell. Yikes. Having confirmation that Hell truly existed was one thing. Hearing all the things we fear are reality? Quite another.

Okay, look. I know I'm a witch. Er, *was* a witch. I know magic exists, spells, all sorts of stuff, etcetera. I know the paranormal exist, too, in a sort of "we are the paranormal world" kind of way. Meaning, I get others exist; I've just not met many of them.

But this? A demon? I didn't know how to respond. So I didn't. I just looked at Coop and blinked again.

Then I took another long gulp of my bottle of wine. Were I a smoker, I'd have lit up the whole pack.

"Do you believe me, Stevie Cartwright?" Coop asked in her straightforward way.

"I…" My mouth slammed shut. In all seriousness, how could I *not* believe her? I was an ex-witch, for gravy's sake. But a demon fresh outta Hell? Rolling my head on my neck to ease the mounting pressure, I entered this new bit of information with caution. "I believe *you* believe you're a demon."

Which did not satisfy Coop. Not one bit. "I am telling you the truth, Stevie Cartwright. I do not lie, and I won't have you say I do." She rose, her knees bent as she spoke, her fists clenched.

But Trixie tapped her on the arm and pointed to the space on to the sofa beside her. "Coop. We talked about this. Sometimes our story's a lot to swallow. Let Stevie digest this information, please. We can't force this on someone. Remember?" Then she turned to me, her eyes compelling me to believe. "What Coop says is true. I'd swear on a stack of Bibles, but I suppose that's not terribly believable since I left the church. I was a nun at a convent in Oregon, which is why Coop calls me Sister Trixie Lavender. To shorten a *very* long story about how all this came to be, Coop saved me from certain death by an evil spirit, and in the process, escaped Hell. We've been together ever since."

"Not so different than our story, eh, Dove?"

Coop looked around the living room and settled

her eyes on the ceiling. "There he is again. The man with the funny-sounding words."

"Winterbottom," he introduced himself. "Crispin Alistair Winterbottom. But you can just call me Win, Coop. A pleasure to meet you both, I'm sure. Please pass those words on to Trixie."

"Nice to meet you, too," Coop chirped and almost— not quite—but almost smiled. Win did that to a woman. Made the unsmile-able smiley.

Trixie, who clearly couldn't hear Win, frowned and whispered to her friend, "Is he talking again?"

"Yes. He said it's nice to meet us and I responded in kind, just like you taught me," Coop assured, clearly pleased with herself.

I was still waiting on words to form when Trixie reached out a hand and patted my knee, her soft eyes sympathetic. "I know this all sounds crazy, Stevie, but we figured it might not sound *as* crazy to someone who truly can hear ghosts. You're the first person we've ever told, and we're terrified to share. But if this is too much, if *we're* too much—and believe me, I get the 'too much' part; sometimes *I* don't even know if I can handle our story—we can leave and we won't bother you ever again."

I ignored her offer to leave and plodded forward, trying to stick to the facts. "So that's why Coop is so strong? Because she's a demon?"

Trixie bounced her head, finally sliding back on the couch and settling into its deep cushions. "Yep, and we've talked about her strength and how people can end up seriously hurt because she's so strong. In Hell... well, let's just say sometimes she had to fight to keep her place. I liken it a little to prison after hearing her stories about what it was like there. It genuinely is everything we fear and more."

Prison.

Hell.

Eep.

I know my shock was seeping into my facial expressions, but I had no clue how to stop them from doing so. Coop had lived in Hell. There was a real Hell. Like, real live fire and brimstone. My next question was to ask what despicable crime had landed her in Hell and whether or not I should be sleeping with headgear and one eye open. Yet, Coop didn't strike me as someone who wanted to hurt you just to hurt you.

Gosh, she was complicated.

"Anyway," Trixie continued, her voice low and soft. "Sometimes Coop forgets her own strength—especially if she feels like someone weaker is being threatened. She felt like Detective Moore was threatening you, Stevie. I have to give her credit for at least asking him to back off *before* she knocked him one in the kisser. She did try. She always tries, and she always will as long as we're a team, but there was a time she would have fought him to a far greater detriment. *His* detriment."

That was fair. She'd clearly asked Starsky to back off. But that wasn't what impressed me about these two; it was the mention of them being part of a team.

That's how I felt about Win, Arkady, and Bel. We were a team. We'd had some really rough times as a team, but we'd had great ones, too. More great than rough, in fact.

And now we were this patched-together earthly/afterlife family, and we were happy. Mostly, anyway.

I wanted to tell Trixie and Coop that. Yet, all I could manage were meaningless words. "That explanation makes sense," I muttered, still wrapping my head around this fantastical story.

"It's also why she has no last name or can't be found online, and why she addresses everyone so formally. She forgets it's unnecessary to use your full name. Coop doesn't always know how to interact with people on a social level just yet. She wasn't taught the things we were—or should I say, *you* were. But she's learning every day, right?" Trixie asked with a smile as she gave Coop one more of those reassuring pats on the back—a pat that touched me. "And she's doing a great job, too."

Somehow, through this crazy circumstance that had thrown them together, Trixie had ended up being Coop's human guide to all things, well...*human*.

And even more ironic, Trixie was an ex-nun guiding what is perceived by most as evil incarnate. They were essentially polar opposites. Which now begged the question, why did Trixie leave the convent with, of all beings, a demon? Didn't that go against everything she'd ever been taught by the church?

"But to be fair," Trixie continued, making me wonder if this was a cleansing of sorts for her—a long-awaited chance to tell her story. "I'm sort of stunted in social nuances, too. I was in the convent a good portion of my late teen years right into my adult life. We didn't learn things like popular slang and such during... prayer. I mean, who knew things like Netflix even existed? *Beverly Hills 9021* would have been a whole different ball game had I been able to watch every episode available. I'd have probably stopped season three."

I almost gasped out loud at that. I couldn't live without my Netflix binges. How did civilized people survive?

Yet, that statement lent to still more mounting questions. I wanted to know why Trixie had left the church. But that only led to another question pile-up.

Before I could remind myself to quash my curious nature in favor of sensitivity, I blurted out, "How did Coop end up in Hell?"

If we were to go by the biblical nature of tales, you had to be evil to end up there, right? Didn't that mean she'd done something heinous?

Trixie twisted her hands together again, meaning the explanation was going to be an unbelievable one, but her answer was tinged with seriousness. "She was created there, as are most minions."

By the time this evening was through, my title was going to be "boozer" for all the chugalugging I was doing.

Taking another sip from my wine bottle, I asked, "Created. Meaning?"

"That means I don't have a mother or father in your earthly traditional sense. Satan is technically my father. He created me for his sole purpose. I'm his property," Coop provided.

His property? I didn't know how to process that, but I can't tell you the relief I felt knowing she hadn't spent her life killing kittens and maiming seniors.

"So you didn't sell your soul to him or do something horrible to end up in Hell when you died, is what you're telling me?"

"Yes, Stevie Cartwright. That's what I'm telling you."

I wiped my brow, noting drops of perspiration on my fingertips. Somehow, her answer was a relief. "But then how did you get here?"

Now Coop smiled, widely, and just like everything else on Coop, it was gorgeous, magical, perfection; her entire face beamed and her eyes lit up like sparklers. "I escaped. When the evil spirit attacked Sister... Uh, Trixie, I took my chances and escaped with my friend, Livingston."

Out of nowhere, Trixie jumped up from the couch, knocking pillows to the floor, her pretty face a mask of worry. "Livingston, Coop! Oh, gracious! How could we have forgotten Livingston? He must be starving by now. We have to go back to the store!"

I jumped up, too, and when I did, I was a little wobbly from all that wine. But I couldn't let them drive in this weather with that old rust bucket of theirs. Looking out the tall windows in our living room, I saw the snow was still falling in white clumps. Surely the roads were slicker than snot by now.

So I gripped Trixie's arm. "Wait, wait, wait! You can't drive your car. It'll never make it without snow tires or chains. Mine has chains. So you drive, Trixie, because I've been drinking. And who's Livingston? Is he another demon?"

Trixie stopped all motion and bit her bottom lip. "Sort of."

Wine made my lips a little loose, and the decorum I tried so hard to hang onto during this whole bizarre conversation slipped away. "Okay, from here on out, no more secrets, ladies. *Please*. We don't have a lot of time to waste, keeping things from each other. Just tell me who Livingston is. Gargoyle? Vampire? Werewolf, maybe?"

Coop's eyes scoured my face. "Don't be silly, Stevie Cartwright. Vampires and werewolves aren't allowed in Hell. Satan says they're sketchy."

"But he's okay with gargoyles?" I found myself asking in wonder.

She shrugged with nonchalant shoulders. "I never asked him."

"You know, the next time you talk to him, you might want to check," I commented. "Surely gargoyles are perfect vessels for evil. I mean—"

"Stephania!" Win barked. "Get to the point. We have no time to waste."

I rolled my eyes and popped my lips. "I was just

being social. I mean, who am I if I don't ask questions, Winterbutt—"

"Stephania!" he howled again with that scowl in his tone.

My sigh was ragged and executed just for Win. "Fine. So what exactly is Livingston, Coop?"

"He's an owl. Livingston is trapped in the form of an owl. A talking owl."

CHAPTER 9

"*H*ah!" Win barked, clearly unable to keep quiet any longer. "The plot thickens."

"A talking owl. Now I've heard everything," I mumbled, scooping up the pillows from the floor as the Coop and Trixie headed to the front door. "An *owl*, for goodness sake."

"You know, Stephania," Win drawled in his coolly British way—the way being the one where he's going to make a point. "I'm seeing a whole new side to you. Dare I say, a discriminating one?"

"*What?* Don't be ridiculous. I don't discriminate." I did, however, have too much wine. Phew, my head was a little spinny.

"Is it so ridiculous? That you have difficulty digesting a talking owl, a demon and an ex-nun when you're an ex-witch who talks to dead people and have your own talking pet says otherwise. You're the OG of the impossible. Yet, you doubt Coop and Trixie at every turn."

True that. Win was right.

"I am surprised at you, too, my little jalapeño. Zero is right. You are being, how you say, stuffy pants."

My cheeks flushed red, and I don't know if that was from the wine or embarrassment for my behavior. "Oh, all right. Enough with the pile-on, boys. You're right. I'm one to talk. I'm just in shock. You have to admit that was quite a tale she told us. I mean, escaping Hell, and demons and tattoos and saving Trixie from an evil spirit. It's a little outrageous."

"And having your powers slapped out of you by a cruel warlock after defending a young boy whose father was a monster, and being kicked out of your coven, is less outrageous, Dove?"

Point, point, point. Win was so right. He was almost always right, and I felt like a total heel for not swallowing Coop and Trixie's story whole.

But listen, *Win* taught me to be skeptical. He taught me to read between the lines. I was just doing what I'd learned from him.

"Okay, guys. I get it. I'm wrong. I just wanted to check off all the boxes. Maybe I'm becoming more human by the day, because you can bet your bippy had they told anyone else this story, they'd be in the psych ward for observation."

"As would you, Stephania," Win crowed.

"What Winterbutt said," Bel chirped from the ceiling as he flew around in a circle.

"Bel! Get down from there. Do you want them to see you?"

He landed on my shoulder with a chuckle. "Because they're going to find me strange when they have a talking owl? Staahhp, Boss. You're killin' me."

I sighed and chucked him under the chin with a gentle finger. "You up to a little recon, buddy? We might need you to get into the store to help this Livingston. You might be the only way to do it."

"Yep. I'm in. But there'd better be a heat lamp and some kiwi in this for me when we're done."

"Deal. Now quit messing with my head and all of you pipe down about my disbelief. That Hell truly exists is a lot to digest in one night."

"Well, it stands to reason, Stephania. Plane Limbo exists, doesn't it? If there's an afterlife for the good, there certainly should be somewhere for the bad. We all have to go somewhere."

"Again, also a valid point. Okay, guys. Let's do this. You two be my eyes and ears up there, please."

I grabbed my purse from the table in our foyer, and another jacket from the stand by the front door, slipping my arms through it. "Hold the phone, ladies. We have to be careful. You're not supposed to go into the store. It's a crime scene, remember? But we'll figure it out. We just have to be very careful, and whatever we do, we can't get caught. If Luis knew I was aiding and abetting, he'd chew me a new one, and if you ever need someone on your side, Luis is your guy—you don't want to make him angry with you."

I'm not sure if it was the wine talking or my deep desire to meet a talking owl named Livingston, but I was rarin' to go despite the potential risks involved.

"Before we leave, there's someone else I'd like you to meet."

"If there's a rhinoceros here, I'm heading for the border," Trixie teased as I handed her the coat she'd used earlier and threw one to Coop, who slipped it on and was left with her long, graceful arms only covered to the elbow.

Laughing, I shook my head and plucked Bel from my shoulder, placing him in my palm and holding him up so they could see him clearly. "This is my familiar. I'll explain what that word means when we get back if you don't already know. For now, this is Belfry. Bel for short. He's one of my best friends in the whole world, and if anyone can get in and out of your store without being seen to find Livingston, it's him."

Bel curtsied. "Nice to meet you both. I'm at your service."

Coop's eyes went wide, glittering like glass marbles as she bent at the waist to eyeball Bel, using a finger to scratch his round-with-more-pomegranates-than-a-familiar-knew-what-to-do-with belly. "It talks," she mused.

"It talks *a lot*," Win joked, making Bel flap his wings.

"*Dah!*" Arkady agreed on a hearty laugh.

Coop almost cracked another smile when she nodded her agreement. "Livingston talks a lot, too. Sometimes, he makes my head noisy."

"Pound, Coop. He makes your head pound," Trixie corrected on a snicker. "And yes, Livingston can be quite a handful. Just a bigger one than your Bel, at almost five pounds. Is Belfry a play on 'bats in the'?"

"It is," I replied, pleased she'd made the connection as I gave Whiskey a scratch on the head and blew him a kiss. "Now, let's go get your handful so *my* handful can meet him and they can be handfuls together, okay? But I'm going to caution you both. You must listen to me. It's imperative. We have to do this right. Coop, if we encounter someone, anyone, no throwing people around like tennis balls. Keep your cool and we'll be in and out like we were never there. Promise me?"

Trixie halted all motion when she threw up a hand and said, "Hold on! I forgot the keys to the back door *inside* the store. I was in such a rush to get to Coop, I must have left them on the counter. Good heavens, I've made such a mess of things!"

"Don't panic," I instructed. "I have an idea. I'll tell you all about it on the way. That said, Coop, I need that promise from you."

She held up two hands and nodded solemnly, her surreally gorgeous face somber. "I promise, Stevie Cartwright, and I never, ever break a promise."

"Good. And Trixie, you, too."

She barked a laugh at me that literally tinkled, and it was a pleasant, almost carefree sound. I suspected that was something she hadn't felt in a long time, and I wanted to know why. But that was for later.

"Just so you know, I'm a big chicken. You don't have

to worry I'll throw even so much as a dirty look someone's way. I'm a lover, not a fighter."

I winked at Trixie, courage coursing through my boozy veins. "Then let's do this, girls!"

As we made our way down the snow-covered stairs, Coop whispered to Trixie, "It speaks, Trixie. It sounds like that toy we saw in the pet store when you crush it in your hands."

"*It's* right here, and it flies, too, and if you guys don't stop talking about me like I'm not two feet from you, I'm going to swan dive right into all your luscious locks, Coop the Demon! Then we'll see who speaks!" Bel chirped, annoyed.

Coop gasped her outrage as she stomped across the lawn and driveway to my car, muttering, "Will not throw anyone around. *Will not.*"

I couldn't help but laugh. "You be nice, Bel. Don't upset the demon, buddy. You did see Starsky's nose, didn't you?"

We all laughed at that as we piled into the car with snowflakes swirling around us and Trixie at the wheel.

~

I tucked my chin into the neck of my coat and shivered at how dark Eb Falls was, even with all the snow. It was almost eerily beautiful with the waves of the Sound crashing about and the stillness of the deserted streets but for the occasional gust of frigid wind. My wine high was fading fast, and without any food in my belly, I was a little lightheaded.

We'd parked a few streets over to avoid being seen, and taken the back alleys to their store so no one would spot us. Not that anyone was out on a night like tonight due to the poor weather, but there were cameras in various spots along the street front. We couldn't afford to be caught on one of them, sneaking around like a passel of bumbling criminals.

As I thought about cameras, I tugged on Coop's arm. She was easily four or five inches taller than me, making it hard for me to look up at her with the wind blowing snow in my face.

I cupped my eyes and asked something I'd thought about on the way over. "Hey, do you guys have security cameras in the storage room at the store? Or anywhere at the store, for that matter? Maybe we could easily solve this murder business by watching the footage to see who killed Hank."

I'd been so immersed in figuring out Coop and Trixie, I'd hardly paid any attention to Hank's murder. I still needed to ask her who she thought might have tattled on her and told the police she'd argued with Hank.

For that, I should be tarred and feathered. Coop would go to prison if we didn't find out who did this and I'd wasted an entire evening playing a game of "My story is nuttier than an episode of *Supernatural*," rather than blowing up the pictures I'd taken and finding an answer to this mess by brainstorming with my spies.

Trixie's shoulders sagged in defeat at my question. "I wish. We only just got our inventory in yesterday. There was some kind of delay in shipping because of the weather in the northeast, and we've been so busy unpacking, I forgot about looking into them, to be honest. It's just another thing I'm going to have to do once we handle this thing with Coop."

A camera would have been way too easy anyway. Why would any of this be easy? I nodded, pulling my knit hat tighter around my ears. "Also, mind telling me about the argument with Hank over the spike in rent? I'm sure you remember Detective Moore telling you an anonymous tip came in about you threatening to kill Hank, Coop."

Coop instantly nodded her head, seemingly not at all affected by the cold. "I did have an argument with Hank. Because he was lying. I told you that."

Shivering, my teeth chattering, I nodded. "Yeah. I get that, Coop. What I want to know is, why you threatened to kill him. Did you hear this argument, Trixie?"

Her teeth chattered, too, but her glance at me was full of remorse. "I didn't. I was out at the time, but he did get into a small confrontation with Coop. She told me about it."

"Where?" I asked. "*Where* did this happen, and did you really threaten to kill him?"

Now Coop looked remorseful. "Right outside the store after he'd already let himself in with his key, but I didn't threaten to kill him, Stevie Cartwright. I said when people lie, where I come from, you could get killed for something like that."

Oh, dear. So she had used the word *kill*, which I'm sure the police would extort to its fullest advantage.

"Did you hit him or touch him in an aggressive manner, Coop?" I asked on a wince, afraid to hear the answer.

"I didn't touch him. I swear." She held up her lean-fingered hand to emphasize as such.

"But you did get intimidating, Coop. You told me you backed him up against the wall of the building," Trixie said. "That's why we've talked about how to handle confrontations. Did you tell the police that?"

Man, this didn't look good. Though, I believed her when she said she didn't touch him.

But Coop stood firm. "They didn't ask me that. They just asked if I threatened to kill him and I said no. They didn't ask me *exactly* what I said."

If Coop didn't end up in prison, she had the makings of a pretty decent lawyer. "Do you remember if anyone saw this confrontation, Coop?"

"A lady with a black hairnet. I saw her from the corner of my eye. But I didn't see her face very well."

Well, that could be half our senior Eb Falls population. Though, a hairnet was pretty specific. "Okay, let's table this for now. My toes are going to break off from the cold. We need to get inside and get your owl. We'll talk more about this when we get back to the house."

Looking upward, I noted the vent to the store's heating system, which I prayed was constructed in the same fashion as ours. A quick peek around the front of the store from Win told us the police had reset the alarm, which meant we were going to have to use Bel to disarm it.

Pulling Bel from my purse, I tucked the tiny scarf I'd found on an old doll during a vintage-shopping spree around his neck. Bel's incredibly adept with his tiny feet. I didn't doubt if he could dial a phone, he could manage to find the key Trixie had left behind and get it into the lock. But it didn't make me any less worried about him.

"You ready, buddy?"

He flapped his web-like wings, gearing up for flight. "As I'll ever be."

"So here's the plan, pal, you're going to have to wiggle your way into the heating vent and down into the duct leading to the store's ceiling. But be very careful. Please. There are fans that'll cut you to ribbons if you get caught up in them, understand? I don't want you to end up chop suey. If it looks like you can't make it, come right back. Don't even try it. Arkady will go with you and relay to me what you see. Got it?" I gave him a kiss on the nose and rubbed his head.

"Got it."

"All I want you to do is locate Livingston, turn the alarm off with the code the girls gave you, and unlock the door with the key Trixie left on the counter. Leave the rest to me. *Please.*"

Thankfully, the back door to Inkerbelle's was nothing more than a pop-lock. One, according to

Trixie, she'd planned to replace but hadn't had time. It should be easy enough for Bel to open.

"Okey-doke, Boss. Here goes nuthin'," he chirped before taking flight, turning into a tiny white dot that blended in with the falling snow.

As he soared up to the roof, I almost lost sight of him in the frosty white of the snow, but Arkady was with him. That much made me feel better.

Pressing myself against the brick façade of the store, my eyes stinging from the cold, I asked, "Arkady? Is he there?"

"Dah. Fluffybutt is looking into vent now."

I held my breath. I think we all did—even Win, until Arkady said, "Belfry, *nyet*! It looks too narrow even for you, tiny ball of fur. You must listen to my lemon drop. She said don't take any—"

I heard a high-pitched squeak and Bel yell, "Bon-saaaai!" before there was nothing.

My heart began to throb in my chest. "Arkady! What happened? Oh, gravy, is he okay?"

"I cannot see him, *malutka*!" Arkady whisper-yelled, and I heard the tremor in his voice. It made my stomach plummet to my toes.

"Bel, good man! Answer us!" Win yelped.

And then, just as I was considering finding a ladder and climbing up the store's side myself, we heard the doorknob jiggle. I leaned against the maroon-painted door and whispered, "Bel, is that you?"

"Yeah, Boss. Just gimme a sec and you'll be in like Flynn."

"Crickety wickets, mate! You frightened me," Win declared seconds before the rusty back door jiggled and I threw it open.

Coop set me aside as though I were nothing more than a feather, then pushed her way past me to get inside.

Trixie was right behind her, making apologies over her shoulder the entire way. "I'm sorry, Stevie. Sometimes Coop doesn't always think before she acts. But I promise you her intentions are good. She loves Livingston like family. They've been together for centuries."

Centuries? "But didn't she say she was thirty-two?"

"That's what I taught her to say because people will surely freak out if she tells them she's been alive for centuries."

That was fair...

I held up both my gloved hands and poo-pooed her, trailing behind. "You don't have to explain. I get it. And as to Livingston, I feel the same way about Bel. I'd plow down the devil himself to get to Bel. So let's go find your owl."

Coop stormed toward the front of the store, her booted feet heavy as she called out, "Livingston! We're here!"

"*Haaalp!*" Bel screamed, his tiny voice filled with panic. "Get off me, you pterodactyl! I'm not the enemy!"

"Belfry!" I yelped, running toward the sound of his

voice, my spinny head pounding and my heart thrashing against my ribs.

"Livingston, noooooooooo!" Coop yelled from another room I hadn't seen upon my first visit, located right behind the cashier's counter at the front of the store. A light flipped on, slightly illuminating the dark store.

Now I was pushing Trixie out of my way and skidding behind the counter to plow through the door—to find Bel hanging precariously by one foot from the beak of a much bigger foe.

He sat upon the back of an old recliner, a red vinyl one with a torn seat and some stuffing seeping from the right arm. He flapped his gray-speckled wings, spreading them out, the span, in all their magnificent glory, easily three feet.

Coop moved so fast, she was almost a blur as she swiped at Bel, catching him in one hand and tapping Livingston on the head with a gentle but admonishing finger. "Livingston! What did Trixie tell us?"

He sighed, expelling a long breath. "What *didn't* she tell us, lass?" he replied, his words dripping sarcasm with a delightful but light Irish accent. "She's always tellin' us sometin'. Livingston, don't do this," he crooned in a pretty darn good imitation of Trixie. "Livingston, don't touch that. Livingston, it's not nice to lick all the icin' off the cupcakes. Livingston, Livingston, Livingston, Li-ving-ston!"

Trixie was right behind me, skirting my side to confront Livingston in all his owlish splendor. Gosh, he sure was pretty with his wide, unblinking brown and yellow orbs for eyes, and his mottled gray feathers. Pretty and cranky.

Hah—I knew someone just like him. Hashtag BelfrycoughBelfry.

Trixie clucked her tongue after chucking him under the chin with a smirk on her face. "Well, it *isn't* nice to lick all the icing off the cupcakes when they're not for you, Livingston. It's also not nice to eat our new friend's familiar. Please don't do it again."

"Wow, Red." Bel flapped out his wings with a ripple, shaking off Livingston's assault. "Nice catch!"

She held him up with two fingers before dropping him on my shoulder. "Thank you, Belfry. I'm sorry Livingston tried to eat you. It won't happen again, will it, Livingston?"

"Roight," the bird agreed.

"Say it," Coop demanded, running a loving hand over the owl's big head and scratching between his fanciful tufted ears. "Use the words."

"Sure, sure, sure. It will not happen again, my beautiful Coopie," he crooned, low and deep, leaning into Coop to accept her affectionate strokes. "Instead, I shall just starve to death the next time ya two crazier-than-the-bedbugs-on-a-Hilton-Hotel-mattress leave me for twelve solid hours without so much as a cricket. Far be it from me to lick the icin' off a cupcake when it might be the only ting standin' between me and death's door."

Trixie patted her arm and offered it to Livingston, who leapt from the back of the old, worn recliner he was sitting on to the safety of his friend. She rubbed the top of his head and cooed, "That was very dramatic. But truly, I'm so sorry, buddy. If you only knew the day we've had. We didn't mean to leave you alone for so long, time just got away from us."

He rubbed his round head against her cheek, despite his next harsh words, "Meanin' ya forgot me, *again*. How could ya forget ya have an owl? It is not like I blend into the walls, for Mona Lisa's sake. I am an *owl*, ladies. Fierce and feathered!"

Coop ran her cheek over the top of Livingston's head before she said sternly, "You are not fierce, Quigley Livingston. You're a fraidy-cat. It's not nice to lie, and you know it. Trixie sai—"

"Said so," he quipped. "Yes, yes. So what's goin' on? I've been asleep all day in me jail cell—I mean, gilded cage. And who is *this* delectable lady?"

"Speaking of cages, how did you get out of yours, Livingston?" Trixie asked, pointing to the large black steel cage on the floor by their bunk beds.

The owl swiveled his head. "Ya forgot the padlock, Dame Gothel. 'Tis easy to get out of there, even without opposable thumbs.

Trixie smiled warmly at him, her eyes lighting up with obvious affection. "It's a subconscious block. I hate locking you up in there, but it's the only way to take you from place to place without someone getting bitten." She glanced at me and explained, "People sometimes get overly zealous with Livingston, and one time a teenager—who didn't really mean any harm—

latched onto him a little too tight. Needless to say, there was a ruckus."

"A Rapunzel reference and a ruckus all in one conversation," I teased, amazed Livingston knew Rapunzel's jailor.

"Now, now. I did not bite him hard, Trixie. I merely nipped. He had me by the feathers, what else was I supposed to do, let him pluck me bald, for pity's sake?"

"I can't believe the police didn't find you in your cage. I also can't believe you didn't wake up while they searched the place—they made a mess out there, pal." Trixie turned to me and held up the bird. "Livingston sleeps all day sometimes," she explained. "He's mostly nocturnal. Or as nocturnal as a demon in an owl's body can be."

I remembered a story Dana'd once told me about an incident with a python they'd found after a drug bust, and how they'd called Horace (who almost singlehandedly ran Eb Falls animal control) to assist, only to find he'd been napping out by the old mill in his animal control van.

"They probably did find him," I commented, eyeing these new surroundings, roughed up by police intrusion. "I'll bet they called animal control and old Horace was too busy napping to come collect Livingston. So they left him here until they can make arrangements to have someone come get him. Let's be grateful for small favors. Had I known he was here, I would have insisted we get him immediately."

"Well, well. A responsible pet owner. Maybe you

can teach the women in my life a ting or two about abandonment and *starvation*."

Coop made a face at him. "Stop telling fibs, Livingston. You know that's not true. We feed you all the time, and you know what happens to people who tell tales."

Livingston hooted his discontent, making me chuckle as I looked around the sage-green room. It had bunk beds with matching patchwork quilts the police had mussed during their search; a small, sparkling white-tiled bathroom with a shower and sink; the tiniest stove known to man and an even tinier refrigerator.

I didn't realize how tiny their room would be. Somehow, I'd imagined it much bigger, like the extra room we have at Madam Zoltar's. You could fit almost an entire apartment's worth of furniture in ours. Starting a business was rough these days, compounded by the idea they were living in the store in such a small space—with an owl, no less. I had to give them credit.

"I'm Stevie Cartwright, Livingston." I held out my hand with a smile, then remembered that was a stupid gesture on my part because, duh, owls have no hands, and stuffed it into the coat of my pocket. "It's really nice to meet you."

"Uh, loves of my life...me darlin's?" Livingston said, his feathers rippling as he shook them out. "I thought I was supposed to be a big secret. Why are we talkin' to the sexy lady? Isn't that one of the two thousand and two rules that're—as ya say—a no-no? We are not supposed to tell anyone I can talk, remember?"

Trixie gasped, narrowing her eyes at the bird. "Livingston! Manners, please! That is not the way we speak to women. No objectifying. Now, be polite, and most especially, be kind. Stevie's been incredibly good to us and you almost ate her familiar."

He swiveled his round head and blinked his eyes the size of saucers at me. "Okay, okay. 'Tis nice to meet ya, too, Stevie. I deeply regret almost eating yer flyin' rat."

"Heeey, now! You watch who you're calling a flying rat, you stuffing-for-pillows lug!" Belfry squeaked a protest. "If you try that one more time, I'm gonna—"

"Bel! Play nice," I chastised, fighting a smile. "It was a simple misunderstanding. You'd have done the same if you thought someone was encroaching on your territory, and you know it. Now, introduce yourself and be polite about it, please."

As Bel buzzed around Livingston's head, chattering incessantly, I decided it was time to take a peek at that darn crime scene. "Ladies, why don't you grab some clothes and pack a bag to bring back to the house? I have plenty of room as you've already seen, and you can't stay here for obvious reasons. Now before you protest, I'm not taking no for an answer. That's off the table. But I'm begging you, please hurry up. We need to get the heck out of here before we're caught red-handed."

That set them in motion, leaving me a way to escape and head toward the storage room.

"Stephania, you know this isn't a good idea, do you not?"

"Of course I know it's not a good idea. However, we need to help poor Coop. *She* might survive prison, but I don't think Hannah the Hammer and her posse will survive *her*. I won't have the death of a perfectly good inmate on my hands. Plus, I really kinda like her, Win. She's a bit in your face, but then I find that refreshing. She holds nothing back. I mean, she wanted to knock Starsky out for being so pushy, so she did. I've wanted to knock Starsky out more times than I care to admit, and I haven't. Props to her is all I'm saying."

Both Win and Arkady laughed. "She can be quite volatile," Win agreed. "But at the risk of being a nag, I suggest you rely on the pictures you took rather than tussle with the actual crime scene, Dove. You can't afford to have anything disturbed."

"I'm not going to disturb it, I'm just going to peek inside. I took those pictures in a hurry. Maybe I missed something crucial," I said as I made my way through the dark store to the storage room, squinting to see where I was going and almost tripping over a random box.

I dug my phone out of my purse and clicked on the flashlight app. As I reached for the storeroom's door, I thought I heard a sound, like the shift of cardboard against the floor. But then I wondered if it wasn't one of the girls moving their clothes around in their tiny room.

So I popped open the door, sticking my head around the corner to peer into the windowless room.

The moment I held up my phone was the moment someone charged me with the roar of a warrior, catching me at the waist and knocking the breath out of my lungs when my back hit the wall behind us before we both fell.

"Stephania!" Win cried out a warning, his alarm filling the air.

As we scrambled on the floor—me trying to hang on to whoever my attacker was by wrapping my arms around his shoulders, and him (at least I think it was a him) trying to get away from me—I simultaneously heard Coop and saw something shiny.

Shiny and deadly sharp.

Holy cauldrons and magic wands.

That shiny sharp thing was a sword.

A big, big sword.

Eep!

CHAPTER 10

"*U*nhand Stevie Cartwright or I'll slice your head off!" Coop hollered seconds before we all screamed (my favorite ghosts included) in unison.

"No, Coop, noooo!"

Just as she was about to take a swing at my attacker, the long, thing blade arcing in the air with a whizzing sound, Trixie was right behind her, grabbing at her arm. "Coop! No!"

But Trixie's action gave the bad guy exactly the millisecond he needed to push off me, hop to his feet and run the ten or so feet to the back door. It slammed after him, leaving a cold burst of air in his departure.

And I was ready and willing to go after him as I rolled to my side and leveraged off the floor with my hands.

But Coop put firm fingers like a vise grip on my shoulder to stop me. "No, Stevie. You're bleeding." She used a finger to wipe at my forehead, her eyes concerned.

I must have klunked heads with my attacker, though I don't remember it, but it could mean he had a knot on his head, too. That would surely help in identifying him.

If it was a *him*, that is.

"Anyone get a look at him? Or if it was a male at all?" I asked, swiping at my head.

"I follow for a little bit, but you know Arkady Bagrov can only go so far without you. I only can go to alley. Also, it was too dark, my *malutka*. I could not see a tree in the park," Arkady complained. "Did you see, Zero?"

"The forest for the trees, Arkady," I corrected, wincing at the throb in my head.

"No, mate. It all happened so fast and I was too concerned for Stephania's well being to attempt to follow. But Stephania, I urge you to summon as much of the experience in your mind as you can. Sight, smell, sound."

"Oh, Stevie!" Trixie cried out, pulling her scarf off to place it at my head to staunch the bleeding. "Coop, get some ice, please."

As Coop stormed off, Trixie pushed the hair from my eyes, peering at me while I tied the scarf around my head like a bandana. "Are you okay?"

I blew out a breath, rolling my head on my neck. "Oh, I'm fine. Believe me, I've been through far worse. This is nothing compared to a broken butt."

Trixie fought a giggle, her gentle hands moving over my scalp to check for further injuries. "You broke your butt?"

"Long story. Someday I'll tell you all about it. Forget that *and* my head. We need to figure out what whoever that was wanted in the storage room. Must be pretty important. I wonder if they were hiding in there the whole time we were out here or came in after. So can you think of anything?"

Trixie shook her head, straightening her cap as she stooped to grab my phone, which thankfully hadn't cracked. "We don't have anything important in there, Stevie. We don't own anything worth much more than a few dollars except the tattoo equipment."

As I shone the light on my phone into the room, I noticed the police tape was broken, so I took a step inside.

But Trixie put her hand on my arm. "Do you think you should do that, Stevie?"

"I don't think I should. I *know* I should. Listen, whoever that was had already broken the crime scene tape. It's not going to kill me to look around."

"But what about DNA and all that stuff they convict you with? I might have missed a lot, living in a convent, but I've binge-watched enough *Criminal Minds* to know they can convict you with almost nothing. I don't want you in trouble because of us, Stevie," she insisted with a tremor in her voice.

Holding the phone higher, I began at the top of the shelves in the room and swept my way down, inching into the space with small steps. "My DNA, or likely my hair strands, whatever, are already in here because I was just in this room earlier today. Don't fret, Trixie. I promise I'm just going to take a peek—" I stopped dead in my tracks and gaped at the floor.

Hank's body was gone, of course, but in its place was something interesting—something in the exact spot where he fell. What the frack?

"Stevie?" Trixie called out. "What happened?"

I shined the light over the floor. "What was here, Trixie?" I pointed to a gaping hole in the floorboards where someone had clearly lifted them—with purpose, I might add—to search for something. It was about three feet long and a couple of feet wide. Easily big enough to hide a box or something substantial. But what? The question was, had the intruder done it or had the police?

Suddenly, Trixie was behind me, her stilted breathing in my ear. "Blessed Mother..." she muttered. "I...I don't know. I didn't even know the floorboards were loose, but I can assure you, we didn't hide anything in there."

"Stephania, take a picture. You need to hightail it out of here. Who knows if someone heard all that ruckus and called the police?"

Win was right—again. I snapped several photos, looking around the removed floorboards with a critical eye before backing away, taking Trixie's hand to guide her out of the room with me.

"We need to blow this Popsicle stand before we get

caught. Get Livingston and Coop and your things and let's get the heck out of here," I instructed.

But Coop was already prepared, a Ziploc bag of ice in one hand, a suitcase in the other, and Livingston on her shoulder. Oh, and that sword. That long, shiny sword, tucked into the loop of the waistband of her jeans as though it had always been there.

I closed the door to the storage room, making sure everything was as the attacker had left it. As we made our way out of the back exit, careful to set the alarm, I wondered about Coop's sword.

I wondered where she got it, why she had it, and if she'd ever killed anyone with it.

Then I wondered if I should wonder any of those things. Because all those questions had answers I was afraid to hear.

~

J took a big bite of my slice of pizza, so grateful to be home in my warm kitchen with Whiskey at my feet, and Strike safely in his bed, downloading those pictures from my phone to my laptop.

My mind whirred with questions about who'd want to kill Hank Morrison, and if he'd been killed over what was in that floor or if the missing boards had nothing to do with this at all.

We mostly ate in silence, each of us lost in our thoughts and all of us starving after going the better part of the day without food. Coop was already on her fourth slice of pizza, making me sick with jealousy at her svelte form as she gobbled all those carbs with nary a care, while I'd have to do a hundred crunches at Win's command just to eat up one slice worth of calories.

"How's your head, Stevie?" Trixie asked, concern riddling her voice as she wiped her mouth and set her napkin on the table.

It only throbbed a little. My back hurt more than anything else after being plowed into the wall. Turned out it was just a smallish knot on my head. No big deal in light of what I'd suffered in the past. I'd almost forgotten about it as I put my hand to my head, the scarf still tied around my skull.

"Like I said, this is nothing. Believe that. I'm more concerned for you two. How are you both? It's been a brutally long day for you."

Trixie punctuated my statement by covering her yawn. "I'm fine, and ready to help you figure this out. Just tell me how I can, and I'm at your service. I don't know much about Hank, other than he was a little money-hungry. But I don't think he should be dead because of it."

Coop placed her palm on her sword's ruby-red handle, tilting it toward her as she took yet another slice of pizza. "I'm ready, too, Stevie Cartwright. What can I do to help? Do you want me to sniff out the bad man who knocked you down?"

Taking a swig of my water, I tilted my head in her direction and let her comment about sniffing out the "bad man" slide. "My, what a big sword you have there, Coop. Care to explain?"

She gave me that look again, the same one she gave me when I'd told her I was a medium. "I don't understand."

"Why do you have an instrument of death, Coop?"

"To protect myself from my enemies."

Well, duh, Stevie. The answer's so obvious. "You do know not everyone has a sword, don't you? It's not like a laptop or a phone, Coop. And most especially not everyone has a sword as deadly looking as that one. So what's the story behind it?"

Her gaze was a thoughtful one as she tucked her hair behind her ears, but as she stroked the handle of her sword, her eyes became possessive. "I brought it with me when I escaped Hell. It's mine and no one else can have it."

Trixie reached out a hand to Coop, tapping her finger. "No one wants to take it from you, Coop. I promise. But you do remember what we talked about, don't you? You can't slice your enemies' heads off here on Earth. It's against the law. That's also why I told you threatening isn't allowed either."

"But he was going to hurt Stevie. No one is allowed to hurt Stevie," Coop defended, her answer straightforward and without malice.

I rose, stretching my arms to the ceiling, fighting a smile at this new alliance I'd cultivated without really trying. "So, new rule, Coop, okay? No slicing heads off of anyone. I realize whoever that was back at the store knocked me down, and I did get hurt, and I sure appreciate you looking out for me, but I don't think he wanted to kill me—which means you can't kill him, okay?"

She chomped on her pizza and nodded as though I'd made a reasonable enough request. "Okay. No killing. Also, incidentally, you say 'no' a lot. You're just like Trixie."

I giggled, unable to stop myself. "I'm just trying to protect you and keep you out of prison, which is probably what Trixie's doing, too. I do realize you're not used to...humans and our ways. And where was that thing, anyway? How did the police miss that weapon of sharp destruction?"

Now Coop grinned, and once more, it was as though the Heavens opened up and hurled all their glowing, mystical light upon her perfect face. "I hid it in the wall behind the bed. Trixie told me I couldn't show it to anyone or I might get into trouble. I don't want to get into trouble, but I don't want to lose my sword either. So I hid it."

I grinned at her, grabbing my paper plate to take to the trash, but not before I slipped Whiskey some leftover crust. "Just keep it hidden, please. We don't need the police finding out you have one of those. It doesn't look good for someone under suspicion of murder."

"I did not kill Hank Morrison. I always admit when I kill someone. I'm not a liar," Coop chirped.

I blanched as Trixie gathered her plate, too, stopping to give Livingston—who happily chomped on some Cheetos—a pat on his round head. It turned out, he was a bird after my own heart. According to the ladies, he didn't eat what owls ate.

There'd be no mice or squirrels for him. In fact, the very idea made him positively squeamish. He was a dyed-in-the-wool junk-food junkie, just like me. After looking up owls on the Internet while we ate, I also discovered he was of the Great Horned variety.

Bel flew around the ceiling, buzzing his way to my shoulder, where he landed to snuggle into my hair, making Trixie ask, "So what's a familiar, Stevie? Coop says it has something to do with witches."

Win barked a laugh. "If Coop only knew."

I dropped my plate into the garbage and turned to smile at her. "She's right on the money. A familiar is a witch's guide."

Trixie gnawed on her lower lip. "So you're a witch?" And then she chuckled nervously. "I can't believe I'm asking such an outrageous question, but after what's happened to us, and finding out about Coop's origins, *nothing* seems outrageous anymore. But you don't have to tell me if you'd rather not. I'd totally understand."

"I don't mind at all. I'm an ex-witch who lost her powers and was booted out of her coven through no fault of my own. When this is all done, and we're sharing a nice spaghetti dinner to welcome you to Eb Falls with the people I plan to introduce you to, I'll tell you all about it. For now, all you need to know is my powers are mostly gone. I've had blips here and there, but none in quite a while."

Which made me incredibly sad. I'd tried not to get my hopes up when my powers made minor appearances, but since the last time, I'd fizzled out—and with that, I found myself working hard to be grateful for what I *did* have instead of moping.

Trixie gave me a light squeeze to my shoulder. "Oh, Stevie. I'm so sorry. We have a lot more in common than I thought, huh?"

"How so?"

"I was kicked out of my convent. I know I told you I left, but that's not the truth. Through no fault of my own, though, and if we ever get to have that spaghetti dinner, I'll tell you all about it. For now, let's focus on clearing Coop's name."

Nodding, I remembered what Luis had said. "Names... We need to get Coop a last name, pronto. We also need to create an identity for her, and it needs to say she's been off the grid or something. Maybe she grew up in a commune setting or something?"

Trixie's sigh was forlorn as she rested her arms on our marble island and lay her head on them. "I don't even know where to begin," she groaned.

"Ah, but I do. Tell Trixie to worry not," Win exclaimed. "We'll have Coop all settled in the matter of an hour. Bel, my good man? Come, we have work to do!"

Bel buzzed off with Win, and I decided, now that my stomach was full of gooey cheese and pepperoni, and my buzz was long gone, we needed to strike while the iron was hot.

I patted her on the back before heading back to the kitchen table and my laptop. "Win says don't worry. Now, c'mon. Let's take a look at those pictures and see what we can find out, okay?"

The doorbell rang then.

Usually a cheerfully welcome sound, it now came across as ominous and worrisome. It was never a good sign when the doorbell rang at almost eleven o'clock at night.

Hopping up, I pointed at the ladies and whispered, "Take Livingston and hide! Don't make a sound. The basement door is just around the corner before the dining room, go down there and stay put. Hurry!"

The women left with nary a peep, taking Livingston with them as I rushed to the door.

Looking at the security camera, I sighed.

Dana. Shoot. I'd forgotten all about our coffee date tonight. But why wouldn't he just text me or call instead of coming all the way out here?

Pulling the door open, I plastered a smile on my face. "Officer Nelson! How delightful you should come all the way out here to check on little old me. If I were a thinking girl, I'd say you were behaving like a friend. Were you sad I missed our coffee date?"

He eyed me with his usual skepticism as the snow poured down in large flakes behind him and his rigid form. "I texted you about our coffee date and told you I couldn't make it because I had to work late."

Dang. Must've missed that in the process of having

my head bashed in. "I forgot to check my phone. Rain check?"

"That's not why I'm here, Miss Cartwright," he replied, his tone dripping authority as he brushed droplets of moisture from his official police-issued jacket.

Of course it wasn't. He only called me Miss Cartwright when he was on official police biz. Yet, I played innocent. "Then why are you here on such a dark and stormy night, Officer Rigid?"

"May I come in?"

I faked a yawn and shivered. "Well, it's pretty late, and I'm just getting ready to go to bed. Can't whatever it is that you need wait until tomorrow?"

Just then, Whiskey drove his nose beside my legs, happily sniffing Dana's scent and wagging his tail with a fury. He loved Dana. Dana played ball with him and brought him the bones from his porterhouse steaks.

Dana reached down a hand with a smile and scruffed the top of Whiskey's head. "Nothing tonight, buddy. But next time, I promise. Now tell your mistress I'd like to speak to her."

Obviously, there was no getting out of this, so I swung the door open and stepped aside. "Fine, but you'd better make it fast, Officer. I have a new facial cream I'm dying to try."

He took one long stride inside and began to make his way toward the kitchen without even asking. He spun around once he was standing near the island and pulled out a stool to sit down. Then he pointed to the scarf on my head with one eyebrow raised. "Why do you have a scarf around your head, Miss Cartwright?"

Boy, was I ever grateful I'd kept the dang thing on, or for sure he'd see my shiner. "Because it's cold?"

He popped his lips. "That's not the real answer, is it?"

"Oh, fine. I was pretending to be the Karate Kid. Wax on, wax off. Remember?" I made the motion with my hands while I stood on one foot, fighting a giggle.

"I remember. I just don't believe you."

Putting a hand on my hip, I made a face at him. "Always coming from a place of no, aren't you, Officer? Listen, I'm a single woman who lives with a dog and a turkey. I'm just shy of crazy by a couple of cats and some knitting needles. I have to do something to amuse myself."

"Miss Cartwright, where are Miss Lavender and Coop?" He gazed intently at me

Uh-oh. That was his I'm-really-serious face.

Tilting my head, I gave him my best confused look. "I have no idea who you mean."

Now his eyes narrowed right at me, glinting under the kitchen lights in their fierceness. "Sure you do, Miss Cartwright. Remember the tattoo lady and her almost freakishly pretty friend? You know, the ladies you were with this morning when we found Hank Morrison *murdered*?"

Scratching my head, I doubled down on my confused look, set on taking it to the next level. "Freakishly pretty friend? Hmmm. I think I'd remember a freakishly pretty friend. Now, if she were just plain-old pretty, that'd be a whole other story altogether. And did you say her name was *Coop*? Like Coop Deville? Coopster? Coop-Coop-Coop-ba-doop—"

"Stevie!" he almost bellowed, his eyes flashing his anger.

I gave him a blank look. "What? You don't like Salt-N-Pepa? I should've known. You're probably more—"

"Cut it out!" he barked, then straightened his spine and took a breath. "Tell me where they are. *Now.* Please."

So I shrugged my shoulders, remaining unruffled by his abruptness. "I have no idea." Less is more. Win always told me that, and I was going to utilize his advice.

He sucked in his cheeks. "Really? Care to explain their car parked outside then?"

I gasped with mock astonishment. "Their car is in my driveway? The nerve of some people, parking wherever they want like I'm running some kind of parking lot! It's unseemly, Officer Stick Up His Butt! Give them a ticket this instant!"

Dana's face hardened and his jaw clenched, revealing that tic that always showed up to the party when he was becoming aggravated with my shenanigans. He looked over his shoulder at the table, still littered with pizza boxes and a stray Doritos bag.

"Are you really telling me they're not here, Miss Cartwright?"

I gave him a coy smile, twisting a strand of my hair

around my finger. "I have no idea what you're talking about."

"So you, little ol' *you*, ate all that food? Two pizzas and a bag of Doritos?"

"Are you calling me fat?"

His glittering hazel eyes narrowed again. "I'm doing no such thing."

"Do you have any idea the kind of appetite one can work up when they're pretending to be the Karate Kid? All that downward-facing dog really gets the endorphins flowing."

"Downward-facing dog is yoga and has nothing to do with the Karate Kid," he said, straight-faced, looking as though he were ready to explode, like when a lit match and an oil tanker collide.

I wrinkled my nose at him. "Picky-picky. Does it really matter how I worked up my appetite? Isn't it sad enough that I stuffed all those meaningless calories into my face while my dog and my turkey looked on in pity? You have to pile on by body-shaming me, too? That's so cruel, Dana Nelson. I can't even believe you're capable of such a thing."

But he ignored me and refused to be knocked off the track of his line of questioning. "And the sword?"

Oh. That. I fought a wince and curtsied. "Sometimes I like to add some spice to my Karate Kid portrayals and I pretend I'm the Karate Kid—*Ninja Warrior* edition."

"Stevie?" he said, cool as a cucumber.

"Oh, now I'm Stevie, but a second ago I was Miss Cartwright? Pick a lane, Officer Nelson."

He drummed his fingers on the counter, clearly trying to keep his patience with me. We rode the line of police officer versus civilian and friends often. "Where are Miss Lavender and Coop?"

I crossed my arms over my chest and gave him a suspicious look. "Why do you want to know, anyway? What difference does it make where they are as long as they don't leave town?"

He slipped off the stool and approached me, his eyes pinning mine. "Okay, here's the score. I'm here on official police business, Stevie. Let's quit playing around, please."

My heart began to race. This wasn't good news. Not good at all. "State your case, please."

He ran his tongue around the inside of his cheek, his eyes growing more intense by the second. "I'm here to bring Coop in as a person of interest in the murder of Hank Morrison. The detectives have more questions for her. Now where are they? Or do you want to go to be hauled in for questioning, too?"

CHAPTER 11

"*S*tephania, don't do something emotionally driven," Win reminded in my ear.

But here's the thing. Sure, Coop might survive jail, because it's evident she could fight her way out of a cage match without so much as a broken fingernail.

But would she survive emotionally? Trixie navigated more than most of her social interactions. I couldn't imagine her in jail—even for a night—picking her way through the network of scum who end up there. She was too honest, too vulnerable in her effort not to lie and be a good person, and I suspected it was all due to her time in Hell. Likely, she'd done bad things to survive because hello, *Hell.*

I couldn't bear the idea she'd be taken advantage of, or tricked into doing something she would end up finding out was the *wrong* thing to do, and it would be to her detriment. I wouldn't allow that.

So I had two choices. Give her up, or keep right on lying to protect her from a far worse fate. If Dana took her in and she said one wrong thing without Luis with her, she wouldn't be just a "person of interest" for long. I knew he knew I was messing with him, but I didn't care.

Now, *my* eyes narrowed, but I kept my cool. "Are you here to arrest her?"

"I'm here to bring her in because I'm the only one the precinct could spare with the weather the way it is. But I suspect they'll likely charge her with Hank's murder."

Then this conversation was over.

I lifted my chin and pushed the tail of the scarf still around my head over my shoulder. "It doesn't matter what you're here to do. I told you, Officer Nelson, they're not here." There. Decision made and out in the universe. I couldn't take it back now.

"And I think you're lying, Miss Cartwright," he insisted, his mouth a thin line of anger.

Believe me when I say, we've been at odds like this before, except this time, the stakes were much bigger. This was a childlike woman's life on the line.

I shot him my haughty, one-eyebrow-raised glare. "I don't care what you think. Now, unless you have a search warrant to tear my place up again while you look for them—which I'm guessing you don't because what judge in Eb Falls is awake past nine o' clock?—I'll simply thank you to be on your way until you can show me something official," I said from stiff lips. We weren't playing a fun game I could talk my way out of anymore. Now I was playing for keeps.

"You're harboring a suspect in a murder investigation, Miss Cartwright. I don't always like my job, but it's my job, and I have no intention of losing it—not even for you."

I wandered my way to the front door, ignoring his words as I did. I pulled it open, grabbing Whiskey's collar to keep him from jettisoning out to play in the snow, which continued to pile up.

"You have no proof I'm harboring even so much as a grudge. It's time you left, Officer Nelson. Good night."

Dana's nostrils flared at my words but he tipped his head and was gone, down the snowy steps, leaving only his footprints in his wake.

Letting out a breath of air, I fought the sting of tears. Dana was my friend, but I knew I was right about not giving up Coop. Knew it in my bones.

"Dove?" Win whispered in my ear. "How fare thee?"

Sniffing, I shrugged. "Thee fares rather poorly, thank you. I just couldn't let him take Coop, Win. And it's not the violence I worry she'd face in jail that made me lie."

"It's her determination to be, as she calls it, 'a good person'. She's tough as nails, but she's also quite vulnerable. I understand and support your choice, Stevie."

"Me, too, *malutka*. This Coop is violent, but not without cause and not without provocation."

"So you guys aren't mad?" I asked in disbelief. "I

thought surely when you told me not to use my emotions, you meant I should give her up, Win."

"Why would I be angry, Dove? You're protecting someone who needs protecting in a way that has nothing to do with strength. What I meant was to simply *think* about your emotions—meaning, when fear is heightened, we sometimes do things we regret. I didn't want you to give in to the fear Officer Nelson would arrest you."

I grinned up at the ceiling. "Wow, you've come a long way, haven't you? You used to be Mr. By The Book, Spy Guy."

"And I still am for the most part. But I also know Officer Nelson, and if he didn't come with a search warrant, he doesn't really believe Coop's guilty. He just wasn't motivated enough, or he'd have suggested getting one before he ever drove out here. I'm sure he knew you'd ask for one. Subconsciously, he believes in Coop's innocence, leading me to believe they don't really have anything on her. I pray that means they didn't find some sort of toxin in the tattoo gun's ink. He's simply following orders. Now he can go back and tell his superiors she's not here. Mission accomplished."

Well, that was one way to look at it. I'd like to believe Dana was being fair, but Dana was Dana. He played by the rules with no regrets.

"So don't be angry with him, Stephania, eh?" Win prompted.

I flapped a hand at the ceiling and made a face. "I'm a

little angry with him, but not enough to sever all ties. I'll get over it. For now, we have bigger fish to fry. We have zero time to find Hank Morrison's killer before they hunt Coop down, Win, and hardly anything to go on. If Starsky can pin it on her, he will. Without a last name and any kind of history, she looks like a vagabond. And it won't be long before they drag Trixie in there, too."

Just then, I remembered Coop and Trixie were still in the basement and rushed to let them know the coast was clear. Coop met me at the top of the basement stairs.

She poked her gorgeous head out of the door. "Is the policeman gone?"

I nodded confirmation with a sympathetic smile. "He is, and we have work to do. So grab your beverage of choice, put on something comfortable, and let's get crackin', girls."

But Coop hesitated, driving her hands into the pockets of her leather pants as she stepped back into the kitchen, her expression now shy and maybe even a little fearful. "Maybe I should go to the policeman's station and turn myself in. That's what it's called, right, Stevie Cart...um, Stevie?"

Trixie was directly behind her with Livingston on her shoulder, her eyes wide and glassy from lack of sleep. "We heard everything he said, Stevie. We're giving you nothing but grief. I don't want you to lie for us. It's the last thing we want you to do. I think we should just get in the car and leave."

"But it's freezin' out there, lass!" Livingston protested, the feathers on his back ruffling.

Coop put two fingers over the owl's beak and frowned. "Hush, Livingston. It's not nice to be ungrateful and complain when someone has been kind to you. We're treating Stevie poorly by staying here in her house and putting her at risk. She told lies to keep us safe, and I know Trixie said sometimes you have to tell white lies, but Stevie could still get into trouble for harboring a…a bad person."

Without thinking, I threw my arms around Coop's neck and hugged her hard while her arms hung awkwardly at her sides and her entire perfect body went stiff. "You're doing no such thing, Coop. Knock it off with that kind of talk. You're here and you're staying here until we figure this out or I find you a better hiding place. You're not leaving this house unless you're free and clear. No outlaws allowed." Drawing back, I patted her cheek before turning toward the kitchen table. "Now, we have work to do. Let's do that, shall we?"

Trixie let out a shaky breath and cracked her knuckles with a smile. "Tell me what you want me to do, and I'm all in."

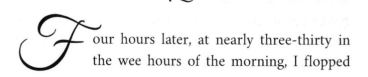

our hours later, at nearly three-thirty in the wee hours of the morning, I flopped down on the table, head in my arms, and groaned. "What, what, whaaat am I missing?" I cried.

Trixie rubbed the heels of her hands to her eyes, now red and glassy. "There's nothing in these pictures, Stevie. I'm telling you, you're not missing anything."

We'd blown up and printed out all the pictures I'd taken of the crime scene, every last one, and spread them all over the kitchen table, but they gave us absolutely nothing to go on. *Nothing.*

"I don't get it. Nothing about the way Hank landed on the floor or the position of his body gives us any hint as to what happened to him. We only have the assumption he was killed with the tattoo gun, but no solid proof as of yet. But there was none or very little, if any, blood on the floor under him. He looks like he just crumpled. Which could mean it was sudden. The only other explanation is poison in the gun. That would explain how everything around him is still mostly in order. For sure it doesn't look like he tussled with anyone. Argh!" I fisted my hands and shook them at the ceiling.

Trixie peered at the picture of Hank's body, squinting her eyes, then shook her head. "It does look just like he fell down. What I'd like to know is how long he was there. We left the store last night for about an hour to grab some dinner at the diner before the roads got too bad. We were only gone an hour and a half or so."

"Did you go into the storage room when you came back?" I asked.

"Nope," Trixie confirmed. "We watched a little Netflix and then we went to bed. It was pretty late by the time we got back in, and of course, if it happened while we were gone, Livingston wouldn't know because he sleeps the sleep of the dead."

The owl's head swiveled in Trixie's direction, his wide eyes droopy. "I heard nothin', lass. Not a peep."

I groaned again and wrapped my arms around my stomach. "Did you go anywhere in the morning?"

"Just to the coffee store," Coop said, trailing her finger over one of the pictures. "But we weren't gone very long."

"Well, it doesn't take long to murder someone, Coop," I reminded her.

"Yes. I know that."

Her concise words chilled me. I didn't want to know how she knew. "Okay, so until we have an approximate time of death, we have even less than I thought, but it had to have happened either when you were out for dinner or when you went for coffee. The locks on that back exit aren't exactly meant to keep much out, so the killer probably just popped it open without much fuss."

"Once this is all over, I'm going to make it a point to put bolts on the door," Trixie assured.

"Do you know if anyone had keys to the store other than Hank?"

Trixie pinched the bridge of her nose. "As far as I know, he was the only one other than us."

I rubbed a hand over my grainy eyes. "Can you guys

think of anything—anyone—who might want to hurt Hank? Did you hear anything from other Eb Fallers about him?"

"You've been over that with them already. I think it's time to call it a night, Stephania. Surely some sleep will refresh all of you," Win suggested with a gentle tone.

Yet, I shook my head with vehemence. "But we have no time, Win. They're going to arrest Coop because that's *her* tattoo gun with her fingerprints on it, and whatever's in that gun probably killed Hank. I know you don't think that's what it is, but it's always the obvious, isn't it? It's the first thing the police considered."

But Coop actually looked offended. "I would never put poison in the ink, Stevie Cartwright! That's wrong and bad."

I clenched my eyes shut and rubbed them, smearing what was left of my mascara on my fingertips. "I know you wouldn't, Coop. But someone else might, and unfortunately, that will make it look like *you* did it. Which suggests premeditation, by any definition, but who would want to murder Hank and frame Coop?"

"He was a bad man. I bet a lot of people wanted him dead," Coop said in her deadpan way.

The question of premeditation led me to something else. "When was the last time you used the tattoo gun, Coop?"

"I haven't used it yet. I only took it out of the box and looked at it. We don't have any clients to use it on."

"Could someone have gotten their hands on it and put something in the ink?"

Trixie's eyes went wide as she twisted her hands together, her knuckles white. "I suppose anything's possible, but it would be pretty tough to get into the store without one of us seeing something."

"I hate to point out the obvious, but someone was murdered—possibly while you were in the store," I commented, feeling positively awful.

Trixie rapped the table with a knuckle. "Touché."

"Okay, then I need you two to write me up a time-line of your comings and goings since you had that tattoo gun delivered. Think back on everything you've done, when you've left the store together, apart, whatever, since the gun arrived," I stressed. "We need answers, and we need them now before they get search warrants, and I know darn well Dana will be back here first thing in the morning with a search warrant."

"While that's likely true, Dove, you'll do yourself no favors without sleep. You do know how cranky you become when you don't get your eight. Dare I say, irrational and overly emotional."

Tears of frustration sprang to my eyes because Win's words were true. As much as I hated to admit it, I'm a schlump without the proper amount of shuteye.

Coop, who looked like she'd just left a photo shoot for *Vogue*, and not in the least tired, pointed to the ceiling. "I think the man up there is right. You'd better sleep, Stevie. I don't like when Trixie is cranky. She gets weepy. I don't think I'll like you that way either."

I shot her a look of sympathy. "But aren't you tired, too, Coop? All that worry with your neck on the line has to be exhausting."

Coop gave me an odd look. "I don't need much sleep and my neck is right here, Stevie. Not on a line." She pointed to her swan-like neck.

Trixie burst out in laughter, jarring Livingston, who'd fallen sound asleep on the back of the kitchen chair, contrary to their claim he was nocturnal. "Stevie means we're in a precarious situation, Coop. It's one of those expressions."

Coop sighed, leaning forward and cupping her chin to look at me thoughtfully. "I don't understand human expressions. Why don't humans just say what they mean?"

Why didn't they indeed? "Because we're all too afraid to say what we mean. So we hide behind innuendo and mixed metaphors. That's why. But I'm not afraid to say we're stewed if we don't find something soon. Trixie, what did you find online about Hank?"

I'd tasked her with looking up and bookmarking every piece of information she could find on Hank. Where he was born, where he went to school, if he had siblings.

"Well, as you know, Abe was his stepfather. His biological father died at the age of sixty-two back in 2004 of pancreatic cancer. His name was John Morrison. And you mentioned you'd met Hank's mother, Francie Morrison Levigne, once or twice, right?"

A picture of Francie Levigne flashed through my

mind. A sturdy woman with thick arms and legs and hair dyed so black, it almost looked blue in the sunlight.

I tapped the table with my finger. "Yep. Met her at bingo not long before Abe passed. Very pleasant, if not super chatty. Not nearly as scary as her imposing image would make her seem. But I've only seen her once or twice since then."

Trixie pointed to the screen and cocked her head. "As sort of an aside, this article from 1987 says in her heyday, Francie was an ax-throwing champion. How unusual."

"Very unusual. I didn't even know that was a thing. I bet Hank thought twice about cutting up with a mother who had those kinds of skills, huh?" I said with a giggle I couldn't help.

"And then there's Hank," Trixie continued, her index finger skirting the screen of my laptop to keep her place. "He never married and has no children that anyone is aware of. All that's left is Hank's sister, Pricilla. She's his older sister by three years, at forty-six. She lives here in Eb Falls with her husband and her two teenage girls. She works at the high school in the cafeteria. Hardly looks murderous." She swung the laptop toward me so I could see her picture.

Pricilla looked nothing like Hank. She was a tall, fair-skinned blonde with a wide smile and overly made-up eyes.

"I didn't even know Hank had a sister…" I said, surprised by that revelation. "But then, I didn't really mingle much with him. Did he have any hobbies or tickets or anything that might lead us to a suspect? Any suspect at all?"

"He liked to golf," Trixie responded, showing me an article from the Eb Falls newspaper. "He's in this picture here—right there in the crowd. But mostly he liked to buy and sell real estate."

I squeezed my temples and watched the snow continue to fall over the Sound. At this rate, I think we could classify this snow as a potential blizzard. My hope was, the terrible weather would continue long enough to keep the police at bay. Eb Falls wasn't equipped for snow like this. We didn't have a large number of plows the way the northern states do. If the roads stayed messy enough, we might catch a break. At least for a little while. I could always find somewhere for Coop and Trixie to go to keep them from the police, but it wouldn't matter if I didn't find something —some kind of evidence that proved Coop wasn't a killer.

Pinching my temples, I asked, "What about a Facebook page? Did he have one? Twitter, maybe?"

"That was my next search." Trixie's fingers clacked on the keyboard while I pondered Hank.

He'd certainly inherited a lot of real estate after Abe passed, and he wasn't exactly making friends if he was raising rents left and right. We needed to look into whether he'd pulled the same fast one on someone else the way he had Trixie and Coop.

"Jackpot!" Trixie yelped, rising to sit up straight in

the chair and reposition herself. "Hank didn't just own our building. He owned the yoga studio, the flower shop, and the beauty salon among several other buildings—and some of those renters were very angry with Hank for raising their rent, too. Look at some of these posts on his business page on Facebook!"

She swung the laptop in my direction once more and pointed to a post about how he'd just acquired another property, and saying he'd post more once the deal was sealed.

As I read the comments, several in particular caught my eye, but one by Burt Freely made me sit up and pay attention, and it had nothing to do with the poor grammar.

Your a cheap no good SOB Hank Morrison. Abe is rolled around in his grave for the way your treating us! You better watch your back!

I clicked on Burt's profile to find he was part owner of the men's barbershop on Main. Hank owned that building too, according to Google. As I perused his page, I noted Burt didn't look anything like a killer. He was more teddy bear than cold-blooded murderer, but he sure was big enough to have been the person who knocked me down last night.

I bookmarked Burt's page as a person of interest to question then read more comments.

One from Enid Gunkle in response to Hank's new property read, *And the rich get richer while the rest of us slugs live paycheck to paycheck! Hell awaits your arrival!*

Now we might be getting somewhere. "Hank had a

lot of people angry with him, didn't he?" I mused. "He must have pulled the same fast one on all these people that he pulled on you two."

"Hank Morrison was a bad man. He told lies," Coop said, her jaw clenched.

I pushed away from the table and stretched my arms again while rolling my head from side to side. "Yes. He sure wasn't a nice one, Coop. But please don't let anyone hear you say that. It only strengthens the case against you."

"Okay, that's enough, Stevie. It's off to bed with you," Trixie insisted. "You've sacrificed your sleep and your time. You need rest. We'll clean up. Just tell us where we're sleeping and we'll take care of the rest."

Normally, I'm not so easily put off, and I know I've been missing a good mystery to pass the time. But this one had, in the mere hours since it had cropped up, become very important to me. Sure, it's always important to me to bring justice to the dead, but I'd become emotionally involved with these women now, and it was crucial I had my head about me when I sought out some of these potential suspects.

So I gave in. Unwrapping the scarf from my head, I gave both women a hug. "I just need a couple of hours of sleep and I'll be good to go. Your bedrooms are up the stairs and to the right. There are fresh towels and soaps and all sorts of toiletries on each of your beds. If you need anything at all, just holler. Please don't hesitate. And Coop? Tomorrow we go over your new identity. Win says his friend's created a really solid background for you, but you'll need to memorize it, okay?"

"I'll do as you say," she assured, moving to clean the table free of the pictures we'd spread out.

"Stevie? We can't thank you enough," Trixie added as I meandered toward the stairs with Strike trailing at my feet and Whiskey leading the way.

"Not necessary," I called back with a wide yawn as I made my way to my bedroom, never more grateful in my life than I was today to see my warm, comfortable bed.

I crawled into it, not even bothering to change into my pajamas. "I'm beat, Spy Guy."

"Then rest well, Mini-Spy," Win crooned. "Tomorrow's a new day, Dove. We shall persevere!"

"Sleep tight, *malutka*. Do not let the bugs bite," Arkady whispered.

Whiskey hopped up and pressed his big body against my back, burrowing his nose in the comforter. And as I closed my heavy eyelids, I said a small prayer that we'd find who killed Hank so I didn't have to drive Trixie and Coop to the border.

~

"*S*tevie…" someone whispered.

I was dreaming, I suppose. I had to be dreaming because I didn't recognize the gravelly voice at all.

But then the voice called me again—a deep,

menacing voice. "Stevie… Wake up. I want to play with you. We can't play if you're asleep…" the voice singsonged, going from menacing to teasing and light.

My brow furrowed as I tried to open my eyes. Using my thumb, I wiped a bit of drool from the corner of my mouth. I always drool when I'm overtired and sleep heavily. Which is what I was doing, thank you very much, and this voice was no longer letting me.

"Steeevie," the voice whispered. "Wake up, Stevie."

"Go away," I muttered, wrapping an arm around Whiskey and tucking back under my comforter. "I just need a couple more minutes."

"Stevie!" the voice hissed in my ear, so close the sound echoed. *"Wake up!"*

Suddenly, the bed shifted violently with the weight of something—or *someone*—and before I knew it, I was forcibly rolled on my back with a hand to my throat, and found I was staring up at…

No. No frackin' way.

As my eyes adjusted and focused on the image on top of me, they widened because indeed, yes. *Yes* frackin' way.

I was staring up at a wild, red-eyed version of *Trixie.*

CHAPTER 12

Trixie—who looked like Trixie but wasn't Trixie, because she sure didn't sound like Mary Poppins anymore—screamed at me, the veins in her neck visible even in my darkened bedroom. "I said, wake up, Steeeviiie!" she bellowed, holding Coop's sword high over her head and preparing to bring it directly down toward mine.

Just as I was getting my bearings, I heard Coop's rebel yell, "Trixie Lavender, no!" seconds before she leapt on the bed and knocked Trixie and the sword to the floor with one swipe of her hand.

Coop pounced on her friend, grabbing Trixie's wrists and holding them above her head while Trixie fought her as though she were possessed, making Whiskey bark furiously.

"Get off me, you stupid half-breed! You just don't want me to tell her that Trixie killed him!" Trixie cried in a voice I never, *ever* want to hear again. It was like something straight out of *The Exorcist*—raw, and black, and hateful. Her face was red, matching her eyes—eyes that bulged from their sockets while spit flew everywhere.

She fought Coop with everything she had, all the while letting eerie, high-pitched wails emit from her throat.

My shock gave way to panic as I watched her really give Coop a run for her money. I mean, this was Coop, for gravy's sake. Coop could take on a football team, and Trixie was trying to knock her off her hips as though she were tissue paper.

Realizing I was rendered immobile by my shock, I scrambled to the edge of the bed, still tangled in my comforter, and fell to the floor with a thunk—and that's when I saw Trixie's nails.

Neatly trimmed and unpolished when we met, now they looked like black, razor-sharp claws.

Terror made my heart crash so loud, I was sure Win and Arkady could hear it, but I grabbed Coop by the shoulders to make her stop as Trixie flailed beneath her. I was afraid she'd kill her friend with such brute force.

"What the heck's goin' on?" Belfry screeched above the howling, buzzing about the ceiling.

I grabbed again for Coop, but she shrugged me off with an angry growl. "No, Stevie! Don't interfere. We have to stop her before she hurts someone! Let me handle this!"

Okay. Now I was terrified. I'd never seen anything like this. I'd seen possession, but *this*? This howling, sweating, spitting, clawing kind of possession? Um, nope.

"Trixie Lavender, listen to me!" Coop demanded, letting one of Trixie's arm go in favor of grabbing her under the chin and forcing her to look her in the eye by squeezing her jaw 'til I thought it might crack. "Listen to my voice, Trixie! You must fight the evil—fight it with all your might!"

Trixie twisted her body with howls and grunts, heaving her hips upward to rid herself of Coop, but the demon held on and gritted her perfect teeth. She leaned in close and soothed, "Listen to the sound of my voice, Trixie. You are good. You are kind. You will not let this evil have you. Listen. Just listen. This is *your* body, Trixie Lavender. You will not let it have your body!"

I had to bite my knuckle to keep from screaming at the top of my lungs as I reached for Whiskey's collar and pulled him close to me. Poor Strike sat frozen in his bed, his feathers quivering, but I couldn't get to him to comfort him without disturbing whatever was happening.

And then Bel did something I'll never forget for as long as I live.

He zoomed down to land at Trixie's ear and nestled in her perspiration-soaked hair. "Shhh, now, Trixie. Easy does it. We're here. Coop is here. Stevie is here. Come back, Trixie. Come back. Don't fight. Shhh,

shhh, shhh," he whispered, and then he began to hum "So This Is Love" in her ear, a tune he'd hummed to me all my life whenever I was stressed or sad.

Little by little, as Coop and Bel crooned to her, quiet, shy, nurturing Trixie-gone-rabid began to settle down until she expelled a long, shuddering breath. Literally, it was as though someone had sucked whatever had been lodged inside her right out.

Instantly, her pretty eyes cleared and she stopped struggling.

Coop cupped Trixie's cheek, pushing her hair out of her mouth. "It's okay now, Trixie."

But then Trixie's eyes went wide with horror and fear as she looked to each one of us. She gripped Coop's forearms, her spine going rigid, and whispered, "No, Coop! Oh, God. I'm sorry. I'm so sorry!" She began to sob, her shoulders shaking.

Coop lifted off her and patted Trixie on the shoulder in her awkward way. "Everyone is okay. No one was hurt. I promised I wouldn't let you hurt anyone and I kept my promise."

And then Trixie saw me, eyes as wide as saucers as she visibly fought a violent tremble. "Stevie! Did I hurt you? Oh, Stevie! I'm sorry. Please forgive me!" she cried, pushing Coop off her to stand up.

I think I was still in shock because I could only manage to shake my head and mutter, "No... I'm...I'm not hurt."

She wobbled a bit, and I suppose I'd wobble, too, if

I'd just thrashed about the floor like a dying fish out of water. But she righted herself and grabbed my hand in her sweaty palm, her eyes watery, her cheeks beet red. "We'll leave right away, Stevie. We can't stay here anymore. Someone will end up hurt. I couldn't bear it if someone got hurt."

But I gripped her fingers and stopped her from leaving the bedroom. "Stop. Don't move. Just give me a second to catch my breath and then we'll talk."

I let her go then and began to right the things she'd knocked over in her fit of histrionics, and then I sat next to Strike, who trembled and cooed softly in his bed. Wrapping my arms around his neck, I cradled him until he stopped shaking.

Then I rose, pushing my hair from my face to get a clear view of Coop and Trixie. I wanted to run out of the room, down the stairs and to the nearest border to get as far away from what I'd just seen as I could, but I didn't. Yes, I've seen some scary things in my time—even from Adam Westfield when he'd come after me once—but it would never compare to seeing someone you genuinely liked being full-on possessed.

I gulped back my fear and kept my voice calm. "Explain, please. What just happened?"

Coop wasted no time when she stood in front of her friend and said, "Sister Trixie Lavender is occasionally possessed by an evil spirit who escaped from Hell."

⌇

"*D*ove! Oh, Dove! How fare thee now?"

"Thee fares pretty freaked out. But I'm okay. It's all going to be okay."

That was a lie. Nothing would ever be okay again. I can't explain why I was so freaked out. I'd seen some pretty crazy stuff, but we were talking *Hell* here. Hell and true evil. Demon evil. It just felt so much darker than what I've faced in the past.

Win clucked his tongue. "I wasn't there for you. I'm woefully sorry, Stephania. But once we bid each other adieu for the evening—"

"You go off and hunt chicks. I know, I know," I retorted, fighting to keep the sarcasm out of my words.

"I do no such thing. I reflect. Sometimes I read. I ponder the state of the world, but I most certainly do not hunt chicks."

We had an agreement we'd stuck to since the beginning of our crazy relationship. When I go to bed, Win no longer has access to my bedroom. We maintain a strict code of privacy, and except for the other night, when he woke me by accident with his tattoo revelation, he's never broken the code.

I always figured while I slept, he went off and did what sexy British spies do on their downtime. Chase exotic women with a dirty martini in one hand and a cigarette in the other. Win says that's not true, and Arkady backs him up.

But if allowed to dwell, my jealousy gets the better of me and I'm convinced he's chasing women. Which is entirely his right whether I like it or not and certainly ridiculous. But jealousy and my overactive imagination are strange bedfellows and can convince me of almost anything if I allow it.

Clenching my eyes shut, I popped them back open and looked out the kitchen windows at the snow that was still falling while I waited for Coop and Trixie to clean up. There was no way I was going back to sleep now anyway. Not after that hellish display.

"Right. Whatever. It doesn't matter, Win. What *does* matter is, I just watched someone I really like and could probably be friends with flail around on the floor, spit, scream obscenities, and threaten death until she was red in the face as her friend held her down on the ground and Bel sang her evil away." I stoked Bel's head and tucked the cloth napkin he'd curled up in tighter around him. "By the way, you were aces tonight, buddy. I don't know if I can ever properly thank you. I love you, Belfry. I just thought you should know."

"No sweat," he mumbled sleepily. "And I love you, too, Boss. Now let me get some sleep. At least one of us has to be aware."

"What in heaven's name happened, Dove?" Win asked, his voice laced with worry.

As I explained to him the events that had just passed, I fought more tears. That it was five in the morning and I'd only had an hour's worth of sleep wasn't helping, but if I tried to close my eyes now, I'd only relive Trixie's suffering, and I couldn't bear that.

"My sweet relish pickle, I wish I was with you right

now, if only to give you great big hug like bear," Arkady said, his words gentle and sympathetic.

I smiled up at him, injecting as much warmth as I could so he'd know how much his support meant. "Thank you, Arkady. I'm fine. I'm not worried about me. I'm worried about Trixie. But we have some exploring to do now. I hate to say it. No, I dread saying it, but—"

"Maybe Trixie, in the state she was in this morning, really *did* off Hank." Win finished my worst fear for me.

"That's what she's afraid of, too," Coop said, making her way into the kitchen with a pale, shaken Trixie in tow.

I jumped up from my chair and rushed to her. "Tell me what I can get for you, Trixie. Coffee? Are you okay? Do you want some water—aspirin?"

Because surely aspirin would take care of a little ol' possession, dummy. Gosh, sometimes I said the stupidest things.

But she shook her head, her eyes still rimmed in red from crying. "So, I owe you guys an explanation. I'm just not sure you're going to believe me. But I swear on all the years I was a nun, what I'm about to tell you is the truth. Not some made-up horror movie idea."

I laughed. I couldn't help myself. Here we were, a demon, a talking bat, a talking owl, two ghosts, and an ex-witch. I was way past the stage of disbelief. "I'm ready when you are. After what I just witnessed, I'm not above wondering what just happened."

We all took seats at the table and as the snow fell, and the night filtered out, leaving a gloomy, very gray dawn in its wake, Trixie explained what had just happened.

An hour later, I poured more coffee into my cup and shoved a mug in Trixie's direction, too—she looked like she needed an intravenous drip of caffeine. "So you're telling me that at the convent, this Father O'Leary—someone you'd known the entire time you lived there, someone you trusted—asked you to retrieve this sacred relic for him, right?"

Her face went crestfallen. "Yep. I wish the convent had videotape of *that*, but unfortunately, they only have the bad parts of that night. Father O'Leary, whom I loved and adored and had followed in good faith since I was eighteen years old, when I decided to become a nun, asked me to get that relic, one that had been in the church for centuries. And I did. And then my entire life blew up," she said, her lower lip trembling.

I took a long sip of my coffee. "And you think he was possessed by this evil spirit, and the evil spirit wanted the relic to use for evil intent." So much throwing the word evil around.

"I have no idea why this spirit wanted the relic. It's just a statue really, but it's alleged to have belonged to the Archangel Gabriel. I'm not sure I ever truly believed that, but then, I don't know that I truly believed in possession either. I don't think any of us did even with the Vatican's guidelines for approving possession. In fact, we used to joke it was mostly made up by movie producers. Yet, look at me now."

Cupping my chin in my hands, I sat silently for a moment, an entirely new batch of questions running through my head. "Okay, so you got the relic for fake Father O'Leary, and then what happened?"

Trixie sighed, tucking her navy-blue sweater under her chin. "Things get a little fuzzy from there on out. But the demon in Father O'Leary cursed me, making me essentially a vessel for Hell. So basically, I'm open season for this spirit to come and go as it pleases."

My mouth fell open. "So…you're cursed. Like this horrible thing can come in and out of your life at random, and you can't do anything about it?"

"That's basically it in a nutshell," she responded, looking away from me and out the window.

Oh, that made me so angry for her! If there was one thing I needed, it was control—of my mind and body. To be at someone's whim was an unspeakable horror. One I sort of got, considering what Adam Westfield had done to me.

"Okay, so where did this relic go and who is doing this to you—or is the question, *what* is doing this to you?"

"Evil," Coop spat, her eyes flashing. "It's evil doing this. There's plenty of it to go around, I can tell you true. And somehow, it wormed its way into Father O'Leary's person. Once it has a body, or a host as we call it down there, it can do as it pleases. "

"I don't know where the relic went," Trixie said, a

helplessness in her voice that cut me to the core. "The video of me and my...poor behavior, or should I say what got me booted from the convent, doesn't show the relic anywhere in my possession. Of course, my fellow nuns think I stole it and put it on eBay, even after they searched my room and all my belongings. If it weren't for Sister Meredith, I'd likely be in jail right now," she said forlornly.

Coop did that almost-smile thing again. "I like Sister Meredith. She's kind—even to a dirty demon like me."

Trixie rasped an aggravated sigh. "You're not dirty, Coop. Stop saying that! You're just as kind as anyone I've ever met. If it weren't for you, I'd have never gotten out of there alive. Give yourself some credit, would you?"

Now I was all about the facts and checking them off my list. "So the relic went missing, and Coop saved you from the evil that had Father O'Leary in its grip. How'd you do that, Coop?"

Coop—beautiful, direct Coop—didn't hesitate with her answer. "When the evil spirit escaped, he left a door from Hell open to the convent. I jumped through it with Livingston riding piggyback. No one leaves Hell without leaving behind a ripple. I waited for the right ripple. I waited many, many years to escape, and I finally did, and I'm never going back. I'll die first."

"Heavens," Win mumbled, probably as entranced by this story as I was.

I really had to fight to stay on task and not stray

from my purpose. I wasn't tired anymore. I was invested, and hearing Coop say she'd die before she'd go back to Hell broke my heart and made me that much more determined to figure this out.

"So this spirit hopped from Father O'Leary to Trixie, and you did what to save her, Coop?"

Clucking her tongue, Coop's look became faraway and distant. "I fought it with my sword, as I've fought many battles before, but he got away. He was a bad, bad spirit. Black and ugly."

Trixie ran a hand over her face, rubbing her eyes. "But in the process, she saved me from total possession. Had the spirit taken over entirely, he would have eaten my soul, and there's no coming back from that."

Ah. Now I understood their bond. It didn't get much more intense than soul-stealing.

Coop's jaw hardened. "But I didn't save you all the way, Sister Trixie Lavender. I couldn't stop him from cursing you."

I held up a finger. "So this curse is what allows this thing to get in and out of your body?"

She nodded, her expression grave, her face chalky. "And makes me do horrible, horrible things—say horrible things—like what you saw tonight, and what I told you I did at the convent earlier. I'm sorry, Stevie. I'm sorry I didn't tell you sooner. It… What happened tonight hasn't happened in a very long while. At least four months. I thought… I *hoped*, it had gone away. I know that's wishful thinking, but there you have it. We even have a calendar where we count down the days since Trixie's last possession."

And I had the nerve to think *I'd* had it bad. I reached across the table and gripped her hand, giving it a hard squeeze. "I don't know what to say. I don't know how to help. Can't you have an exorcism or something? Why wouldn't the nuns help you? Isn't that their whole purpose?"

Now Trixie barked a laugh. "Because they didn't believe me. Not after the stunt I...or should I say, the stunt my evil spirit pulled. The church has a stringent guideline for possession, and because I was sometimes vocal and challenged scripture at every turn, no one believed me. In essence, they thought I was faking it. So until we can find the relic, or find out what's so special about the relic, there's nothing to be done."

Clenching my fists, I fought a scream of rage. "And Coop, *you* don't know what it means?"

Coop clapped a hand on the table, making me jump, her reply as fierce as she was. "I swear on my new soul, I don't know why anyone would want the relic or why this spirit wants Trixie, other than the fact that it can enter this realm through her. I swear this to you, Stevie Cartwright! But we can't allow it to take her over or she's as good as dead. I will not let that happen. Not at any cost. That's why I can't go to jail. Trixie won't have anyone to protect her."

So that's why she'd said all those things about not letting the spirit "have" Trixie's body. I wanted to cheer

Coop's steadfast loyalty. I wanted to tell Trixie how lucky she was to have someone as amazing as Coop, someone who would help her fight her demons to the bitter end. She could have left Trixie to her own devices after getting what she wanted, but she didn't.

I'd lucked out with Win and Arkady, and it made me breathe a sigh of relief that Coop and Trixie had each other. But now wasn't the time for kudos because I was getting around to asking a very touchy question. But it had to be asked.

First, I needed more coffee and a Twinkie. I went to the coffeepot and poured more, grabbing my favorite spongy cake on the way. "Do you know when this possession is going to happen to you? Can you feel it coming? Do you get any warning?"

Trixie's shoulders sagged, and I hated the defeated look on her face and in her body language. "No. None. Though, sometimes, I see what's happening in sort of a hazy way, but I have no control over it. Not one iota. And sometimes, I don't even remember it."

"That's what we're trying to learn," Coop said with determination all over her face and written in her eyes. "We must learn how to control this bad, bad spirit until we can cleanse ourselves of it and regain Trixie's freedom."

I looked to Trixie, whose eyes were downcast, her fingers entwined. "Do you think that's possible?"

"I suppose anything's possible, right? I mean, who would have believed one could truly be possessed? Like screaming, kicking, red-eyed, malicious possessed. I know millions of people do, but I'm pretty sure I didn't. You know what's funny?"

Not possession, that's for sure. "What?" I asked.

"Even though I was a nun, I never really believed in evil, per se. I don't necessarily believe everything the Bible says, or believe in the horrors that will befall you if you break a commandment. In fact, I often challenged the nuns on scripture—sometimes daily. But I do believe in being the best person you can be. Yet, there really is a Hell, and it grabs hold of me and uses me as a shield to the outside world."

That made me wonder something. "Why did you become a nun, anyway?"

"Drugs," she said on a nervous laugh, running her fingers over the handle of her coffee mug. "I was addicted as a teen. My parents sent me to their very dear friend, a nun, at the convent I ended up pledging my life to. This nun helped me free myself of addiction and I, in turn, became a nun in her honor, and even though I'm not bound to the church anymore, I try to uphold every lesson about being a good person she ever taught me."

My heart clenched in my chest. "And where are your parents now?" I asked.

Trixie's eyes went sad, her posture slumping. "They're gone. Both from cancer, and not too far apart, unfortunately. But we'd made amends long before they died. They often came to see me at the convent. I'm so grateful for the time I had with them, to try to make up for how difficult I was when I was on drugs. I miss them every day."

"Now Trixie has us for a family, right?" Coop asked, giving her that awkward pat on her hand she'd clearly been taught was a sign of consolation.

Trixie grinned and patted Coop's hand in return. "That's right, and I wouldn't have it any other way. Anyway, we've been gone from the convent for a while now. We sort of drifted until we came up with a plan, and that plan was to open a tattoo shop. Not end up accused of murder."

My lips flatlined. Now onto the uglier bits of this mess. "Murder... I don't like asking this, Trixie, but I don't have a choice. Do you think you could have killed Hank while possessed? Because the spirit or whatever it is said you did."

Horror washed over her expression and her eyes filled with angry tears. "I... I have to be truthful. I don't know, Stevie. *I don't know...*"

"Oh, Stephania. Whatever shall we do if this is the case?"

But I shook my head, angry with the notion this sweet, gentle woman was being forced to live this way. "I'm not sure I believe that's the case, Win. Now, listen, Trixie. I realize this thing is evil and likely lies for the sheer pleasure. In fact, I get the impression it wants you to give in so it can find a mortal host. I don't know why or to what end, but you can't ever give up. *Never.* That said, we have to consider the possibility."

She threw her hands in the air as though she *were* giving up. "And how will I explain that to the police? Sorry I killed Hank, but it wasn't my fault, Officer. I was possessed."

But I wasn't going to give up so easily. Nay. In fact, I was going to question everyone who I thought looked even remotely suspicious, because I couldn't let it be Trixie. It just wouldn't stand.

"We're not there yet. I have a whole list of suspects to chat up still." Speaking of, I needed to get a move on. I was hoping to catch some of the people I'd considered today so I could begin a process of elimination. I imagined it would be tough with the weather being so poor, but I was going to do whatever I had to in order to clear Trixie's name. For sure, the cops were a dead end for information. I'd be lucky if Dana ever spoke to me again. I was going to have to go this one all alone.

Turning to the ladies, I cracked my knuckles. "No one gives up—not on my watch. Now, you two, stay here. Do not leave this house. Don't answer the door. Don't look out the window. Stay put. I'll move faster alone, and I don't want the police getting to you before I've had the chance to ask around."

Trixie peered at me from her end of the table. "Do you think anyone will even talk to you, Stevie? Don't people usually clam up at a time like this? That's what happens on *Criminal Minds*."

"This isn't *Criminal Minds*, and they don't have me. I'm pretty good at getting what I want. Don't you worry. I'm going to grab a shower and head out. It's going to take me a little while to get into town with all the snow, but I'm hoping the weather works in our favor and keeps everyone busy with other things. While I'm gone, you guys memorize the stuff Win had prepared for Coop—especially her new last name."

"Weather providing, supporting documents should be here within a day or two," Win assured.

"Who did you get to help you anyway, Win?" He'd been a spy. I'm sure that meant he had tons of contacts that could produce fake documentation, but I was curious.

"Never you mind, Stephania," he said on a chuckle. "All you need to know is I've handled everything necessary to create a believable past for Coop."

Coop looked up at the ceiling. "Thank you, uh... Winterbottom," she said, her eyes turning oddly shy.

I smiled at her. She was too darn cute—even if she *was* a little over the top. "Okay, I need to motor."

"But you've hardly slept, Stevie," Trixie pointed out. "And Google says they've officially called this a blizzard. You need your wits about you if you're going to drive in this. I can't let you do that."

I smiled as I rose and grabbed my coffee cup to put in the sink. "You say that a lot, and I keep telling you, you don't have a choice. But just one more thing?"

Trixie began clearing the table and pushing in chairs. "What's that?"

"Did you really moon all those nuns while you were possessed? Is that really what got you booted out of the convent?" I still couldn't believe it.

Trixie fought an impish smile as she took one last sip of her coffee before she said, "Oh, I really did, and there's video to prove it."

I couldn't help it—because it was almost too absurd —but I laughed like a loon all the way to the shower.

CHAPTER 13

"*S*tephania, the roads are atrocious. The last thing I want is for you to join me here on Plane Limbo over this impromptu investigation."

The roads sure were atrocious. It had taken me over an hour just to get to Main Street with the hope Burt Freely or Enid Gunkle, two of Hank's most vocal haters on his Facebook page, would talk to me. A drive that usually takes all of five minutes.

Now my dilemma was where to start. At their places of business or their homes? But I had to start somewhere. This snow couldn't last forever, meaning, time was running out.

Pulling over to the curb by Burt's Barbershop, I saw lights on inside, leaving me hopeful I'd catch him, but it looked like Enid wasn't at her sewing machine repair shop and yarn store, Sew Ready (does anyone even have a sewing machine anymore?), or if she was, there were no lights on announcing her presence.

Some of the shop owners here in Eb Falls lived in their stores—like Madame Zoltar had, and the way Trixie and Coop were—leaving me hopeful I'd find both my prime suspects, and maybe someone else who'd seen something.

The problem was, I had next to no information about Hank's death. No time of death, no cause of death, no stalkery girlfriends except for his Facebook haters—nothing. And seeing as I'd burned my bridge with Dana last night, not to mention Starsky with my defense of Coop, I doubted I'd be able to wrangle any information out of anyone in the Eb Falls Police Department.

Though, I kept Melba in the back of my mind. She wasn't an ace in the hole by any stretch, but she was definitely an iffy possibility. I hadn't offended her yet. As for Sandwich, I'd tricked him one too many times. Thus, if I said "boo," he was running in the other direction these days. If I went to the police station, I'm pretty sure Dana would corner me, and if he didn't, someone else would. Therefore, I had to fly low under the radar for as long as I could.

But first up, Burt. I swiveled my head to look at his shop and everything outside it, all covered in wet snow. "I can't believe we made it here. Those chains were the best idea you've ever had, Win."

"And to think you balked at me when I suggested them."

I literally pushed my way into a parking space, the snow crunching under my tires as I did. "That's because you suggested them in mid-July. I was too busy windsailing and sunbathing to think about tire chains. Plus, like I said, we hardly ever get this kind of weather here. Anyway, I'm glad I bought them or we'd be stuck at Mayhem Manor without a way to get anything done. We have to hit this one hard because we don't have much time before this storm clears and they come looking for Coop."

"Before you talk to Burt, *malutka*, have you give thought to what Trixie tell you? Have you think about what happened last night?"

I stared at the console of my car, noting the time was just nine in the morning and I'd had maybe an hour's worth of sleep. Still, I laughed ironically. "It's all I've thought about, Arkady. But if you're asking if I think Trixie murdered Hank while possessed? I don't know. That's my honest answer. I have no gut feeling about that. What I'm praying for is another solid suspect to at least throw them off Coop's trail for a bit. I know it's wrong of me, but if it *was* Trixie, my first instinct is to find a way to cover it up."

"Stephania, you simply cannot!" Win admonished, stuffy tone of voice and all. "If she harmed Hank, she could harm others. How can we have that on our conscience?"

Yet again, Win was right, logically, but my heart ached for her and all she'd lost. "But it's not her doing the harming, Win! How can I let her serve time—hard time—if she was possessed? We know it exists. We're very clear it happens. You've possessed a couple of bodies in your time. So is it right to ship her off to prison for something she has no control over?"

"Bah! This is dilemma, apple strudel! I do not wish to see Trixie go to big house any more than you, but Zero speaks the truth. She can hurt innocent people."

I smoothed my gloves over my hands. "But then there's this... The one thing that keeps me from thinking she's a real suspect is whoever knocked me down last night at the store. It sure wasn't Trixie. So what did that person want? What was in that hole in the floor in the storeroom?"

"Speaking of the assault on your person last night, remember anything, now that you've had some time away from immediate danger? Scent, maybe?"

Sighing, I shook my head and gripped the steering wheel. "Not a darn thing. It all happened so fast, and I was hungry and tired. My reflexes were so off, and I know as spies, you guys think that's a bunch of hooey, that my senses should always be on, but I can only remember being knocked around. I don't know if I could even tell you how big the person was."

"As you're not a spy, and you've had very minimal training in such, it's understandable. Sometimes, like in the case of me and the hand with the tattoo, things take time to marinate before they make their appearance," Win offered.

I smacked the steering wheel with my hand. "Shoot, Win! I forgot all about investigating the tattoo! I'm sorry."

"Nay, Dove. No apologies necessary. Coop's

dilemma is far greater than mine. This takes precedence."

Then something else came to me. "Here's another thing. We don't even know Hank's death has been labeled a murder. Maybe we're doing all this work for nothing? Maybe he just had a heart attack or his arteries were clogged. I mean, he did frequent the fried chicken and waffle food truck, right?"

"There's one way to find out. Check the *Eb Falls Herald* website, Stephania. Surely, if something's been announced, the *Herald's* on it."

I took a look at my phone and typed in the URL for our local newspaper, hoping against hope Hank's death had been ruled anything other than murder. But my hope was short-lived.

The front page hit me like a shot to my kidneys. *Local Real Estate Mogul's Death Ruled a Homicide.*

"Crud on a cracker," I mumbled as I read the story. "So much for hope. It says here that the coroner's report hasn't come in yet and cause of death is unde-termined. But they're calling it a homicide."

"All the more reason to get your backside in gear, Dove."

Lifting my eyes to the car's ceiling, I reached for my purse. "Listen, you guys say a prayer, cross your fingers, do whatever it is one does when they need a miracle, that I'm able to find the person who did this before the police get to Coop. Now, let's go question Burt. And by all means, if you can think of anything I miss while I chat with him, speak up. I know I usually ask you two to be quiet, but I'm so tired, I'm afraid I'll forget something."

"Consider it done, Dove."

With that thought in place, I took one last look at the eerily deserted Main Street, the sidewalks empty but for the snowdrifts, and inhaled a long breath. I had to do this. I *would* do this.

I pushed my door open and hopped out into the snow, now at mid-calf and still falling. I really should take a peek at my phone to see if there was going to be any end of this blizzard in the foreseeable future, but I didn't have time to do anything but hit the bricks.

Trouncing through the powdery white, my breath visible in small white puffs, I made it to the door of Burt's shop, complete with candy-striped poles and that old-timey feel of a barbershop from days gone by. Just as I was about to knock, I caught sight of Burt, who frowned at me and waved me off, pointing to the sign that read they were closed.

But I knocked harder, shivering as the wind cut right through my cute waist-length parka. "Mr. Freely! Please open the door. It's an emergency!"

His big body quivered when he huffed, clearly not pleased with me for interrupting him. We'd never formally met. I'd only seen him in passing at various places of commerce and a few Eb Falls events.

His eyes narrowed at me as he made his lumbering way toward the glass door. He wore one of those throwback white smocks all barbers used to wear, and his face, while on his Facebook profile page was cheerful and smiling, looked just shy of murderous.

"Didn't you see the sign?" he growled, pushing the door open with a beefy hand, giving me a whiff of his heavy aftershave. "It says closed!"

It was time to improvise and appeal to his chivalrous side. Surely someone who celebrated days gone by with an old-fashioned barbershop would rise to the occasion.

I made my best sad Panda face as I slipped one foot in the door and sort of danced from foot to foot. "I'm sorry, Mr. Freely. My car is stuck," I said, pointing to my vehicle over my shoulder. "And I really, really need to use the ladies' room. I saw your lights on and, well, I just thought maybe you'd be willing to help a girl out? *Please?*"

Instantly, his face went from a hard mask of perturbed to the gentle teddy bear I'd seen on his Facebook page. He pushed the door wide open with a welcoming smile full of white teeth. "My apologies, Miss...?"

I smiled wide, fluttering my eyelashes in a foolish attempt to woo him with my charm. "Cartwright. Stevie Cartwright. I own Madam Zoltar's just down the block here, but I forgot my keys to the shop and it's going to take forever to get back to my house by the edge of town and no one else looks like they're open. I'm so sorry to inconvenience you, but..."

"Of course," he blustered with a cheery smile,

letting me pass into the store. "It's just been one of those days. You know, when it rains it pours."

I nodded my head and looked to the end of the store where the sign read "restrooms." Much like the outside of Burt's, the inside was a throwback to the day when getting a shave and a haircut were commonplace.

There were eight chairs all told, with matching mirrors and big jars of green solution used to disinfect combs and mustache brushes. The floor was a checker pattern in red, black and white, and clean as a whistle with the lack of customers on a day like today.

As I made my way to the bathroom with my legs almost crossed to keep up the act of having to use the facilities, I paid special attention to my surroundings. A little lame, I know. I mean, what killer would leave evidence behind in his place of business? Still, as tired as I was, I did my best to stay extra observant.

Once inside the bathroom—also sparkling clean, with white subway tiles and burgundy walls—I turned the faucet on and waited a minute before I flushed the toilet. Then I washed my hands with some fruity soap and hit the button with my elbow for the air dryer and waited another minute more.

I needed to strike up a conversation with him in such a way as he'd give me information willingly without realizing he had. But as tired as I was, I wasn't sure how to do that...

Just as the air dryer's cycle ended, I heard Burt's voice, making me press my ear to the door.

"I told you, I don't know anything, Martha!" he

shouted, his voice clearly filled with dismay. Then he lowered it. "The police were here today asking a bunch of questions because of that stupid Facebook post I made. I overheard 'em talking and they were saying stuff about tetra something-or-other in his bloodstream. I didn't want 'em to catch me eavesdropping, so I pretended I didn't hear. I can't even pronounce whatever they were talking about, but the one said it had to do with his cause of death. That means somebody really killed him, Martha. Maybe that looker and her friend who rented the store, but it wasn't me! I swear!"

"Tetra something..." I whispered against the bathroom door.

"The moment you leave this store, you must look up deadly poisons beginning with the prefix tetra, Dove. Surely, the police have found something if they mentioned it in correlation to Hank's bloodstream."

I nodded, keeping my ears open in the hopes Burt would say more.

'That's right, Martha. *The police!*" he stressed with a frantic hiss. "I almost bit the head off that nice kid from down the road who owns that crazy psychic place because they had me so scrambled. I haven't seen or heard from Hank since he told me he was raising my stinkin' rent, and I told that detective with the broken nose the same thing. I don't know anything about what happened to Hank. He was a mean son of a gun, for sure. But I wouldn't murder him for it."

There was a pause, and then I heard Burt say, "All right, Martha. I'll get some on my way home. I'm gonna close up shop once this kid leaves. There's no business to be had on a day like today. See you soon."

That was my cue to exit, and that phone call had just made breaking the ice easier.

As I made my way back to Burt, I held out my hand to him. "Thank you, Mr. Freely. You're very kind."

He winked with a rumbling chuckle. "No trouble at all, young lady."

"I hope you don't think me nosey, but I overheard you on the phone. Have you been questioned about Hank's death, too?" I asked with as much innocence as I could inject into my question.

Burt looked surprised. He planted his hands on his round hips and leaned back on his heels. "Did they come sniffin' around your place?"

I would neither confirm nor deny. Instead, I hedged. "I hear they're asking all the store owners if they saw anything yesterday. Especially people who rented from him."

Burt clucked his tongue and scrunched his face up. "You know, funny thing. Coulda sworn Abe said he was going to leave all his worldlies, like his property and buildings, to his wife. I don't understand what the heck happened. Like I was tellin' my wife Martha the other day, Hank was taking advantage of Abe's goodwill."

My heart began to race. Now we were getting somewhere. "Abe told you that himself? He actually told you he was leaving everything to Francie? When?"

Burt's cheeks puffed outward in dismay. "He sure did. Just before he died. Swear it. Maybe as little as a week before he kicked the can. Used to play poker together sometimes. Abe was a good guy. Darn shame about his heart attack. Him and Hank…well, they didn't get along all that great. But I guess he figured Hank'd take care of his mother, and seeing as she's gettin' on in years, too, the best thing to do was leave all that property with someone who had experience in property management. Buildings here are worth a fortune if you can rent 'em out. Especially during the tourist season. You should know that as a business owner yourself."

Tucking my purse under my arm, I looked at him thoughtfully. "And you rented from him, didn't you?"

Burt's wide face went grim. "Didn't most everybody on this block of buildings? Hank was a greedy SOB. Abe was a decent guy, and he was going to take his stepfather's legacy and trounce all over it by raising our rent and charging us for sewerage when that had always been part of our rental agreement. Do you know how much water a barbershop uses?"

"Do you know anyone who'd want to…murder him?" I asked, keeping my voice fearful and hesitant.

Burt coughed a laugh and reached for one of his warming towels on a countertop under one station's mirror, throwing it over his shoulder. "I can think of a lot of people who might have wanted to hurt him. He wasn't very nice, and he had no business raising our rent so high, but murder? That's not like a punch in the nose. So, I dunno."

"I think we're at a dead end here, Stephania. In light of our time constraints, we should move onward."

Pulling my cap down over my head—the one I was using to hide my shiner—I ran a hand over my coat and smiled. "Thank you, Mr. Freely. I'll let you get on with your day."

"You need help getting out of all that snow?" he asked, genuine concern on his round face.

But I waved a hand at him to dismiss the notion and smiled warmly. "Nah. If I have to, I'll leave a note on the car so they won't tow me and stay at my store for the night. It's not far to walk if necessary. Now, you've been very kind, Mr. Freely. If you ever want a free reading, pop on down the block. I'd be happy to give you one."

Burt cackled a phlegm-filled laugh, his round belly jiggling. "Do you really think I believe you talk to dead people?"

Now I winked. "I guess you'll just have to come by and see for yourself. Bye now," I said over my shoulder as I made my way to the door and headed for my car.

Beeping the door, I piled in and turned it on, putting my head on the steering wheel so I had a chance to absorb what Burt had told me while I pulled my phone out and Googled the word tetra.

As I scrolled the meanings for the word, none of which had anything to do with poison, I said, "Burt wears enough aftershave to choke someone out. I don't think it was him who tackled me in the store last night. I'd remember that scent."

"And you're finding nothing for the word tetra?" Win asked.

"Not unless he means a fish or an antibiotic, as in tetracycline—which won't kill you, by the by." Letting my head hang to ease the tension in my shoulders, I grit my teeth. I would not give in to the fear of failure, but it sure was trying hard to latch onto me. "Listen, Burt's an older guy, maybe he didn't hear what the police were saying correctly. But don't you find it interesting that Abe allegedly told him he was leaving everything to Francie?"

"*Dah*, banana cream pie. Very interesting. Maybe it is like Burt said and he change his mind at the last minute. People do things like this all the time."

The snow continued to fall, adding to my feeling of defeat. The weather was making everything so much harder. "Okay, so who's next? Enid Gunkle, I suppose. I don't see her lights on in the store, but maybe she's just hiding in the back. Also, Trixie gave me the keys to her store. If I can get in without being seen, I'd like to get back in there and do some more poking around."

"That doesn't seem wise, Stephania. The place is probably crawling with Eb Falls' finest."

"In this weather? Surely they've collected all the evidence they can at this point. They have the body, and the potential murder weapon. What else is there?"

"Exactly my question to you. What else is left to see?"

I couldn't say. I just had this feeling. "I can't say for

sure, Spy Guy. I just have this feeling I missed something—somewhere."

"I vote we talk to Enid before you go to tattoo shop. Maybe Hank's mother and sister, too," Arkady said. "Maybe we find out more personal information, like who didn't like Hank. If anyone would know, would it not be his family?"

Nodding, I pulled out of the space and moved down several more to smush my way toward the curb at Enid's store. "They're on my list but in a vague way. They must be broken by Hank's death, and I don't want to be the one who goes in both guns blazing. First and foremost, we need to clear up the incidentals like Enid. It's only just nine thirty in the morning right now. We have plenty of time to squeeze in the others if we don't get anything from Enid."

More snow crunched under my tires as I parked and used the emergency break as a just in case. Since I'd been in town, I hadn't seen a single car, and definitely not a snow plow in sight. Time was still on my side.

I said another prayer it would stay that way for just a while longer.

～

Ten minutes later, after knocking repeatedly on Enid's shop door and asking her fellow shop mates where she lived, I found out she'd gone to

California to visit her daughter—three days *before* Hank was killed.

Dead ends sucked rotten eggs. I hated them, but I had a knack for running into them.

Now, when defeat tried to worm its way in, I found it harder than ever to squash. "I'm trying not to get discouraged, but I feel like I set the ladies up for disappointment. I said I'd help and I'm doing anything but. We have very few suspects, gentleman. What now?"

"Hank's mother?" Win suggested, though he did so with tentativeness to his voice that meant he was as uncomfortable talking to her as I was.

Wincing, I massaged the spot near my temple where I'd been knocked in the head. "I think I should just pay my respects and let it be. I'd do that whether Hank was murdered or died of natural causes. It's what all Eb Fall-ers do. I'm going to see if the bakery's open, and I'll grab some pastries to bring to her and her family. But to pry after something so awful would just be heinous on my part, don't you agree? Not to mention, they're not really suspects. They're more like vessels of information on Hank's background. So let's be gentle."

"I agree wholeheartedly. Pastries it is then, Dove," Win agreed in his husky tone.

Before I got out of the car to walk to the bakery, rather than drive, I had a thought. "As our time with this storm ticks away, I have an idea. Maybe we could find a place for Coop and Trixie to hide? Like, in plain sight?"

"Whatever do you mean, Dove?"

I stopped on the sidewalk, stuffing my hands in my pockets. "Madam Zoltar's. We'll just bring them there. They can't stay at the house. It won't be long before the police show up with a search warrant. At least at Madam Z's, they have everything they need—food, stovetop, a bed. This way, if the police manage to get to us today in all this bad weather, we can let them search away. But the way things are stalling, we're taking a huge chance they'll get that search warrant, and I want to be prepared."

"Bravo, Dove. Bravo."

I beamed with pleasure at Win's approval, even though I wanted to hate that I beamed because I shouldn't be beaming over anything concerning Win. But truth be told, his approval meant everything to me.

I looked up at the sky, still swollen with bruised blue and gray clouds and the never-ending snowfall. "Okay then, in this order. The bakery, Francie's, and back home to grab the ladies and Livingston, then bring them to the store to get settled—all before this weather gets any worse. We're going to have a heck of a time getting back and forth with any degree of ease the way this snow keeps coming down."

"Then let's make the moves!" Arkady encouraged, making me laugh.

"It's bust a move, Arkady," I teased. I loved correcting him. I'm not sure why I bothered. It's not as if he'll ever have the chance to use the correct metaphors with anyone but us, but it kept me smiling.

"If you're making the moves, you're likely courting a special lady.

"Why would one bust the move? This make no sense, candy cane. I will tell you why it make no sense…"

But Arkady's voice drifted off as I focused on the problem at hand. Keeping Coop from the police for as long as possible.

CHAPTER 14

"*P*lease, don't make a fuss over me, Mrs. Levigne. I just wanted to drop these off to you and hopefully offer my help with anything you need," I protested as she offered to make me some tea with honey.

I'd managed to make it to her house safely, a one-level ranch in a mixture of brick and eighties blue siding. Well cared for, no doubt, with its trimmed hedges covered in thick snow and arborvitaes lining the drive, but definitely in need of some updating.

For such a large, imposing woman, Francie wasn't nearly as scary in person as her angry scowl on Facebook (I'd looked her up before coming to pay my respects) or her ax-throwing championships suggested. And indeed, she was an ax-throwing champion. She had an entire glass and gold curio cabinet devoted to her medals and trophies. She even had a bronzed ax to commemorate her triumphs.

People milled about her living room, still decorated with a flair for the seventies. Gold shag carpet adorned her floors and an avocado-green refrigerator sat proudly in her kitchen, outdone only by the brown wall oven. She had a collection of wooden cows displayed all over her countertops; so many, she could rival a good dairy farmer. It was safe to say, not much had changed in the Levigne household since 1972.

Hushed whispers swirled around the room as people came and went to offer their condolences—even as poor as the weather was, the people of Eb Falls had found a way to bring comfort in the way of casseroles and condolences.

"Miss Cartwright?" Francie peered at me with hawkish eyes and raven-black hair.

"Oh, no thank you, Mrs. Levigne."

"If you're sure," she said with a fleeting, close-mouthed smile. "But I'd be glad to get you something else, if you'd prefer."

"Oh, no, no. I'm really fine. I just came by to give you my condolences and bring you some pastries. Nothing more."

"Did you know Hank?" she asked, eyeing me with startlingly coal-black eyes.

I kept my answers vague enough to keep suspicion at bay. "I met him a time or two. We didn't travel in the same social circles, of course. But we chatted here and there. Either way, he was an Eb Fall-er, and you know what we do best in Eb Falls when there's a tragedy."

But Francie didn't appear too broken up about

Hank's death. In fact, I hadn't seen her shed a single tear, and that was after several mourners had come and gone.

Maybe she wasn't the wear-her-heart-on-her sleeve type? I tried to remember if she'd cried at Abe's funeral, but I couldn't. Yet, this was her son, for goodness sake. If she was an emotional woman, she sure was doing a great job of keeping it under wraps.

Francie's bright red lips puckered, making her face look even wider as she smoothed a hand over her black shirtwaist dress. "Did he own your building, too?" she asked, as though anticipating I'd come to complain, but I wanted to reassure her that wasn't the case.

I placed a hand on her forearm. "No. I own Madam Zoltar's."

Francie's lips flatlined then and she backed away ever so slightly, wiping her hands on her white apron with the ruffled trim. "You're that lady who says she can talk to ghosts, eh?" Her penciled-in eyebrows rose with the furrow in her brow.

I decided to look her directly in the eye. It isn't like I don't get flack for my conversations with the dead, but for some reason, her question annoyed me because it smacked of visible disapproval.

Still, I admitted, "*I am.*" And I said it with pride, lifting my chin. I didn't care who believed or didn't believe. I knew the truth.

Francie crossed her large, unusually toned arms over her ample chest. "You do know that stuff's all a bunch of hooey, don't you? Like that woman with all the big, ratty blonde hair and fake nails in Long Island who's on TV? She needs to see a shrink before she sees any more dead people."

Okey-doke. A nonbeliever. I could live with that. I gave her my canned reply—one I'd practiced almost since birth. "I believe we're all different, and we all have different beliefs. I respect yours, as I'm sure you respect mine. That's what I believe. Now, I won't keep you any longer, Mrs. Levigne. I realize you have guests to tend to. I just wanted to lend my support. My best to you and yours." I patted her hand and slipped into a small gathering of people who were chatting.

As I made my way to the front door, past the old buffet table crowded with pictures in frames of all shapes and sizes, I stopped to glance at the ones of Abe with Francie's children. Looking at them, you'd never know Abe and Hank didn't get along. They certainly looked happy enough at a Fourth of July party, arm in arm, smiling for the camera, their faces tanned, their eyes bright.

But if one were to believe the buzz in the room and the story from Burt, Abe disapproved of Hank and his shady real estate transactions. I wondered what that meant, and decided it was worth looking into.

I'm not sure why I decided to do it, but in light of the dire circumstances, it couldn't hurt to eavesdrop on some of the conversations for a little while, on the off chance something valuable would pop up.

One conversation I found particularly interesting was the one two middle-aged men, both in crisp black suits, were having about how Hank should have gone to the doctor.

"He was having trouble breathing, said his heart kept pounding out of control for no reason. Flew out to Florida to play some golf and had to go to the emergency room for it, you know," the man with the dark blue tie and slick comb-over said.

The second man, lean like a runner and quite handsome with his thick chestnut hair, nodded as he fiddled with his tie. "Yeah. He mentioned that at our last meeting at the agency. Said he was planning to go see the doctor next week about it."

The agency must be the real estate company Hank worked for, but I didn't know he'd been having health issues. Definitely something to note. Though, the article I'd read in the paper said plainly it was murder. So if his heart played a role in his death, the police didn't think it was the reason he'd died.

Both men moved on, as did I, trying to stay inconspicuous. Surely there were people here who'd been shafted by Hank's rent increase?

But as I circulated, grabbing a deviled egg from a platter being passed around, I didn't get much gossip at all. Thankfully, it appeared everyone was keeping any resentment they harbored, if any, quiet.

"Another dead end," I mumbled under my breath, just as the heavy wood front door blew open and a very stylish older woman swept in with a blast of cold air.

Her hair was bleached almost white-blonde and styled in side-swept fashion to cascade along her neck and over the very top of her shoulder, and held in place with a sparkling rhinestone barrette.

Her makeup was a tasteful mix of glamorous and classic with a lighter-colored lipstick on her mouth, and heavily made-up eyes in smoky brown, accenting her round blue eyes. For sure, she was in her early sixties if she was a day, but it was evident, she had preserved herself well via the aid of a plastic's surgeon's knife. She had that slick, shiny look to the apples of her cheeks, the skin stretched over them a little too tight, and her lips, while not unattractive, surely has seen some Botox fillers.

I found myself mesmerized by her. The woman didn't just enter the room, she fell into it with a graceful pause as everyone's eyes turned to her before she glided her way to the center of the space in black heels and a navy-blue trench coat.

How she'd made it up the steps to Francie's house in those heels was legend, as far as I was concerned. She didn't have a single snowflake on her black shoes, and that, in and of itself, was worthy of praise.

The room went very quiet very fast, though to note, it was mostly the older generation whose mouths fell open. The younger groups of folks my age, or even Hank's, while interested, didn't appear as shell-shocked as the others.

Well, now. I couldn't leave just yet. This woman was someone. Someone who'd made an obvious impact, good or bad, and I wanted to know who the heck she was.

So I hovered and moved over to the table where a plate of cold cuts and creamy potato salad sat in a fluted bowl. Making myself look busy by putting together ham, cheese and salami on a hard roll, I positioned myself near a woman around the same age as Francie, and whose mouth was moving a mile a minute as she whispered animatedly to her friend.

"I can't believe she showed up," the woman hissed, taking a bite of a croissant with a snap of her teeth.

Her friend wiped the crumbs from the corner of the woman's mouth. "Shush, Maura! Don't let Francie hear you. She'll just get upset all over again. That Luanne doesn't give a fig about Francie's loss. She's just putting on a front so we all won't talk about her tomorrow when she goes back to that fancy house of hers in Beverly Hills."

So, the pretty older lady's name was Luanne and, apparently, she had some kind of beef with Francie Levigne. This was definitely worth sticking around for. I didn't know if it was going to help my investigation into Hank's death, but the tension in the room was as tangible as pea soup.

This Luanne meant something. But did she mean something to Hank's case—now labeled a murder?

I squirted some spicy mustard on my sandwich and heaped a lump of potato salad on my paper plate while I watched Luanne make her way toward Francie. She slipped through the groups of people, never once addressing them or even meeting their eyes.

Instead, she latched onto Francie's arm and pulled

her close, her eyes glistening with tears. "Oh, Francie," she whispered in the raspy voice of someone who'd had a cigarette or two. "I'm so sorry, Francie. *So sorry.*"

But Francie Levigne didn't look like she was terribly interested in how sorry Luanne was. She gripped the woman's slender wrist and pulled her down the short, carpeted hallway just off the living room without saying a word.

However, Francie didn't have to say anything. Everyone could see how she felt, and it had nothing to do with goodwill.

Plopping a forkful of potato salad in my mouth, I leaned into a conversation by the refreshment table. A man and his wife, also probably about the same age as Francie, were engaged in a heated debate.

"That woman is *disgusting*," spat the white-haired lady with crisp trousers and a black sweater tied around her shoulders. "I hope she leaves as fast as she came."

But the man, a portly gentleman with pudgy, pock-marked cheeks, ruddy weathered skin and a wisp of white hair atop his bald head, admonished her. "Don't be so judgmental, Lenore. She left a long time ago. It's long over."

Now my ears were on fire. *What* was over?

"But not before she stole all of Francie and John's money! She's Francie's sister, for pity's sake! And after that, she went off and married some rich man and took all *his* money. She's on her third husband now," the woman said with a sneer.

Wait. Two things. Luanne was Hank's aunt? And wasn't John Francie's first husband, Hank's biological father? So this grudge went quite a way back then.

But that only meant Luanne was a gold digger. Not a murderer. This didn't help me at all. Not that I'd wish Hank's aunt were his killer, it was unthinkable, but I was giving in to my penchant for gossip, and that made me uneasy. I dropped the rest of my sandwich on the plate, my appetite gone.

"Francie, please listen to me!" Luanne cried from the hallway, startling everyone into complete silence.

"Get out of my house, Luanne!" Francie demanded, her voice tight and angry.

Time to go. I wasn't going to stick around for the drama while everyone else spoke ill of Luanne as though she weren't even in the room. Worse, I wasn't going to watch a mother who'd just lost her son argue with her sister when she should be mourning the death of her child.

As Francie stormed out of the darkened hallway with Luanne hot on her heels, tears streaming down her face, Pricilla, Hank's sister, came out of nowhere and grabbed Luanne's arm as the women barreled toward me.

"Please, Aunt Luanne! This isn't the time or the place!" she cried, her blue eyes, much like Luanne's, riddled with worry.

But Luanne pulled away from her and headed toward the door, pushing me out of the way. She rushed down the steps, with Pricilla following close behind, kicking up snow the entire way.

I slinked out the door and tried to make myself very small. I wanted no part of whatever was happening, but Pricilla caught up with Luanne and forced her to turn around.

"Why did you come today of all days, Aunt Luanne? You should have just stayed home!" Pricilla cried, her gaunt cheeks turning red from the frigid temperature as her long fingers wrapped around Luanne's slender wrist again.

But Luanne shook her coiffed-to-the-nines head, snowflakes swirling all about her and mixing with her tears. "He was mine, too, Prissy! Hank was mine, too!"

"What a strange thing to say," Win commented as I made a wide arc around the two women, hunching down behind some big SUVs to get to the end of Francie's long driveway.

"Yep. It sure is," I agreed. "And I don't know what it means, and I don't want to know what it means." I beeped my car open and jumped in with a shiver. "Whatever's happening there, it's not good. Did you hear the bit about the money Luanne supposedly stole?"

"I did. Money is the root of all evil."

"You bet it is. I can attest to that. Either way, it's none of our business. Though, everyone inside that house appeared to know whatever that Chatty Cathy was talking about." Then I shook my head. "I'm not here for the gossip. I am, however, ready to get Coop and Trixie moved over to MZ's. We're going to have a heck of a time getting home and back into town if we put it off much longer. The temperature's only going to drop and the roads will be far worse than they already are." Pulling out my phone, I sent Trixie a text and asked her to pack up, explaining my plan.

"You're absolutely right, my sweet cornbread stuffing. I do not wish to see you splat all over the road like slushy."

"I don't wish to see that either, Arkady," I said with a smile then I frowned. "I don't know what to do next, boys. I'm at a loss."

And that left me feeling incredibly sad. I hated that we were no closer to finding Hank's killer than we were yesterday. How long could I hide Coop and Trixie before this passed? *Would* it pass, or would they rail-road Coop into a conviction?

She was an easy target. Too easy.

The very notion made me that much more determined to find Hank's killer.

CHAPTER 15

J'd gone back to the house, which took me not one, but two solid hours, collected Trixie and Coop and company, drove back to the store, which was not only another hour-and-a-half journey, but stuffed to the gills with people and animals piled on top of each other. And now we were all happily safe and warm at MZ's. For the moment, this was the best I could do.

I set a plate of cold cuts and rolls on Madam Z's reading table and gave the girls a sorrowful look. "I'm sorry I didn't find anything today, ladies. But we're not giving up. I just need some fuel in my belly, and then we go hard."

"And by fuel, our lovely Stevie means food fit for a third-grader," Win teased, trying to lift my spirits.

"Oh, you hush, International Man of Mystery. Baloney and turkey are very adult. Look, I put some

Havarti cheese out. How much more grown-up do you get than that?"

Trixie giggled, passing the plate of rolls to Coop, who took three. "First, I don't think I'm ever going to get used to you talking to the ceiling, and what do you mean by International Man of Mystery? Isn't that James Bond?"

"Hah!" Win barked with sarcasm. "As if some fictional character could ever live up to the life a true spy leads."

"You're just jelly because Sean Connery's so smexy," I teased, taking a roll and a few slices of turkey.

"Really, Stephania. As if."

I chuckled and turned to Trixie to explain. "I sort of mean like James Bond. Crispin Alistair Winterbottom was once an elite spy for MI6 before he died. But he's also my best bet when it comes to facing off with a killer. He taught me everything I know."

"Did he teach you how to use a sword?" Coop asked, piling some baloney on her plate.

"No swords as of yet, but I'm pretty good with a knife and a gun. I've learned a lot from Win and Arkady."

Trixie popped a chip in her mouth and smiled. "He's the other guy you talk to, right?"

"He's a Russian spy. He and Win were rivals at one time, and now they're BFFs, aren't you?"

I heard Arkady chuckle. "*Dah*, Zero is my BFF. Wouldn't Russian Spy Central be happy to hear that?"

"I can teach you how to use a sword, Stevie

Cartwright," Coop offered, pushing a piece of her sandwich into her mouth.

"Too roight!" Livingston confirmed, his head swiveling in my direction. "She's the master, me darlin'! Beautiful and deadly, she is."

Apparently, he and Belfry had spent some time bonding today, and now, as Bel happily munched on some fresh kiwi, he and Livingston laughed and joked with each other. Seeing them together made me happy.

Bel refused to hang around any of his old familiar friends due to their shunning of me, and it made me sad. He needed to be with his own kind, but he staunchly refused to even consider doing so until they all came to their senses and allowed me back into the coven.

Which was never going to happen.

"You know, I don't know when I'll ever have the need for a sword, but I'll never say no to a fencing lesson. You can never have enough tricks in your arsenal, Coop. So thank you." I reached over and gave her smooth cheek a pinch, making her almost smile.

Trixie pushed her plate away and wiped her mouth with a paper napkin. "So, where are we, Stevie, and how can I help? I felt like the slug of all slugs, sitting around your gorgeous house today while you were out in this horrible weather, hunting down suspects."

Yeah. That was the part of this I wasn't looking forward to. "I don't know. I've never felt so helpless in all the time I've been sticking my nose where it doesn't belong. I heard a bunch of conversations at Francie

Levigne's house today, some not so pleasant, and the only one that might even remotely have to do with this murder investigation is the one I overheard about Hank's health. Apparently, he was having trouble with his breathing and heart racing, and he mentioned it at a meeting at his real estate agency. Though, I can tell you true. No way will his doctor give me any information on why he was having trouble breathing. Believe that."

"So you think maybe his heart had something to do with his death?" Trixie asked, slumping in her chair.

She looked so tired. Heck, we were all looking pretty haggard. Except Coop. Coop looked like she should hit the runway in Paris—even in ratty jeans and an old T-shirt.

"I *hope* it had something to do with his death. If he was having heart problems, maybe he died because of them while he was rooting around in your storeroom. Makes sense, right?"

"It makes complete sense," Trixie agreed. "But the police must have something else or they wouldn't have called it a murder."

Nodding, I felt my stomach took another nosedive, making me push my plate away, too. "Yeah. There's that. Burt mentioned he overheard the police say something about *tetra* in his bloodstream, but I can't figure out what the heck tetra is. I did a Google search and everything, but it brings up a type of fish and tetra-cycline, which is an antibiotic." I sighed, circling the wood table's knots and divots. "Maybe Burt just heard them wrong. I don't know. But what really disturbed me was Hank's aunt Luanne. What could she have meant by *Hank was mine, too*? Isn't that a strange thing to say about your nephew? I can't guess they were very close. I mean, Francie didn't even want her in her house."

Trixie pulled my laptop to her side of the table and flipped the lid open. "That *is* peculiar, and strangely sad. Either way, maybe I can find something you didn't? You're so tired, Stevie. What you need is a good night's rest. Please, let me help. I'm pretty good at research. Just ask Coop how long I searched for some answers to the mess that stupid relic from the convent left me in."

"Did you find an answer?"

She gave me a sheepish look. "Um, no. But! That's not to say I can't use my Google-Fu in other ways. Just let me take a peek. Maybe I'll see if this Luanne has a Facebook profile while I'm at it. Got a last name for her?"

"Nope. And she's been married three times, I think. So it could be under anything. But check some friends lists. Look at Hank's page or even Pricilla's. Maybe they're Facebook friends with her?"

Trixie smiled and rolled up the sleeves of her shirt. "I'm on it."

I was happy to hand something off to Trixie. This whole case had my head spinning. Nothing was connecting for me, or even Win and Arkady. Maybe I just needed to clear my head with some fresh air. Plus, it was still snowing, and Whiskey would love a good run. His chances for snow in this part of the country were rather slim. I wanted my sweet guy to have a moment to enjoy it while he could.

"While you do that, I'm going to take Whiskey for a walk and clear my head. You're right, Trixie. I *am* tired, and nothing's coming together for me. I need to think."

Coop frowned, leaning forward to rub Strike's head, and revealing the most amazingly gorgeous tattoo on her shoulder of an angel, glorious and so detailed, it took my breath away. "But the weather is very bad, Stevie Cartwright. People get lost in snowstorms of this nature. I heard it today on the television."

I smiled at her concern as I dug Whiskey's leash from my purse and clipped it to his collar, giving Strike a stroke on the head as he rested by Coop's side. "I'm pretty familiar with Eb Falls, Coop. I know my way around here like I know the back of my hand. Plus, I'll stick to the sidewalk, where some people have shoveled. But Whiskey's been cooped up all day and he really loves the snow. The opportunity for him to play in it doesn't come up often here in Washington. I won't be long, promise. You guys stay here and lay low, okay?"

Coop gave me the thumbs-up sign. "What do you consider low enough, Stevie Cart... Um, Stevie? Should I lie on the floor?"

Coop made me laugh. She was almost as bad as Arkady when it came to expressions but in a drier way. "Laying low's an expression, it means staying out of sight of the police. You don't actually lie down while you do it. Well, not unless they come knocking. Then you hide. But I think we're safe for now. The weather's really bad and probably hanging this whole investigation up. You guys should be good—at least for tonight. I'll bring my phone in case I need you or in case you need me, okay?"

Coop gave me another thumbs-up sign. "Okey-dokey. I learned that 'expression' on the television today, too."

"Every day you grow, Coop," I praised.

She wrinkled her nose. "No, I do not. I'm the same size as I was yesterday."

"I meant emotionally, Coop." Then I shook my head. "Never mind. You're just awesome, and that's that."

Trixie was too busy buried in her research to acknowledge much else but a quick "Be safe," to me before she had her head back down, clicking away.

"Mind if I join you, Dove?" Win asked, his warm voice invading my ears.

"Not at all."

I made my way through the front of the store, past our displays with healing crystals and postcards, smiling at how happy being here made me. I could use a little happy right now because I felt a whole lot of sorrow coming on if we didn't get to the bottom of this.

Bundling up, I dressed in layers to keep the dropping temperatures at bay. My head still ached just a little, but overall, even with my lack of sleep, I didn't feel too bad.

Pushing open the door of Madam Z's, I inhaled the damp air. I'd lived in the Texas heat for a very long time, and I'd missed the change of seasons. Like Whiskey, I, too, loved the snow.

"'Tis truly beautiful, is it not, Dove? Rather Dickensian, yes?"

Sighing, I nodded my head as the first snowflakes blew at me sideways, hitting my nose when I began to walk. Whiskey anxiously tugged me along, and I tried to forget how pleading Luanne had sounded, and those words—*Hank was mine, too.*

There was so much emotion in them, but then, I had to wonder if Miss Luanne wasn't a bit of a drama llama. Her entrance to Francie's alone said as much.

I shook my head. Clearing my brain meant letting the case go for a while, so I turned my eyes to how beautiful Eb Falls was at this very moment. "It is Dickensian. I love how it blankets everything. I don't love driving in it. But for now, we're warm, and safe, and together, and the world is a peaceful place."

"How are you, Dove? What can I do to make you feel better?"

Plodding along behind Whiskey, who cut through the snow with his big paws like steel blades on a sled, I shrugged. "Find me a killer for Hank that isn't Coop or Trixie."

"Nay, Dove. You know that's not what I mean.

You've been quite melancholy as of late. What troubles you so?"

Oh, no. No way was I divulging what troubled me. I wasn't ready to voice my feelings to him. How would that make him feel when there was nothing he could do about them?

"I think it's just the end-of-winter blues. I'm sure I'll perk up once we start seeing some signs of spring. You know, tulips and daffodils?"

Win was silent for a moment. He knew I wasn't being truthful, but he couldn't figure out how to make me spill the beans. "Why don't we talk about our plans for the gazebo out back?" he suggested. "Surely the idea of a summer project will cheer you."

Smiling, I huffed out a breath as Whiskey pulled harder, dragging me behind him. We'd discussed his wish to have a gazebo in the back, with trailing roses and wisteria adorning the façade.

I'm not sure where Win comes up with some of his ideas, or even why. He can't enjoy them the way I can, but even though he considered his money mine, I never turned my nose up at his desire for any item. He'd earned all of it and then some.

He'd died earning that money. Doing as he asked was the least I could do.

Fluttering my eyelashes, I giggled girlishly. "Oh, definitely. A gazebo is sure to wash away my blues. Who doesn't want a gazebo? Every girl should have a gazebo."

"You're mocking me."

I stopped for a moment to catch my breath, tugging on Whiskey's leash as we grew closer to Trixie and Coop's store. "*Moi?* Mock *vous?* That you would use that word in a sentence with me is just plain crazy. I would never mock you."

He chuckled, warm and raspy. "You live to do such."

"Do not. I live to have a gazebo," I said on another giggle, my breath coming out in a puff of condensation.

"Are you happy, Stephania?" he asked, his warm aura embracing me and enveloping my senses.

When unsure what your conversation partner is getting at, always deflect with a question. "Are you?"

"As happy as one can be when the world is down there and I'm up here. But you didn't answer my question. Are *you* happy? Would things be easier if Arkady and I weren't always interfering in your life?"

The very idea terrified me. What if someday, I couldn't hear Win and Arkady anymore? What if the last of my witch powers slipped away? What if they left me alone to face life's everyday challenges without them? I couldn't even bear to touch the subject—but I couldn't let him know that. Because what if, one day, Win wanted to go into the light? To leave Plane Limbo and see what's on the other side?

There isn't a chance in H-E-double-hockey-sticks I'd keep him from that. But the very thought stung and left an empty ache in me that nothing could fill.

I strolled along the sidewalk, casting my glance into shop windows to avoid Win seeing a single tear fall, but my eyes filled up quickly anyway. "Define easier?

Do you mean, would it be easier if you didn't keep hassling me to build a gazebo?"

"Stephania, you're not being serious—"

"Whiskey! Stop!" I ordered as, for no reason at all, in the middle of our conversation, he took off at a gallop, with me trying my best to run behind him.

Win whistled and yelled, "Whiskey, old man! Stop this instant!"

But he wasn't stopping. He yanked so hard on his leash, I lost my grip, slipping in the hard-packed snow on the sidewalk, and I sure couldn't run the way he could in this mess. "Win, keep as close as you can while I catch up!!"

"Whiskey! Come here, boy! No, Whiskey! No! Don't go down there! Argh!"

I stopped for a moment, leaning against the door of the flower shop and gasping for breath. I'd been working out on the reg, and still, I was huffing as if Win The Exercise Enforcer wasn't insisting I run on a treadmill for an hour every day.

Bracing my gloved hands on my knees, I gasped. "Don't lose him, Win! What the heck's gotten into him?"

"I don't know, but he's heading down the alleyway by Trixie and Coop's."

I pushed off the building and let out a ragged breath, my chest tight. "When I get my hands on him, I'm going to kill him!" I began to trot through the thick snow, crossing the street dividing each block of stores.

"Whiskey, no pig knuckles for you, buddy, if you don't get your butt back here!"

"Bah! He's taken to the back alley, Dove!"

I growled and ran down the side of the building, making a left into the alleyway where it was pretty darn dark and scary. "Whiskey!" I shouted, not even bothering to stay quiet. Snow beat at my face and the wind whipped around my head in frigid circles.

"Whiskey!" Win bellowed again as I ran along, following his paw prints, which stopped at Trixie and Coop's back door.

And that back door was open just enough for Whiskey to have slipped inside. I heard his big feet tromping around as though he owned the joint. A shiver slipped along my arms, making me break out in a cold sweat.

Aw, c'mon. "What the heck is he doing? He usually only takes off like that when food's involved—or a cat. You know he loves a good cat."

"I have no idea, Stephania, but what I'd truly like to know is why the door is open. You locked it last night. Surely the police, if they came back to collect more evidence, aren't that careless?"

Another shiver skittered up my spine. A cold, clammy shiver. But I couldn't just leave Whiskey in there. He'd wreak havoc. Or if someone was in there, they'd wreak havoc on *him*.

Poking my head in the door, I let my eyes focus on the dark hallway before the storeroom. "Whiskey!" I whisper-yelled. "Get your butt out here now!"

He barked. Yes, he did. He had the nerve to bark, and it was a playful bark, which eased my concerns someone could be in the building. He was playing a fine game of hide-and-seek with me—we did it all the time. This just happened to be the wrong time, with a blizzard raging and a crime scene that shouldn't be mussed.

Feeling more confident no one was inside due to Whiskey's playfulness, I stepped over the threshold and pulled my phone from my jacket pocket when it vibrated. Trixie had sent me a text that read, *"I think I figured out what Hank's aunt meant after seeing her Facebook page. I don't think Francie is Hank's biological mother! Finish your walk and I'll explain when you get back."*

Francie wasn't Hank's mother?

Holy cats! What did this mean?

"Stephania?" Win interrupted my thoughts as they whirled out of control.

"Sorry!" I said, holding up the phone. "Just got a text from Trixie, and I think we're onto something. No time to explain. Let's go get our dog."

"Whiskey, boy—come on out!" Win called as I peered into the darkness.

"Whiskey?" I called, too, but this time he didn't bark…and that worried me. "Maybe he's hurt?"

That thought spurred a move I'd sorely regret.

Inching down the hall just past the storeroom, I squinted into the pitch-black space but I couldn't see my beast anywhere. "Whiskey, where are you, buddy?

Okay, I take it back, you can have pig knuckles for days, if you'll just get out here!"

There was a sudden creak, and then the back door slammed shut, probably from the gusts of wind. As I tripped forward, stumbling to find my flashlight app, I glanced upward—and that was when I saw something rather rectangular in shape and shiny coming straight for me.

"Stephania, duck!" Win ordered with an urgency I couldn't ignore, and I reacted, dropping to my knees and covering my head—only to find Whiskey on the floor, too, unmoving.

My hands instantly went for his muzzle, stroking it to see he was still breathing. But I didn't have time to thank the universe when I found he was, before Win was yelling another order.

"Stephania, get out of the way!"

As large feet came thundering toward me, I dove through a doorway, onto the store's floor, sliding on my belly and grateful I'd worn a nylon jacket, enabling me to skid forward with ease.

"Roll, Stephania, roll to your back and to the left!" Win bellowed, his voice laced with panic amidst the calm he always brought me when I was in a pickle like this.

"What's going on?" I yelled, doing as I was told and rolling to my back and to the left, only to crash into a stack of boxes.

"Get to your feet, Stephania! Do it now! Hurry, Dove!"

I exploded upward, grateful for all those stupid, gut-busting crunches Win made me do to keep my core strong, but rather than land on my feet solidly, I wobbled.

Okay, so I didn't stick the landing, and in not sticking the landing, it gave my unknown nemesis the opportunity to come at me full steam. I heard a grunt and then a scream, low and feral, and just as my assailant came at me, I caught a glimpse of their face by the streetlight shining in through the big picture window.

And you'll never guess who it was. I mean, clearly, I didn't guess who it was, so why should *you* have all the fun?

Know who it was?

Francie Levigne!

CHAPTER 16

"*Y*ou nosy meddler!" francie screamed, her rage rife and thick as she took a swing at me with—guess what?

An ax. Yes, I was being hunted down like a small woodland creature by a woman more than twice my age. And she was coming for me, guns…er, axes blazing.

Man, for a woman of her maturity, she sure was in good shape. I wondered if she ate a lot of Wheaties, because she swung the ax up in the air, winging it around her head before rushing toward me with impressive precision.

I screamed and held up my hands, envisioning my brains splattered all over Inkerbelle's. "Stop, Francie! Stop!" I cried out.

"It's okay, Mom! I've got her!" someone else said from behind me, grabbing me around the neck and pulling me backward toward the big picture window until I thought my throat would burst open from the pressure.

Mom...? Oh, come on. Seriously? Pricilla was in on this, too?

As I struggled to tear her arm from around my neck, I dug my fingers into the flesh of her forearm, but she had a heck of a grip. Squeezing harder, she forced my chin upward.

"Pricilla, why are you doing this?" I rasped, lifting my chin to ease the strain. "What's going on?" I pleaded, and she only gripped tighter, her heavy breathing whispering through my ears.

Then she laughed, ugly and rich with hatred. Why is it that perfectly normal people turn into rabid lunatics when trying to kill someone? And why does it always involve maniacal laughter and heavy breathing?

"Why couldn't you just stay out of it? Why did you have to come back here?" she asked, her words angry.

"Stephania, easy does it. Don't rile. Remember what I've taught you. I beg of you," Win demanded in his calm, take-charge voice

"Come back here?" I blurted without thinking about Win's words of caution. "That was *you* who rammed me into the wall?"

Shoving me forward until I twirled around, Pricilla and I came face to face with each other for the first time while her mother flanked my back. I saw her eyes clearly now via the streetlight outside the picture window, and they were glazed and angry.

"Yes, that was me, you nosy Nellie! I came here

looking for something because of that idiot Hank. Do you know he *laughed* at us when he found out Abe left everything to him? He laughed harder when he told me I'd never be able to open my own store because *he* had all of Abe's money. He hated me as much as I hated him, the big bully! He taunted me my entire childhood, and he just kept right on taunting! He knew how much I needed to get out of that stupid cafeteria at the high school where I barely make enough to pay my bills—while *he* rides around in a sports car and uses money that was never meant to be his!"

I can't say why or even how, but the bit about someone wearing a hairnet seeing Coop arguing with Hank hit me like a freight train, making me forget all about the reasons Pricilla had come back to the store. After all, don't most cafeteria workers wear hairnets?

"It was *you* who called in and left that anonymous tip to the police about Coop, wasn't it? You wear a hairnet at the school cafeteria, don't you?" I asked, backing up carefully so as not to get too much closer to Francie, still trying to figure out how I was going to get out of the middle of this sandwich of doom.

She nodded her head, tears streaming down her face, her body visibly trembling beneath her pink sweatshirt. "Yes, it was *me!*" Then she shrugged. "Besides, she was easy to blame, as violent as she is. She shouldn't be wandering the streets anyway. I did Ebenezer Falls a favor!"

Win's voice hit my ear with a calm, rational, yet urgent approach. "Look for a weapon, Stephania. Keep her talking while you look for anything to stop them. Play dumb if you have to. It's two against one. You must think!"

"But how could you?" I asked, my voice raw and hoarse. "How could you frame an innocent woman? How will you live with yourself?" Gosh, that sounded stupid.

If she could live with murdering her own brother, she could live with framing someone for his death.

However, at least I'd succeeded in keeping her talking...and what she said next made me want to vomit.

Pricilla's voice hit me like a ton of bricks, right in the gut. Her eyes were suddenly dry, and as calm as the day is long, she said, "Someone had to go down for it, right? It might as well be a violent piece of work like that one."

A chill, so foreboding, so cold, flitted its way along my spine as some of the pieces began to fall into place in my brain, and despite Win's warning, I had to keep them talking until I could find a weapon. *Any weapon.*

Gulping, I licked my lips. "How could you be so cruel, Pricilla?" I asked, hoping to goad her into talking just a little longer so I could find a way out of this.

"Like they say, only the strong survive," she offered simply, her eyes, even in the dark store, now utterly vacant—devoid of any emotion.

"Stall, Stephania..." Win warned again.

"But to let someone as nice as Coop go to prison— possibly be *executed* for a crime she didn't commit?

How do you sleep at night?" I whispered, fighting the tremble in my throat.

Pricilla lifted her chin and looked directly at me. Now her eyes glittered in the dark. "I'll sleep just fine knowing *we* didn't end up in prison for Hank's murder."

My eyes scoured her thin face as my heart crashed in my chest. Hearing her say those words, hearing them out loud, made them that much more horrifying.

"Then answer me this. Why would you murder your own brother, Pricilla? *Why?*" I asked, my legs shaking, making it hard to stand my ground.

"She wasn't alone, you know! I helped her—because Hank was a horrible, horrible man!" Francie hissed from behind me, her voice seething with hatred and frustration. "He was going to take everything Abe said he was leaving to *me* after he found out about Hank's dirty real estate dealings. But Abe never had the chance to change his will before he had a heart attack—and left me with that heartless swine in charge of my purse strings!"

My eyes scanned the room as I fought to find something to say. What *did* you say to a mother who'd killed her son? What, I ask you?

"So you helped Pricilla kill Hank?" I squeaked, trying to keep my eyes on Pricilla but listen to Francie's answer. "*You killed your own son?*"

The horror of it seeped into my bones, deep and driving. I mean, I had my troubles with my flighty, irresponsible mother, but she'd never tried to kill me, and even though Trixie's text left me suspicious of Hank's origins, Francie had *raised* him, for heaven's sake! That made Hank hers.

Francie scoffed with a snort, her breathing becoming rapid. *"Hank wasn't my son!"* she screamed, as though their lack of biology excused the fact that she helped murder him.

My eyes popped open wide. Gone was the grainy feel to them from lack of sleep, and in its place was my own revulsion as I confirmed the last piece of the puzzle.

Hank was mine, too.

Holy kittens and puppies, Luanne really was Hank's mother. My suspicions about Trixie's text were right.

"Stephania, I know you've already figured this out in that razor-sharp mind of yours, but you need to stall! Ask who Hank was to Francie and take note of the tape gun to your right on the small table by the stack of boxes. If you distract, you can make it, and then you come out swinging, understood?"

I nodded numbly, still too shocked to absorb what I was hearing. But I cleared my throat as the two bore down on me with menace.

"Wait!" I shouted. "Who was Hank to you, Francie, if not your son?"

"He was my nephew!" She howled the answer as though it brought her agonizing pain. "But I raised him like my own, just like I promised John I'd do when he begged me to take him back, after he'd slept with my lying, cheating *sister*, Luanne! After he got her *pregnant*!

And after everything I did for her, keeping her from prying eyes so no one would know she was having a baby out of wedlock, waiting on her hand and foot. Do you know what she did then? After she had the baby, after we moved her to Ebenezer Falls with us for a fresh start? She stole our money and never looked back! Ran off to Beverly Hills and found herself someone else to deceive!"

Eyeing the tape gun, I kept my voice steady, despite my inner turmoil. Honest, I sometimes wonder how a killer doesn't hear my heart pounding up a storm for all the crashing it does in my chest.

As I processed what Francie said, as I let the idea that she'd catered to her sister in order to keep her marriage intact, that she'd lived with a woman who'd slept with her husband, was forced to see them together every day, I asked, "But *murder*, Francie? How did you murder Hank?"

But Pricilla noted how irritable Francie was becoming, and said as much. "Mom, we have to do something with her, and we have to do it now!"

"Waaait!" I cried, moving toward the wall to my right in a nervous hop, keeping one eye on the tape gun. "At least tell me this before you whack my head off! How did you kill him?"

Now Francie cackled, as though she'd pulled off the great escape all on her own. "We poisoned him with Visine! So we wouldn't have to hear him bragging anymore about how he was going to raise rents and make another million," she spat. "Do you know what it was like to make nice with him after my Abe died? Knowing what he was doing? Abe was a good man! He was good to his renters. That money was supposed to be *ours*, once Abe found out Hank was a lying cheat, just like his mother!"

"It's true," Pricilla declared with equal pride in her voice, the tremble almost totally gone as she appeared to gain courage. "I found it on the Internet. Visine has a compound called tetrahydrozoline, and it constricts your blood vessels. Hank had trouble with his heart and his circulation. The doctor *told* him to lay off all those hot dogs and chicken and waffles at the food truck. But like always, Hank didn't listen, which worked in our favor. Over a long period of time, and with a lot of it, Visine can kill you."

Ah, the infamous tetra had nothing to do with medication, per se. Good to know for future reference. If I made it out of this alive, that is.

"Stall, Stephania! You must stall. Stall and inch. Talk and inch your way to that table!"

Heart in my throat, I said the first thing that came to mind. The first question I'd ask, were I allowed to interrogate them in an official capacity.

"What did you put the Visine in?" I asked with fake curiosity. And I inched in tiny baby steps toward the table.

Pricilla snorted, derision dripping from her next words. "Hank was always mooching a free meal, because who else would want to eat with that cheap-skate? At least three or four times a week, he was at one of our houses, knife and fork in hand, all while we pretended there were no hard feelings that he'd stolen *everything* from us. *Everything!*"

"You put it in his food?" I squeaked, taking more tiny steps, praying I wouldn't trip over my clumsy feet.

"Nope," Pricilla said with a shake of her bleached-blonde head—and then she looked me dead in the eye, her words sly. "We put it in his drink. Boy, did Hank love good bourbon, which we made sure we had plenty to offer. Once he was good and buzzed with his first glass, we poured him another with a little something extra added, didn't we, Mom?"

Francie's breathing grew shallow, the smell of sweat filling the room, even though it was freezing, and I wasn't sure if it was mine or theirs. "That's *exactly* what we did. It sure took a long time, but it finally paid off!"

I kept hoping against hope that someone would walk by that big picture window, framing Pricilla in such an eerie light, but it just wasn't happening. There was nothing but swirling snow out there.

And the more I hoped someone would walk by, the edgier Pricilla and Francie became. I heard it in there breathing, felt it in their body language, in the soft tap of their feet, rocking back and forth.

As I stood between them, both of them ready to pounce me, I eyed the tape gun one last time.

"And now that you know everything, Miss Cartwright, you really do have to go," Pricilla said, her voice filled with deadly determination.

"You can just call me Stevie," I assured as calmly as

possible, even though my stomach was now in my throat. "Why be so formal when we're at this stage of the game? It's all fun and games until someone gets killed, right?"

And that was that. Francie Levigne snapped. "Shut! Up!" Francie screeched, the whiz of the ax sounding behind me, tearing through my ears.

And that was my cue to make a break for it. The second the words were out of Francie's mouth was the second I made a dive for the tape gun, grabbing it up with a decent amount of precision, if I do say so myself.

"Well executed, Dove!"

As chaos ensued, and both women came charging at me, I crashed over the top of the small table, breaking it into little pieces and slamming to the floor. The wind was knocked out of me, but I somehow managed to get to my haunches and lurch to the side before Pricilla made a grab for me, luckily missing.

Thwack, thwack, thwack. The sound of the ax slicing the air made my knees turn to mush, making me zigzag and back up until I was almost pressed against the picture window. As Pricilla came at me full steam, catching me in the gut, I gave her a jab to the ribs I don't think she'll get over too soon, due to the fact that it made her cry out in pain and crumble to the floor.

And that was when Francie steamrolled me, enraged like a crazed bull.

It happened so quickly, I had no time to prepare, so when she crashed into me, knocking me backward, she knocked me right out the glass window, landing on top of me with all of her weight. I hit the snow-covered sidewalk like a ton of bricks, glass shards splintering and falling all around us.

And then I heard Win yell, ragged and raw, "Coop! Coop, help! Stevie needs you! Go, Whiskey, go get Coop!"

Which I thought was really strange, but I had no time to dwell upon it because while Pricilla was semi-neutralized, Francie was straddling me, and when she took her next swing, she only missed the top of my head by a hair before I grabbed the handle of the ax.

I managed to keep a firm grip—briefly. But in my panicked state, I lost my hold on the ax, and as the snow battered my face, that's when Francie took the opportunity to raise the ax high in the air.

Her face distorted with rage, her eyes demonic and wild, her hair plastered to her skull by the wet snow, scared me almost like nothing else. I knew I had one chance and once chance only to catch that ax before it cracked my head open.

In that split-second before she lowered the blade of steel, with the hard, cold sidewalk at my back, and after several unsuccessful attempts to shake her off me by bucking my hips, I said a small prayer I'd see another day.

And miracle of miracles, I heard Coop shout at the top of her lungs, "Do not hurt Stevie Cartwright!" A half second before she knocked Francie to the ground by throwing herself right at her.

Francie landed with an ugly thump, her head

cracking against the unforgiving concrete curb. From the corner of my eye, I saw the glint of steel when Coop dragged that sword of hers from her belt loop and readied it for the kill.

For the second time in as many days, every last one of us, earthbound or otherwise, yelled, "Coop, *noooo*!"

I launched myself up off the ground, snow lashing at me in cold splotches, and hobbled to this strange, beautiful, totally innocent creature and grabbed her by the shoulder. "Coop, no! I'm okay. Look. See?"

And then Trixie was running toward us and police sirens were blaring, filling the air. "Coop! Put the sword away!" she ordered, her feet crunching against the ice on the ground.

The sword clattered to the earth with the clank of heavy metal and solid ice connecting, as Coop threw her most prized possession away from her.

In that moment, just when I thought everything was safe, Pricilla rose like a Phoenix from the ashes with a feral howl, flying out of the broken window like a cannonball, aimed right at Coop. She roared her anguish as she barreled toward her, scooping the sword up and aiming directly for the top of Coop's head.

And then there was "I'm a lover, not a fighter" Trixie, her eyes filled with horror—who, in a split second, made a choice.

Anyone who witnessed the look of determination in her eye would know it was a choice she made out of love for her friend, and therefore she didn't consider it a choice at all.

That choice was to protect Coop by using her body as a human shield.

Her scream rang in my ears, so piercing and so loud my teeth chattered. Trixie's a heck of a lot braver than she thinks. A heck of a lot braver than maybe *I* even thought, as gentle a soul as she appears.

She hurled herself into the path of that sword, hands stretched outward, reaching for Pricilla's neck, mouth open wide. "Cooop! Look out!" Trixie bellowed, the echo of her words ringing through the street.

There, but for the grace of whomever rules this universe, Pricilla slipped on the snow and lost her grip on the handle...and it fell to the snow, never touching Trixie.

However, Trixie also fell into the snow, after crashing right into Coop, who let out a grunt and knocked *me* over as she fell on top of Francie Levigne, who grunted, too.

And that's how the police found us—in one big people pile with Whiskey barking happily, running in circles around us in the freshly fallen snow.

I groaned when I rolled to my side, the crunch of glass leaving me nicked and in some places cut, my head throbbing out an incessant drumbeat, my limbs frozen and achy.

Officer Nelson looked down at me with concern in his eyes as he held out a hand to help me off the ground. He looked around at the mess, the crushed boxes inside the store, the litter strewn from one end to the other, the endless shards of glass from the window on the street.

I moaned, looking up at him, splotchy snowflakes falling as I took his hand and let him haul me upward. His face wasn't nearly as hard and unyielding as it had been the other night.

"Miss Cartwright?"

"Officer Crabby Patty? How can I help you today?" I managed to get out on a cough while someone threw a heavy blanket around my shoulders.

"Care to explain what happened here?"

"Only if you promise not to tell me I've taken my Karate Kid role too seriously…"

And that was when Dana Nelson laughed so hard, he had to hold his stomach and wipe the tears from his eyes.

～

*A*s we sat in the back of the ambulance after giving our statements, hot coffee in hand, blankets around our shoulders, we listened to Dana and Sandwich while the snow continued to fall and they talked to the other officers at the crime scene.

Peering over the steaming Styrofoam cup, I turned to Trixie, her sweet face with the clearest skin ever, now a bit bruised and scratched from her scuffle. "What did you find on Luanne's Facebook page?"

"Holy sinners and saints! You won't believe it. It was

this longwinded post, a thinly veiled diatribe I guess you'd call it, about how family was family, and she couldn't believe how she was treated by her own sister."

"Aha!" I said on a laugh. "I should have known vague-booking was Luanne's bent. She's very dramatic. Should have seen her sweep into Francie's earlier today. Very grande dame-ish"

"Well, my first clue it had something to do with today at Francie's was the timestamp. She posted it after she left Francie's, if the timestamp is correct. But some of the comments in support of her dramatic display were suspect, too."

I tugged the blanket tighter around me. "Like?"

"One person, some guy in Santa Clarita, said, and I quote, *'You were tricked into doing what you did, Lu-Lu. We all know it. Tricked by that hag Francie and her husband John to give him up.'* The second I saw that, I compared Luanne's photos to Hank's. They look so much alike, it's eerie when you put their photographs side by side."

I held up my fist to her for a fist bump. "Nice job, Detective Lavender! You're right. Luanne is Hank's biological mother, and according to Francie, she left him and never looked back."

Trixie snorted and sipped her coffee. "I didn't hang up my habit for this line of work, but I have to admit, when I found that clue, I was pretty excited. It felt good to feel useful."

I gasped in outrage, giving her arm a squeeze. "*Useful?* Helllooo, Sister Trixie. You took some hit for

Coop. Never, ever tell me you're not a fighter. Because you were amazing tonight."

"Coop's done it for me," she said in her quiet way, never allowing herself the credit she deserved. We'd have to work on that.

I bobbed my head. "You saved me tonight. I can't ever thank you enough for that. Francie was going to lop my head off with that ax. So, I don't know about you, but I like my brains on the inside. You're my hero. Which makes Miss Coop amazing, too. Right, Coop? "

Coop lifted her head and gazed intently at me. "Right. Trixie is amazing. I'm amazing. You're amazing."

I grinned from ear to ear. "That's exactly right. Women supporting women is what it's all about. No matter how sick with jealousy they make us with their perfect faces and perfect bodies. Never forget that. Now, remember what I showed you?" I held up my fist. "Gimme one, Gorgeous."

Coop gave me a fist bump.

I nodded again. "Now blow it up, Coop."

And she did by splaying her fingers wide. And then we laughed. Well, *I* laughed. Coop sort of smirked. But whatever. We were getting there.

Trixie cupped her hands around her coffee. "Here's something I've been wondering since I considered Luanne might be Hank's mother."

"What's that?"

"Did Hank know Francie wasn't his mother? Is that

why he took all of Abe's money and wouldn't share with his sister? As some sort of weird payback?"

Sandwich poked his head inside the interior of the ambulance, his big body made larger by his parka. "He didn't know. Not for all his life, but according to Francie, she made sure she told him while he was dying. Gotta tell ya, never thought Mrs. Levigne had a cruel bone in her body, but jeez Louise."

I stabbed a finger in the air. "Which proves my point. You can never really know a person. Here's something that's been bugging me since we've been sitting here, Sandwich. Why was Hank here at the store the night he died, anyway? And how could Francie have told him about Luanne when he was dying? I mean, how could she have known that was the night he was going to die if it took so long for the Visine to work?"

Dana approached with a grim look on his chiseled face. "Dumb luck. Pricilla says they followed him to the store that night to confront him about the money. They were getting tired of waiting for him to die. Her words, I swear." He flipped open his notepad and read whatever he'd jotted down. "But also, in Pricilla's words, just as they confronted him, 'He fell on the ground. Deader than a doornail'."

"Why was bad Hank Morrison here at the store, Officer Dana Nelson?" Coop asked, nary a scratch on her, her hair silkily falling around her face in cascades of dusky red.

He cocked his head at her for a moment with a

strange look on his face at the way she'd addressed him.

But I distracted him. "Yeah. Why was Hank here at Inkerbelle's, Officer Dana Nelson?

"What do *you* think he was up to, Miss Amateur Sleuth?" Dana joked.

I shrugged. "Practicing his vocals because the acoustics in the store are the bomb. No, wait. Meeting a secret lover? No. It's not terribly romantic in there, is it?"

Dana sighed. "Always with the comedy act, huh? He was looking for a diamond ring buried in the floor of your storeroom, Coop. Looks as though Abe loved to hide things, and he'd bought a ring for Francie's birthday, which was just two days after his death. He hid it in the store and drew a diagram of its hiding place because he was a forgetful old coot, according to Francie. But he died before he could collect it, and you ladies moved in before Hank found the diagram."

"So he was going to steal her birthday gift, too? Jeez! *Creep.*" I wasn't sure whom I should feel sorrier for. Dead Hank or murderess Francie. Then I slapped my thighs. "How did Hank find Abe's diagram anyway?"

Dana rocked back on his heels, the snow beating at his police officer's cap. "When he was helping pack away some of Abe's clothes for donation. Abe was a generous guy, according to Pricilla. Hank found the diagram tucked away in an old shirt. When they came to Inkerbelle's to confront Hank that night, he taunted them with the drawing of the ring's hiding place. Just another thing to steal from them, if you listen to Francie Levigne tell it. But it was worth over twenty thousand dollars."

I whistled, my eyes wide. "So is that why Pricilla came back here last night and almost knocked me out?"

Dana's eyes narrowed. "Speaking of coming back here...to a crime scene...where you're *not* supposed to be..."

Ah. One of the two women must have ratted me out. Murderers and snitches, the both of them!

But I shook my finger at him. "You listen here, Officer Rigid. There was a living animal in this store and you numbskulls just left him without a word to Coop and Trixie. He could have died, Dana! We were merely doing the job you guys should have done in the first place."

"Nice way to gaslight, Miss Talks To Dead People," Dana said, clucking his tongue. "I agree it was a poor choice, but we couldn't get in touch with animal control, so it was the *only* choice. As much as I love animals, you don't think I looked up how long the owl could survive without food? You know me better than that, so quit talking crazy. Not to mention, how was I supposed to know he wouldn't eat my hand off if I tried to take him?" Then he smirked.

"Fine, fine," I joked, letting my legs dangle and swing at the edge of the ambulance. "So why did Pricilla come back here? For the ring? Did you guys find it?"

Now he grinned, his handsome face lighting up.

"We did. Pricilla said they didn't have time to look for the ring because Trixie and Coop came back seconds after Hank died. So they slipped out as fast as they could. But Pricilla came back last night for her *earring*. She lost it the night they confronted Hank in Inkerbelle's. She knew it would put her at the store the night of Hank's murder. Why else would she be in someone else's store after hours? You just managed to catch her off guard in the middle of her search."

Rubbing my forehead, I nodded. "Um, yeah. I have the shiner to prove it, buddy." I paused then and wondered out loud, "Then why were they here tonight?"

"To keep looking for the earring. Pricilla was afraid we'd found it. She was right, too. But Pricilla's cousin is Duncan Levitt, one of Eb Falls' finest. He told us both Francie and Pricilla had been behaving strangely, asking him a lot of questions. He didn't like it, but he's a good cop so he gave us a head's up. And because family is almost always suspect, we told him to let slip that we had very little physical evidence to go on. Nothing but Coop's tattoo gun to show for our efforts."

I smiled knowingly and jabbed him in his bulky arm. "Nice play, Officer By The Book!"

But Trixie was the one who found this news most exciting. She hopped out of the ambulance and said, "So you had Duncan drop a crumb, leading them to believe Pricilla's earring might still be at Inkerbelle's. I bet they thought the ring might still be here, too!"

"Aw, man," Dana groused with a chuckle. "You've

been hanging around our Miss Cartwright a little long for my comfort. But yes. You're absolutely right, Miss Lavender. Duncan contacted us about an hour ago, right after finally getting in touch with Francie and Pricilla. We'd planned to do a stakeout and wait to see if they'd take the bait—but naturally, Miss Cartwright got herself mixed up in the middle of everything before anyone could do anything."

I hopped off the ambulance, too, and shook my head. "Oh, no you don't, pal. I was walking Whiskey, minding my own business. Is it my fault they left the door open to Inkerbelle's like the bumbling criminals they are, and he rushed inside? No, siree. No, it is not."

Whiskey, hearing his name, poked his head out of the truck and barked, making us all laugh.

Coop ran her hands over his big head, and it was nice to see her warming to him when she whispered, "You're a good boy, Stevie Cartwright's dog. A very good boy," before dropping a kiss on the top of his head.

I turned to Dana, giving him a light punch in the arm. "Hey, I'm sorry again we missed our coffee date. Was it anything important you wanted to talk about?"

"Nope. Just wanted to catch up."

I wasn't sure I believed him, because he'd been very specific when he'd invited me out for coffee…but he didn't look as though he were ready to share, so I winked at him. "You'd better be careful, Officer Nelson. I might think we're friends. You don't want to give me the wrong impression, do you?"

"Heaven forbid," he teased with a wink of his own.

I shivered. It was time to take everyone back to the house and pack it in for the night. "So are we cleared for takeoff now, Officer Nelson?"

"For the moment. But don't you three go too far. We may have more questions for you in the next few days as we sort the rest of this out. Are we clear?"

I sighed, letting my shoulders slump as I looked at the two women. "Shoot, girls. I guess that means we'll have to delay our trip to Australia to see the *Thunder From Down Under* strippers."

Coop jumped out of the ambulance, pulling Whiskey with her, her beautiful face made more beautiful by the swirling red and blue of the police cars flashers. "What are strippers down under, Stevie Cartwright? We didn't have any strippers anywhere down under," she said plainly, giving me that direct gaze. "Oh, and what are strippers?"

"Yeah, Stevie Cartwright, what are strippers?" Trixie asked, and then she began to laugh…laugh so hard, she had to hold her belly and bend at the waist.

And I laughed with her as we made our way back to Madam Zoltar's in the falling snow.

Just three women and a dog, laughing and chatting —a true testament to girl power at its finest.

EPILOGUE

One Week Later...

"You guys have everything?" I asked Coop and Trixie as they packed up their car with the last remaining boxes from the store.

A week had passed since the death of Hank Morrison, and Coop had been cleared of all charges. Dana was able to share with us more evidence they'd found against Pricilla and Francie. Namely, the searches done on Pricilla's laptop about the substance in Visine that was so harmful to Hank due to his heart issues. After that last visit from the police, we all breathed a sigh of relief.

Some of the finer details of that night when I'd battled it out with Francie and Pricilla emerged in increments. One of which was why Win had called out Coop's name in the middle of such chaos. Seems we'd both forgotten she could hear Win, and when he remembered she could at just the right time, he'd decided it was worth a shot, and I can't tell you how grateful I am for that.

Poor Whiskey had a knot on his head after Francie had clocked him with the handle of her ax because he wouldn't stop jumping on her. But the vet said he was just fine, and he'd recover fully.

Because the girls had no place to stay while they figured out their next step, they'd stayed with us—and it had been a week of many things.

Mostly, it had been a week of blossoming friendship. I'd grown quite fond of these two women, and Livingston for that matter. He could call me a pretty lady with that Irish accent all day, every day.

Trixie had promised, once they'd settled, to see if she could find out any information about the artist who'd inked the tattoo Win described to her—and she'd sketched for him in glorious detail. She truly was gifted. And I had a standing invitation with Coop if I ever wanted a tattoo of my own.

I was going to miss them terribly when they were gone, Livingston included. Sadly, the girls had opted to leave Ebenezer Falls. The store was a mess, and with it now in probate until the courts could decide who it should be given to for management, it forced Trixie and Coop to make a decision.

So last night, to show them what being a part of a community rich in love and support (even if we had our differences) was all about, we had a big spaghetti dinner with Enzo, Carmella, Dana, and Melba. We'd laughed. We'd toasted new beginnings. We'd drunk too much wine. We'd laughed some more.

And today, with the warm sunshine beating down on our heads, and the sounds of Whiskey playing fetch on the lawn with Bel in the background, they were leaving, and I was woefully depressed.

But I plastered a smile on my face and said, "So I guess you're leaving me for that life you talked about wanting, huh? Fine friends you are."

We all stood out in the driveway by their newly fixed car, the Puget breeze blowing in our hair. Sailboats floated by in a colorful array, and the waves passed, frothy and rolling.

Trixie burst out laughing under the noonday sun, her chestnut hair glimmering, her eyes bright "After seeing you, Stevie. After watching you live your life, even with all the hardships you've suffered getting here, with all the adversity, and witnessing all the people and love you've accumulated since you lost your powers…it gives me hope. You know that, right?"

My throat tightened at Trixie's words. No one knew better than I how hard it was to start over again —to leave everything you loved and try to make it on your own. We'd both been forced to do just that. Me from Paris, and her from the convent.

I winked. "I'm glad you found hope, Sister Trixie Lavender. What's the point of life if there's no hope?"

She grinned. She'd done that a lot this week, and it made my heart happy. "And that's all because of you. You didn't just clear Coop's name, my friend. You gave us an eyeful of what living really is, and we want that. *I* want that. I want to live, and experience, and laugh, and make friends. I want to be a part of a community, and have people over for spaghetti dinners the way you do. Lots and lots of people."

Coop nodded, rubbing her nonexistent belly. "I want spaghetti dinners, too, Stevie Cartwright. Yes, I do. Spaghetti is delicious."

I looped my arm through Coop's and gave her a squeeze. "I wish you a thousand spaghetti dinners, Coop the Demon, and then a thousand more."

She gave me her point blank stare as the wind blew her gorgeously silky hair around her face. "I like you, Stevie Cartwright. I like you very much. You're a very nice human. Will you always be my friend?"

I threw my arms around her neck and gave her the tightest hug I could summon, and whispered, "*Always, always*, Coop."

And wonder of all wonders, Coop hugged me back before firmly setting me from her, and then she gave me that awkward pat on my shoulder to let me know she appreciated me.

I held out my arms to Trixie, my eyes welling with tears. "I wish you guys would reconsider staying. It would be so nice to have people living right here in Eb Falls who really understand what it's like to have those two men in my ears all the time and won't call me crazy for the having."

Trixie gave me a hard squeeze before leaning back and cupping my elbows. Her smile was watery and her voice full of emotion. "I wish we could, too, Stevie. You've been so kind to us, and I'll never forget everything you've done. But I think too much has happened here in Eb Falls for us to stay—we need a fresh start. Plus, the store is kind of a mess with all the broken glass. We can't afford to fix that, and the police told us they didn't know how long the store would be tied up as evidence or who it would belong to in the end. But we won't be far. Just in Portland. So I expect to see you at one of *my* spaghetti dinners really soon, okay?" she whispered, a tear falling down her porcelain cheek.

I wiped it away with my thumb and grinned, fighting my own tears. "I'll bring the wine. Now off with you both before I change my mind and beg you to stay. And I warn you, I can be *veeery* persuasive. I'll cling to Coop's leg, and cry and plead, and things will get really ugly, really fast." I gave Livingston a kiss on the top of his head and scratched him between the ears.

Stepping away from their car, I shooed them off as Trixie got into the refurbished rust bucket Caddy and started the engine. It turned over with a purr, just like Win had promised when he'd offered to have it fixed for them.

"Godspeed, Coop," Win said, his husky voice full of emotion. "May your journeys always fare thee well."

Coop broke out in one of her very scarce, but certainly infamous grins and saluted the sky. "Aye-aye, Captain. Thank you, Crispin Alistair Winterbottom. Thank you very much for all your help."

With that, she hopped in the car, pulled Livingston

to her lap, and then they were gone, leaving nothing behind but the scent of gas fumes and the sound of Trixie's tinkling laughter.

Sighing, I looked up at the sky. It was a beautiful day, easily seventy and climbing, puffy clouds smooshed together, and the sun was a ball of butter. How quickly the weather had turned from last week's blizzard. But I felt an empty space in my heart where Coop and Trixie had grown, and I couldn't enjoy it.

"Don't be sad, Dove. We'll see them soon enough."

I walked to the front steps, once covered in snow, now covered in planters filled with pansies, courtesy of Chester and Enzo. "I know we will. It was just nice to have people who truly understand what it's like to live in a human world when you know the paranormal exists. It's not like I can confide in anyone here in Eb Falls, you know?"

"Ah, but you can confide in me, Stephania. I'll always listen."

And I knew that was true, but I was still sad. "Yep. I know. But you're not here-here, you know what I mean?"

"Well, someday, I hope to be there-there. What say you to that?"

Stuffing my hands in the pockets of my vintage Jordache jeans, I rose and turned toward the front door. "I say you'd better not do anything stupid. I can't understand a darn thing about the plans for that gazebo, and I'm pretty sure, control freak that you are, you'll want to be here to explain when Enzo builds it or we'll end up with, heaven forbid, a tree house."

"The horror," Win teased.

Heading inside, I inhaled deeply the sweet scent of home, where I'd placed daffodils that had finally bloomed in a glass vase on the table by the entryway. "Indeed."

"So do tell, Dove, are you mysteried out for the time being?"

"You know, I know you guys think I love this mystery business a little too much, but this one? This one was tough. I never really figured out who the killer was. I didn't have time with everything going on with Coop and Trixie. It was all just handed to me in confessional fashion."

"Ah, so the challenge is digging around and finding your own answers, eh?"

I bobbed my head with a smile. "I guess so. Either way, I think I'm good for a little while. So what say we go wash away Stevie's blues with a couple of Twinkies and a tall glass of milk?"

"Ugh, Stephania. Can't we wash it away with something more sophisticated? Say a lovely zinfandel and some tea cakes?"

I stopped in the entryway and looked up at the ceiling. "What the heck are tea cakes? Is that anything like spotted dick?"

Win garbled a laugh. "Nay, Stephania. Nothing at all."

"Still sounds fishy to me. I'm settling for Twinkies,

and you'll just have to like it. Besides, I thought this was a wash-Stevie's-blues-away party. Don't you want to see me happy?"

"Always, always. Dove. *Always.*"

The End

(Thank you so much for joining Stevie and gang for another Witchless in Seattle installment! I know you waited a long time and your patience is much appreciated. I hope you'll look for Trixie and Coop in their own story, *Then There Were Nun*, the first edition of the Nun of Your Business Mysteries. Until then, happy spring—may all your journeys fare thee well!)

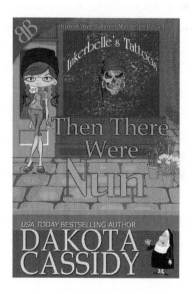

Chapter 1

"So, Sister Trixie Lavender, how do we feel about this space? Open concept, with plenty of sprawling views of the crumbling sidewalk from the leaky picture window and easily room for eight tat chairs.

"Also, one half bathroom for customers, one full for us—which means we'd have to share, but there are worse things. A bedroom right up those sketchy stairs with a small loft, which BTW, I'm calling as mine now. I like to be up high for the best possible views when I survey our pending tattoo empire. A tiny kitchenette, but no big deal. I don't cook anyway, and *you* sure don't, if that horse pucky you called oatmeal is any indication of your culinary skills. Lots of peeling paint and crappy plumbing. All for the low-low price of...er, what was that price again, Fergus McDuff?"

Short and chubby, a balding Fergus McDuff, the landlord of the current dive I was assessing as a candidate for our tattoo parlor, cringed and visibly shuddered beneath his limp blue suit.

Maybe because Coop had him up against a wall, holding him by the front of his shirt in white-knuckled fists as she waited for him to rethink the price he'd quoted us the moment he realized we were women.

Which was not only an outrageous amount of money for this dank, pile-of-rubble hole in the wall, but not at all the amount quoted to us over the phone. It also looked nothing like the picture from his Facebook page. I know that shouldn't surprise me. He'd probably used some Snapchat filter to brighten it up. But here we were.

A bead of perspiration popped out just above Fergus's thin upper lip.

Coop's dusky auburn hair curtained his face, but his stance remained firm. "Like I said, lady, it's three grand a month—"

Cutting his words off, Coop tightened her grip with a grunt and hauled Fergus higher. His pleading gray eyes darted from her to me and back again in unadulterated fear, but to his credit, he tried really hard not to show it.

Coop licked her lips, a low hum of a growl coming from her throat, her gaze intently focused on poor Fergus. "Can I kill him, Sister Trixie Lavender? Please, please, pleeease?"

"*Coop*," I warned. She knew better than to ask such a question. "She's just joking, Fergus. Promise."

"But I'm not. Though, I promise I'll clean up afterward. It'll be like it never happened—"

"Two thousand!" Fergus shouted quite jarringly, as though the effort to push the words out pained him. "Wait, wait, wait! I meant to say two thousand a month with *all* utilities!"

That's my demon. Overbearing and intimidating as the day is long. Still, I frowned at her, pulling my knit cap down over my ears. While this behavior worked in our favor, it was still unacceptable.

We'd had a run-in with the law a few months ago back in Ebenezer Falls, Washington, where we'd first tried to set up a tattoo shop. Coop's edgy streak had almost landed her with a murder charge.

Since then (and before we landed in Eb Falls, by the by), we'd been traveling through the Pacific Northwest, making ends meet by selling my portrait sketches to people along the way, waiting until Coop's instincts choose the right place for us to call home.

Cobbler Cove struck just the right chord with her. And that's how we ended up here, with her breathing fire down Fergus McDuff's throat.

Coop, who'd caught on to my displeasure, smirked her beautiful smirk and set Fergus down with a gentle drop, brushing his trembling shoulder with a careful hand to smooth his wrinkled suit.

"That's nice. You're being nice, Fergus McDuff. I like you. Do you like me?"

"Coop?" I called from the other end of the room, going over some rough measurements for a countertop in my mind. "Playtime's over, young lady. Let Mr. McDuff be, please."

She rolled her bright green eyes at me in petulance and wiped her hands down her burgundy leather pants, disappointment written all over her face that there'd be no killing today.

Coop huffed. "Fine."

I looked at her with my stern ex-nun's expression as a clear reminder to remember her manners. "Coop…"

She pouted before holding out her hand to Fergus, even though he outwardly cringed at the gesture. "It was nice to meet you, Fergus McDuff. I hope I'll see you again sometime soon," she said almost coquettishly, mostly following the guidelines I'd set forth for polite conversation with new acquaintances.

Fergus brushed her hand away, fear still on his face, and that was when I knew it was time for me to step in.

"You do realize she's just joking—about killing you and all, don't you? I would never let her do that," I joked, hoping he'd come along for the ride.

But he only nodded as Coop picked up his tie clip and handed it to him in a gesture of apology.

I smiled at her and nodded my head in approval, dropping my hands into the pockets of my puffy vest. "Okay, Fergus. Sold. Two grand a month and utilities it is. A year lease, right? Have a contract handy?"

Fergus nodded and scurried toward the front of the store to get his briefcase. It was then Coop leaned toward me and sniffed the air, her delicate nostrils flaring.

"This place smells right, Trixie Lavender. Yes, it does. Also, I like the name Peach Street. That sounds like a nice place to live."

I looked into her beautiful eyes—eyes so green and perfectly almond-shaped they made other women sick with jealousy—and smiled, feeling a sense of relief. "Ya think? You've got a good vibe about it then? Like the one you had in Ebenezer Falls before the bottom fell out?"

And you were accused of murder and our store was left in shambles?

I bit the inside of my cheek to keep from bringing up our last escapade in a suburb of Seattle, with an ex-witch turned medium named Stevie Cartwright and her dead spy turned ghost cohort, Winterbottom. It was still too fresh.

Coop rolled her tongue along the inside of her cheek and scanned the dark, mostly barren space with critical eyes. Any mention of Eb Falls, and Coop grew instantly sullen. "I miss Stevie Cartwright. She said she'd be my friend. Always-always."

My face softened into a smile. I missed Stevie and her ghost compatriot, too. Even though I couldn't actually hear Winterbottom—or Win, as she'd called him—Coop could, and from what she'd relayed to me, he sounded delightfully British and madly in love with Stevie.

Certainly an unrequited love, due to their circumstances—him being all the way up there on what they called Plane Limbo (where souls wait to decide if they wish to cross over)—and Stevie here on Earth, but they fit one another like gloves.

Stevie had been one of the best things to ever happen to me; Coop, too. She'd helped us in more ways than just solving a murder and keeping Coop from going to jail. She'd helped heal our hearts. She'd shown us what it meant to be part of a community. She'd helped us learn to trust not just our instincts, but to let the right people into our lives and openly enjoy their presence.

"Trixie? Do you think Stevie meant we'd always be friends?"

I winked at Coop. "She meant what she said, for sure. She always means what she says. If she said she'll always be your friend, you can count on it. And I miss Stevie, too, Coop. Bet she comes to visit us soon."

Coop almost smirked, which was her version of a smile—something we worked on every day. Facial expressions and body language humans most commonly use.

"Will she eat spaghetti with us?" she asked, referring to the last meal we'd shared with Stevie, when she'd invited her friends over and made us a part of not just her community, but her family.

"I bet she'll eat whatever we make. So anyway… We were talking the vibe here? It feels good to you?"

"Yep. I can tattoo here."

"Gosh, I hope so. We need to plant some roots, Coop. We need to begin again Finnegan."

We needed to find a sense of purpose after Washington, and this felt right. This suburb of Portland called the Cobbler Cove District felt right.

Tucking her waist-length hair behind her ear, Coop nodded her agreement with a vague pop of her lips, the wheels in her mind so obviously turning. "So we can grow and be a part of the community. So we can blend."

"Yes, blending is important. Now, about threatening Fergus…"

Her eyes narrowed on Fergus, who'd taken a phone call and busily paced the length of the front of the store. "He was lying, Trixie Lavender. Three grand wasn't what he said on the phone at all. No, it was not. I know what I heard. You said it's bad to lie. I was only following the rules, just like you told me I should if I wanted to stay here with you and other humans."

Bobbing my head to agree, I pinched her lean cheek with affection and smiled. "That's exactly what I said, Coop. *Exactly*. Good on you for finally listening to me after our millionth conversation about manners."

"Do I win a prize?"

I frowned as I leaned against the peeling yellow wall. I never knew where Coop was going in her head sometimes. She took many encounters, words, people, whatever, at face value. Almost the way a small child would—except this sometime-child had an incredible figure and a savage lust for blood if not carefully monitored.

"A prize, Coop?" I asked curiously, tucking my hands in the pockets of my jeans. "Explain your thinking, please."

She gazed at me in all seriousness as she quite visibly concentrated on her words. I watched her sweet, uncluttered mind put her thoughts together.

"Yep. A prize. I saw it the other day on a sign at the grocery store. The millionth shopper wins free groceries for a year. Do I get something for free after our millionth conversation?"

Laughter bubbled from my throat. Coop didn't just bring me endlessly sticky situations, she brought me endless laughter and, yes, even endless joy. She's simple, and I don't mean she's unintelligent.

I mean, sometimes she's so black and white, I find it hard to explain to her the many levels and nuances of appropriate reactions or emotions for any given situation, and that can tax me on occasion. But she's mine, and she'd saved my life, and I wasn't ever going to forget that.

And I do mean *ever*.

She'd tell you I'd saved *hers*, but that's just her innocent take on a situation that had been almost impossible until she'd shown up with her trusty sword.

I gazed up at the water-stained ceiling and thought about how to explain the complexities of mankind. I decided simple was best.

"Trixie? Do I get a prize?" she inquired again, her tone more insistent this time.

"No free groceries. Just my love and eternal gratitude that you restrained yourself and didn't kill Fergus. He's not a bad man, Coop. And when I say *bad*, I mean the kind of bad who kicks puppies and pulls the wings off moths for sport. He's just trying to make his way in the world and get ahead. Just like everybody else. It might not be nice, but you can't kill him over it. Them's the rules, Demon."

"But he wasn't being fair, Sister Trixie Lavender."

"Remember what we discussed about my name?"

Now she frowned, the lines in her perfectly shaped forehead deepening. "Yes. I forgot—again. You're not a nun anymore and it isn't necessary to call you by your last name. You're just plain Trixie."

Plain Trixie was an understatement. Compared to Coop, Angelina Jolie was plain. My mousy, stick-straight reddish brown (all right, mostly brown) hair and plump thighs were no match for the sleek Coopster. But you couldn't be jealous of her for long because she had no idea how stunning she was, and that was because she didn't care.

"Right. I'm just Trixie. Just like Fergus isn't Fergus McDuff. He's just plain old Fergus, if he allows you to call him by his first name, or Mr. McDuff if he prefers the more formal way to address someone. And I'm not a nun anymore. That's also absolutely right."

My heart shivered with a pang of sadness at that, but I'm finally able to say that out loud now and actually feel comfortable doing so.

I wasn't a nun anymore, and I'm truly, deeply at peace with the notion. My faith had become a bone of contention for me long before I'd exited the convent, so it was probably better I'd ended up being kicked out on my ear any ol' way.

In fact, I often wonder if it hadn't *always* been a bone of contention for the entire fifteen years I'd lived there. I'd always questioned some of the rules.

I'd never wanted to enter the convent to begin with —my parents put me there when they could no longer handle my teenage substance abuse. They'd left me in the capable, nurturing hands of my mother's dear friend, Sister Alice Catherine.

But after I'd kicked my drug habit, and decided to take my vows in gratitude for all the nuns of Saint Aloysius By The Sea had done for me, I came to love the thick stone walls, the soft hum and tinkle of wind chimes, and the structure of timely prayer.

They'd saved me from my addiction. In their esteemed honor, I wanted to save people, too. What better way to do so than becoming a nun in dedicated service to the man upstairs?

Though, I can promise you, I didn't want to leave the convent the way I did. A graceful exit would have been my preferred avenue of departure.

Instead, I left by way of possession. Yes. I said *possession*. An ugly, fiery, gaping-black-mouthed, demonic possession. I know that's a lot of adjectives, but it best describes what wormed its way inside me on that awful, horrible night.

"Are you sad now, Trixie? Did I make you sad because you aren't a nun anymore?" Coop asked, very clearly worried she'd displeased me—which did happen from time to time.

For instance, when she threatened to kill anyone who even looked cross-eyed at me—sometimes if they just breathed the wrong way.

I had to remind myself often, it was out of the goodness of her heart she'd nearly severed a careless driver's head when he'd encroached on our pedestrian right of way (the pedestrian always has the right of way in Portland, in case you were wondering). Or lopped off a man's fingers with a nearby butter knife for grazing my backside by accident while we were in a questionable bar.

Still, even while Coop's emotions ruled her actions without any tempered, well-thought-out responses, she was a sparkling diamond in the rough, a veritable sponge, waiting to soak up all available knowledge.

I tugged at a lock of her silky hair, shaking off the memory of that night. "How can I be sad if I have you, Coop DeVille?"

She grimaced—my feisty, compulsive, loveable demon grimaced—which is her second version of a smile (again, she's still practicing smiling. There's not much to smile about in Hell, I suppose) and patted my cheek—just like I'd taught her. "Good."

"So, do you think you're up to the task of some remodeling? This place is kind of a mess."

Actually, it was a disaster. Everything was crumbling. From the bathroom that looked as though it hadn't been cleaned since the last century, to the peeling walls and yellowed linoleum with holes all throughout the store.

Her expression went thoughtful as she cracked her knuckles. "That means painting and using a hammer, right?"

I brushed my hands together and adjusted my scarf. "Yep. That's what that means, Coop."

"Then no. I don't want to do that."

I barked a laugh, scaring Fergus, who was busily rifling through his briefcase, looking for the contract I'm now positive changes with the applicant's gender.

"Tough petunias. We're in this together, Demon-San. That means the good, the bad, and the renovation of this place. If you want to start tattooing again, we can't have customers subjected to this chaos, can we?

Who'd feel comfortable getting a tattoo in a mess like this?"

I pointed to the pile of old pizza boxes and crushed beer cans in the corner where I hoped we'd be able to build a cashier's counter.

Coop's sigh was loud enough to ensure I'd hear it as she let her shoulders slump. "You're right, Sis...um, *Trixie*. We have to have a sterile environment to make tattoos. The Oregon laws say so. I read them, you know. On the laptop. I read them *all*."

As I said, Coop's a veritable sponge, which almost makes up for her lack of emotional control.

Almost.

I patted her shoulder as it poked out of her off-the-shoulder T-shirt, the shoulder with a tattoo of an angel in all its magnificently winged glory. A tattoo she'd drawn and inked herself while deep in the bowels of Hell.

"I'm proud of you. I'm going to need all the help I can get so we can get our license to open ASAP. We need to start making some money, Coop. We don't have much left of the money Sister Mary Ignatius gave us, and we definitely can't live on our charm alone."

"So I've been useful?"

"You're more than useful, Coop. You're my right-hand man. Er, woman."

She grinned, and it was when she grinned like this, when her gorgeously crafted face lit up, I grew more certain she understood how dear a friend she was to me. "Good."

"Okay, so let's go sign our lives away—"

"No!" she whisper-yelled, gripping my wrist with the strength of ten men, her face twisted in fear. "Don't do that, Trixie Lavender! You know what happens when you do that. Nothing is as it seems when you do that!"

I forced myself not to wince when I pried her fingers from my wrist. Sometimes, Coop didn't know her own demonic strength. "Easy, Coop. I need my skin," I teased.

In an instant, she dropped her hands to her sides and shoved them into the pockets of her pants, her expression contrite. "My apologies. But you know I have triggers. That's what you called them, right? When I get upset and anxious, that's a trigger. Signing your life away is one of them. We have to be careful with our words. You said so yourself."

She was right. I'd poorly worded my intent, forgetting her fears about the devil and Hell's shoddy bargains for your soul.

As the rain pounded the roof, I measured my words and tried to make light of the situation. "It's just a saying we use here, Coop. It means we're giving everything we have to Fergus McDuff on a wing and a prayer at this point. But it doesn't mean I'm giving up my soul to the devil. I promise. My soul's staying put."

At least I thought it was. I could be wrong after my showdown with an evil spirit, but it felt like it was still there. I still had empathy for others. I still knew right from wrong—even if all those morals went directly out the window when the evil spirit took over.

Coop inhaled and exhaled before she squared her perfectly proportioned shoulders. "Okay. Then let's go," she paused, frowning, "sign our lives away to Fergus McDuff." Then she smirked, clearly meaning she understood what I'd said.

Our path to Fergus slowed when Coop paused and put a hand on my arm, setting me behind her. There was a commotion of some kind occurring just outside our door on the sidewalk, between Fergus and another man.

A dark-haired man with olive skin stretched tightly over his jaw and sleeve tattoos on both arms yelled down at Fergus, who, after Coop, had probably had enough of being under fire for today. But holy crow, this guy was angry.

He waved those muscular arms—attached to lean hands with long fingers—around in the air as the rain pelted his sleek head. His T-shirt stretched over his muscles as he gestured over his shoulder, and his voice, even muffled, boomed along our tiny street.

I couldn't make out what they were saying, but it didn't look like a very friendly exchange—not judging by the man's face, which, when it wasn't screwed up in anger, was quite handsome.

Yet, Fergus, clearly at his breaking point after his encounter with Coop, reared up in the gentleman's face and yelled right back. But then a taller, leaner, sandy-haired man approached and put a hand on the handsome man's shoulder, encouraging him to turn around.

That gave Fergus the opportunity to push his way past the big man and grab the handle of our door, stepping back inside the store with a bluster of huffs and grunts.

Coop sniffed the air. She can sometimes smell things the rest of us can't. It's hard to explain, but as an example, she smelled that our friend Stevie isn't entirely human. She's a witch. Or she was. Now, since her accident, she only has some residual powers left.

But Coop had smelled her paranormal nature somehow—which, by definition, is crazy incredible and something I can't dwell on for long, for fear I'll get lost in the madness that demons and Hell and witches and other assorted ghouls are quite real.

"The man outside is not paranormal. He's just normal, as is the other man, and Fergus, too. If you were wondering."

I popped my lips in Coop's direction. "Good to know. I mean, what if he was some crazy hybrid of a vampire who can run around in daylight? Then what? We'd have to keep our veins covered or he might suck us dry."

Coop gave me her most serious expression and sucked in her cheeks. "I already told you, you don't ever have to worry anyone will hurt you. I'll kill them and then they'll be dead."

Ba-dump-bump.

"And I told *you*, no killing." Then I giggled and

wrapped an arm around her shoulder, steering her past the debris on the floor and toward a grumpy Fergus, feeling better than I had in weeks. We had a purpose. We had a mission. Above all, we had hope.

We were going to open Inkerbelle's Tattoos and Piercings. I'd pierce and design tattoos, and Coop would handle the rest. We'd hopefully hire a staff of more artists as gifted as Coop. If the universe saw fit, that is.

And then maybe we'd finally have a place to call home. Where I could nest, and Coop could ink to her heart's desire in her tireless effort to protect every single future client from demonic harm with her special brand of magic ink.

During her life under Satan's rule, Coop had tattooed all new entries into Hell. She'd been so good at it, the devil left her in charge of every incoming sinner. But it was a job she'd despised, and she eventually escaped the night she'd saved me.

Lastly, I'd also try to come to terms with my new status in this world—my new freedom to openly share my views on how to get through this life with a solid code of ethics. Oh, and by the way, it has more to do with being the best person you can, rather than putting the fear of scripture quotes and fire and brimstone into non-believers.

I don't care if you believe. I know that sounds crazy coming from an ex-nun once deeply immersed in a convent and yards and yards of scripture. But I don't.

You don't have to believe in an unseen entity if you so choose.

But I do care deeply about the world as a whole, and showing, not telling people you can live your life richly, fully, without ever stepping inside the hallowed halls of a church if you decide that's what works for you.

I want anyone who'll listen to know you can indeed have a life worth living—even as a low-level demon escaped from Hell and an ex-communicated nun who suffers from what Coop and I jokingly call demoniphrenia.

Also known as, the occasional possession of an ex-nun cursed by a random evil spirit.

And I was determined to prove that—not only to myself, but to this spirit who had me in its greasy black clutches.

NOTE FROM DAKOTA

I do hope you enjoyed this book, I'd so appreciate it if you'd help others enjoy it too.

Recommend it. Please help other readers find this book by recommending it.

Review it. Please tell other readers why you liked this book by reviewing it at online retailers or your blog. Reader reviews help my books continue to be valued by distributors/resellers. I adore each and every reader who takes the time to write one!

If you love the book or leave a review, please email **dakota@dakotacassidy.com** so I can thank you with a personal email. Your support means more than you'll ever know! Thank you!"

ABOUT THE AUTHOR

Dakota Cassidy is a USA Today bestselling author with over thirty books. She writes laugh-out-loud cozy mysteries, romantic comedy, grab-some-ice erotic romance, hot and sexy alpha males, paranormal shifters, contemporary kick-ass women, and more.

Dakota was invited by Bravo TV to be the Bravo-holic for a week, wherein she snarked the hell out of all the Bravo shows. She received a starred review from Publishers Weekly for Talk Dirty to Me, won a Romantic Times Reviewers' Choice Award for Kiss and Hell, along with many review site recommended reads and reviewer top pick awards.

Dakota lives in the gorgeous state of Oregon with her real-life hero and her dogs, and she loves hearing from readers!

OTHER BOOK BY DAKOTA CASSIDY

Visit Dakota's website at
http://www.dakotacassidy.com for more information.

***A Lemon Layne Mystery, a Contemporary Cozy Mystery
Series***

    1. Prawn of the Dead

    2. Play That Funky Music White Koi

    3. Total Eclipse of the Carp

***Witchless In Seattle Mysteries, a Paranormal Cozy
Mystery series***

    1. Witch Slapped

    2. Quit Your Witchin'

    3. Dewitched

    4. The Old Witcheroo

    5. How the Witch Stole Christmas

    6. Ain't Love a Witch

    7. Good Witch Hunting

Nun of Your Business Mysteries, a Paranormal Cozy Mystery series

1. Then There Were Nun
2. Hit and Nun

Wolf Mates, a Paranormal Romantic Comedy series

1. An American Werewolf In Hoboken
2. What's New, Pussycat?
3. Gotta Have Faith
4. Moves Like Jagger
5. Bad Case of Loving You

A Paris, Texas Romance, a Paranormal Romantic Comedy series

1. Witched At Birth
2. What Not to Were
3. Witch Is the New Black
4. White Witchmas

Non-Series

Whose Bride Is She Anyway?

Polanski Brothers: Home of Eternal Rest

Sexy Lips 66

Accidentally Paranormal, a Paranormal Romantic Comedy series

Interview With an Accidental—a free introductory guide to the girls of the Accidentals!

1. The Accidental Werewolf
2. Accidentally Dead
3. The Accidental Human
4. Accidentally Demonic
5. Accidentally Catty
6. Accidentally Dead, Again

7. The Accidental Genie

8. The Accidental Werewolf 2: Something About Harry

9. The Accidental Dragon

10. Accidentally Aphrodite

11. Accidentally Ever After

12. Bearly Accidental

13. How Nina Got Her Fang Back

14. The Accidental Familiar

15. Then Came Wanda

16. The Accidental Mermaid

The Hell, a Paranormal Romantic Comedy series

1. Kiss and Hell

2. My Way to Hell

The Plum Orchard, a Contemporary Romantic Comedy series

1. Talk This Way

2. Talk Dirty to Me

3. Something to Talk About

4. Talking After Midnight

The Ex-Trophy Wives, a Contemporary Romantic Comedy series

1. You Dropped a Blonde On Me

2. Burning Down the Spouse

3. Waltz This Way

Fangs of Anarchy, a Paranormal Urban Fantasy series

1. Forbidden Alpha

2. Outlaw Alpha

Made in the USA
Monee, IL
03 June 2023

35216426R00171